Enrollment Form

☐ *Yes!* I WANT TO BE A *P*RIVILEGED *W*OMAN.
Enclosed is one *PAGES & PRIVILEGES™* Proof of
Purchase from any Harlequin or Silhouette book currently for
sale in stores (Proofs of Purchase are found on the back pages
of books) and the store cash register receipt. Please enroll me
in *PAGES & PRIVILEGES™*. Send my Welcome Kit and FREE
Gifts -- and activate my FREE benefits -- immediately.
More great gifts and benefits to come.

NAME (please print)

ADDRESS **APT. NO**

CITY **STATE** **ZIP/POSTAL CODE**

PROOF OF PURCHASE ONLY

NO CLUB!
NO COMMITMENT!
*Just one purchase brings
you great Free Gifts and
Benefits!*

Please allow 6-8 weeks for delivery. Quantities are limited. We reserve the right to
substitute items. Enroll before October 31, 1995 and receive one full year of benefits.

Name of store where this book was purchased_____

Date of purchase_____

Type of store:
   ☐ Bookstore ☐ Supermarket ☐ Drugstore
   ☐ Dept. or discount store (e.g. K-Mart or Walmart)
   ☐ Other (specify)_____

Pages
& Privileges ™

Which Harlequin or Silhouette series do you usually read?

Complete and mail with one Proof of Purchase and store receipt to:
U.S.: *PAGES & PRIVILEGES™*, P.O. Box 1960, Danbury, CT 06813-1960
Canada: *PAGES & PRIVILEGES™*, 49-6A The Donway West, P.O. 813,
    North York, ON M3C 2E8

▼ DETACH HERE AND MAIL TODAY! ▼

SSE-PP6B

"He's my son," *Ryan had said.*

Sarah closed her eyes against a wave of sickness. Recent memories hurtled through her like a series of explosions, each one crashing with more horrifying impact. She could feel angry tears burning her throat, but she wasn't going to let them spill.

Why had she never noticed how much alike Ryan and her beloved nephew were? Why had she always assumed the only reason young Jesse walked and stood and even gestured like Ryan was that he admired the man?

Why had she ever let this drifter, this adventurer, become part of Jesse's life?

And why, *why*, had she let him into her heart?

Dear Reader,

There's a lot in store for you this month from Silhouette Special Edition! We begin, of course, with October's THAT SPECIAL WOMAN! title, *D Is for Dani's Baby*, by Lisa Jackson. It's another heartwarming and emotional installment in her LOVE LETTERS series. Don't miss it!

We haven't seen the last of Morgan Trayhern as Lindsay McKenna returns with a marvelous new series, MORGAN'S MERCENARIES: LOVE AND DANGER. You'll want to be there for every spine-tingling and passionately romantic tale, and it all starts with *Morgan's Wife*. And for those of you who have been eagerly following the delightful ALWAYS A BRIDESMAID! series, look no further, as Katie Jones is able to say she's *Finally a Bride*, by Sherryl Woods.

Also this month, it's city girl versus roguish rancher in *A Man and a Million*, by Jackie Merritt. A second chance at love—and a secret long kept—awaits in *This Child Is Mine*, by Trisha Alexander. And finally, October is Premiere month, and we're pleased to welcome new author Laurie Campbell and her story *And Father Makes Three*.

Next month we're beginning our celebration of Special Edition's 1000th book with some of your favorite authors! Don't miss books from Diana Palmer, Nora Roberts and Debbie Macomber—just to name a few! I know you'll enjoy the blockbuster months ahead. I hope you enjoy each and every story to come!

Sincerely,

Tara Gavin, Senior Editor

Please address questions and book requests to:
Silhouette Reader Service
U.S.: 3010 Walden Ave., P.O. Box 1325, Buffalo, NY 14269
Canadian: P.O. Box 609, Fort Erie, Ont. L2A 5X3

LAURIE CAMPBELL

AND FATHER MAKES THREE

Silhouette®

SPECIAL EDITION®

Published by Silhouette Books

America's Publisher of Contemporary Romance

For Pete,
the inspiration for every romantic hero
I've ever written

 SILHOUETTE BOOKS

ISBN 0-373-09990-8

AND FATHER MAKES THREE

Copyright © 1995 by Laurie Schnebly Campbell

LAURIE CAMPBELL

spends her weekdays writing brochures, videos and commercial scripts for an advertising agency. At five o'clock she turns off her computer, waits thirty seconds, turns it on again and starts writing romance. Her other favorite activities include playing with her husband and son, teaching a catechism class, counseling at a Phoenix mental health clinic and working with other writers. "People ask me how I find time to do all that," Laurie says, "and I tell them it's easy. I never clean my house!"

Dear Reader,

Stars. Birthday candles. Wishbones. Every chance I've gotten over the past few years, I've made the same wish: that my Route 66 book will get published, and that people will remember Ryan and Sarah and Jesse.

For a long time my list of "things I'd love to write about" included a photographer who could turn reality into art. A woman torn between her child and her love. A teenage rebel who couldn't wait to hit the road. When those three characters came together, the idea exploded. And when my husband suggested we celebrate our tenth anniversary by driving Route 66, I realized there was magic in this story.

Even so, when the first part of my wish came true, I was stunned. You know how when you dream about something for a long time, it seems like it'll always stay a dream? I still can't quite believe that readers all over the world will get to know these characters I've come to love like my own family. It's thrilling to know that you'll travel "the road to paradise" with people who mean so much to me…and I hope you'll enjoy the trip as much as I have!

Laurie Campbell

Chapter One

Next time he found himself in some roadhouse at the back of beyond, he would have a great story to tell.

Watching with curiosity as the police conferred around the desk outside his cell, Ryan tried a few opening lines. "So, I'm in this little town outside of Chicago...."

No. Too flat.

How about, "Ever try driving a rental car that looks just like the one a bank robber used half an hour ago?"

That might work. This would be a terrific story, Ryan knew, as soon as the cops realized they had the wrong person. Once that happened he could probably make some trouble if he wanted. Threaten a lawsuit for false arrest or something. Make them wish they had never pulled over a relatively law-abiding photographer on the road into Gilroy.

But at least it was cool in here. There were worse ways to kill an afternoon than camping out in some two-bit jail at a small-town police station. He had no plans, no commitments until Bunker showed up with the Winnebago and he could start putting his life back together. Meanwhile, his nostalgic journey through Gilroy might as well take in the police station as anywhere else.

Apparently not everyone felt the same way, though, because from outside came the sound of a scuffle.

"Forget it! No way am I ratting on anybody!"

The hoarse, defiant voice sounded a little young for a place like this, Ryan thought, straining for a glimpse of what was causing the commotion near the door. To some kid out there, this was no longer just a lazy afternoon in a Midwestern jail. This was a crisis, a struggle. This was raw desperation.

"We'll let you think it over, Jesse," one of the policemen announced, ushering the boy into the room. "Maybe you just need a couple hours to get the smoke cleared out of your head."

"How come you're not asking Myers?" the kid demanded, shaking the restraining hand off his shoulder and facing his captor head-on. "You think his old man might not like it or something?"

From the way the policeman tensed, Ryan could tell the boy had hit a sore spot. He wished he had his camera: the scene before him was a classic. The gray-haired, paunchy cop versus the hotheaded teenager with the dark hair swinging past his collar and the blaze of anger in his steel blue eyes—they could have come right out of a movie. *Rebel Without A Cause,* maybe. But before Ryan could envision the proper focus, the policeman recovered, shook his head and reached for a ring of keys.

"Don't worry about the Myers boy," he told Jesse. "We know there've been kids at your school growing marijuana for a while now, smoking at the old Reardon place. All we need are a few names from you, and we're gonna stop it." He unlocked the door to Ryan's cell and the boy stepped in, his shoulders stiff. "You've been headed for trouble a long time now, Jesse. Not much surprise there, with a mother like yours. But if I were you, I'd do some pretty serious thinking."

For a moment the boy stood frozen, as if gathering himself together, and yet the anger, the desperation in him looked almost hot enough to touch. Then, as the steel-barred door clanged shut behind him, he turned away from the policemen out front, faced Ryan with unseeing eyes and took a long, unsteady breath. When he spoke, his voice was tight.

"I gotta get out of here."

Take it easy, Ryan wanted to say. *It's okay, kid.*

But the boy didn't need anyone talking down to him, he knew. Instead he moved over on the cold metal bench, making room for Jesse if he chose to sit down, and addressed him with a casual question.

"They call somebody to come get you? Shouldn't be too long."

Jesse started, almost as if he hadn't realized there was someone else in the cell with him. He squinted at Ryan, giving him a look of quick assessment, and then turned away. "Yeah, I guess. That's not what . . . It's this town, is what I mean." He clenched his fists around the bars for a moment, his knuckles white, then suddenly released his grip. "I gotta get out of this town."

"Yeah. I know." Maybe the kid's intensity was rubbing off on him, but Ryan remembered the feeling all too well. The frustration of being trapped in a too-small town where everyone knew you, knew you were headed for trouble and had already written you off as worthless. The chafing vexation of being hemmed in by rules, of watching kids from the town's leading families get away with stunts that would land you in jail, and of knowing there was no way out. "You still in school?"

The kid shrugged, and as he turned back from the bars, Ryan could see a flash of humor cross his face. "Probably not after today," he said, flexing his arms behind him as if to reassure himself of the freedom to move. "Anyway, it's a waste of time. I could be working. I could be *doing* something."

"How old are you?" Ryan asked.

"Seventeen. I—"

"Mr. Ryan?" Another policeman—a rookie by the looks of him—stepped up to the cell door with a sheaf of papers in hand. "We're ready for fingerprinting. Right over here."

The fingerprinting routine was just as he remembered it, although he hadn't been arrested in quite a few years now. Not since that time back in Shreveport, or Baton Rouge, or wherever the hell it was. Somewhere in the South, he knew, because of the humidity. But that was the only clue. There had been so many cities, so many alleys, so many nights alone....

"Okay, that oughta do it," the policeman concluded, startling him out of his reverie. "This shouldn't take much longer. We're just gonna check for any outstanding warrants."

There wouldn't be any, Ryan knew, which meant they'd have to let him go. At least he couldn't think of any, although it was hard to say for sure what might have happened during those few agonizing months after—

For God's sake, don't think about it!

"Take your time," he said flatly, and he felt the policeman's wary suspicion at his tone of voice follow him all the way back to the cell.

Jesse seemed more at ease, Ryan noticed as he returned to the bench where the kid had finally settled. His look of rebellion had given way to a watchful calm. Apparently he had decided to hold up his end of the conversation, man-to-man, because he offered a question of his own.

"What're you doing here, anyway?"

The kid had a lot to learn about jail conversation, Ryan thought, before remembering that most people would never need or even want to know the etiquette of asking a fellow prisoner about his offense. Well, this was as good a way as any to pass the time. He sat down on the other end of the bench, careful to match the boy's man-to-man tone, and tried out his tale.

"Ever try driving a rental car that looks just like the one a bank robber used half an hour ago?"

Jesse's jaw dropped. He had a winner of an opening, Ryan decided. Too bad he hadn't thought beyond his first line.

"This'll make a great story one of these days," he continued. "What happened is somebody in Afton robbed a bank and got away in a car that matches mine. It wasn't me, kid," he added hastily when he saw the flicker of concern on Jesse's face. "They're checking with the car-rental people now, and as soon as they compare my driver's license with the rental office I'm out of here. But until then, I figure this'll be an interesting way to spend a couple hours in Gilroy."

Jesse looked as though he could argue that point, but instead leaned back against the concrete wall, determinedly nonchalant. "Why'd you want to spend any time in Gilroy?"

Good question, Ryan had to admit. "Sentimental journey, I guess," he said, knowing that such a notion would make no sense to a kid that age. Hell, until recently it wouldn't have made sense to him, either. "I was here maybe fifteen, twenty years ago. Just thought I'd see if any of the same people are still here."

"Gotta be," the kid muttered. "Nothing ever changes in this town."

Ryan hoped that was true. He'd enjoy seeing the photographer who had taken him on as a summer assistant all those years ago, when he'd drifted through Gilroy while waiting to report for basic training. "You know if Larry Bailey's still around?"

Jesse squinted, as if trying to place the name. "Oh, the photographer on Main Street? He died last year."

Bailey probably would have been in his eighties by now, but Ryan couldn't help feeling a tug of disappointment. The grizzled photographer had introduced him to a set of skills he'd used ever since, and it was thanks to Bailey that he'd so enjoyed that long-ago summer in Gilroy.

Well, and thanks to Adele.

"Guess I should've come back sooner," Ryan said. Adele was probably married now, with four kids and a station wagon, but the memory of her legs could still make him hot. "Anyway," he added hastily, "I'm meeting my researcher in Chicago on Friday, so I figured I'd come through this way and look up Bailey. Too bad I didn't do it a few years ago."

"Research? Like science or something?"

"No, like for a photo shoot." Ryan stretched his legs out, scuffing his bootheels against the concrete floor. Might as well get comfortable; this could be a long afternoon. "We're driving from Chicago to Los Angeles on what's left of Route 66. You know, the road to paradise? It's for *Odyssey Magazine.*"

"No kidding." The boy looked impressed—whether at the name of the magazine or the freedom to drive cross-country, Ryan wasn't sure. "You're one of the *Odyssey* photographers?"

With any luck, he would be once they saw this story. "Yeah," Ryan said. "They've got their own writers, so I don't need to worry about that. But the research will help sell the piece." Then, with an *Odyssey* sale to his credit, he'd be back on the national track again. Back where he'd been before—

Don't think about it!

"Wow." Jesse sounded genuinely awed and a little envious. "You're driving clear across the country, huh?" For a moment he looked younger, his face lit with wonder. Then, before he could launch another question, the gray-haired policeman stepped up to the cell door.

"You come up with any names, Jesse?"

The boy stiffened. Ryan could almost feel the weight that descended on his shoulders as the youth stared deliberately across the room, then slowly shook his head.

There was a long moment of almost-electric tension as the two faced off against each other, and Ryan found himself breathing more softly as the policeman threw out a warning.

"We can make it tough on you, you know."

Their gazes locked. Jesse stayed silent, not moving a muscle until, with a sharp sigh, the policeman walked away.

But the showdown had cost the boy, Ryan could tell. His back was still rigid, his stance defiant, but his eyes were bleak. He had nowhere to go, and he knew it.

Ryan cleared his throat. "You know something? I've been thinking, every now and then, it'd be handy to have someone who could help with the gear. Loading film, hauling equipment, that kind of thing."

Jesse swallowed.

"I don't know if you'd be interested," Ryan added, wondering what Bunker would say if he suddenly turned up with an assistant. "But if you want to talk it over with your folks—"

"Ryan! You're all clear."

The sergeant couldn't have picked a worse time to announce the good news, Ryan thought. He could feel Jesse tensing up, torn between begging for more information and maintaining a watchful reserve. Well, this probably wasn't the time or place to offer the kid a job, anyway. As the sergeant unlocked the door, he stood up and nodded to Jesse.

"Why don't you think about it and give me a call if you're interested? I'm at the Gilroy Inn. Name's Ryan." Before the door clanged shut behind him, he turned back to offer a final salute. "Hang in there, kid."

It took only a few minutes to sign for his wallet and keys, accept the sergeant's apology for mistakenly detaining him—the guy was good at this, Ryan noted; he had just the right touch for averting lawsuits—and get directions to the courthouse parking lot, where they had stowed his rental car. But before he left, he wanted to make sure of one thing.

"That kid in there," he said to the sergeant, who seemed like the best source of information. "Has he got someone coming to pick him up?"

The cop looked surprised at the question, but glanced at the clock above his desk. "Yeah. Oughta be here any minute."

"All right. Thanks," Ryan added, before realizing he didn't owe this guy any thanks. He went outside, noticing that the late-afternoon air was as cool as he'd remembered. The kid was probably right about nothing ever changing in this town.

Two blocks down Main Street he could see the courthouse roof shading the gravel lot where his car was parked. Ryan took a shortcut across the long, shallow steps that surrounded the courthouse and almost tripped as someone came around the corner from the other side.

It was a woman, a fast-moving woman wearing a lavender dress of some woven fabric that scratched at his fingers as he grabbed her shoulders, steadying them both.

"Sorry," he began, diving for the folder he had knocked out of her hands and hoping he hadn't knocked the wind out of her. But as he straightened up and saw her face, her full lower lip, her wide-set eyes, her dark blond hair slipping loose from its soft, thick knot, he suddenly felt as though his breath had been stopped in his throat.

"My God," he said. "Adele."

This was the last thing she needed.

"Excuse me," Sarah Corcoran said, trying to step around the man who was staring at her in astonishment. She didn't have time to deal with anyone who had known Adele, not when Jesse was locked up in the police station.

"You haven't changed at all," he said in wonder, lightly resting his hand on her shoulder. "I was just thinking about you and—"

Sarah backed away. "I'm not Adele!" In a way, she almost regretted that she wasn't, because the man had such a captivating smile. But it would vanish as soon as he learned who she was. "Adele was my sister."

He stared at her for a moment longer, then moved down one step so he could look at her more directly. The fascination still hadn't left his eyes, which was unusual for one of these mistaken encounters. "Twins, huh? I didn't even know she had a sister."

None of Adele's two-week-long boyfriends had, Sarah almost answered. Her sister hadn't spent much time talking about family whenever an attractive man came through town. But there was no reason to go into that now, not when Jesse needed her so urgently. She gave the stranger a quick smile and started edging away, just as he blurted, "Did you say *was?*"

"Adele died six years ago," she told him, waiting for the inevitable look of annoyance that accompanied every such explanation she'd given her sister's unending parade of old lovers. This man, though, surprised her. His face softened in sympathy, and he reached to take her hands in his.

"I'm sorry. Really." He sounded genuinely concerned, as if he regretted having opened an old wound. "That must've been hard on you."

"It was," Sarah admitted, startled at his response. Maybe they hadn't been lovers, if his first thought was for her rather than Adele. "I never . . . Did you know her?"

That was a silly question, she realized as soon as she'd asked it. But he didn't seem to think so. "Not that well," he said. "I used to work for the photographer next door to her doughnut shop."

Adele must have been involved with someone else at the time, Sarah thought, because this was the kind of man any woman would find appealing. He had a solid, muscular presence that spoke of hard-fought days and harder nights, and his square jaw was shadowed by the stubble of a beard that matched his tousled, dark hair. Still, she had the feeling there was more to this man than just the earthy sensuality her sister always coveted. His steel gray eyes were tempered with compassion, and that unexpected warmth contrasted oddly with his rough-hewn, rugged face.

"Well," she said a little breathlessly, taking a step back, "it's been six years. Now—"

"Can I buy you a cup of coffee?"

For a moment she let herself enjoy the temptation before realizing what an irresponsible idea that was. Just because this stranger's touch left her skin tingling with awareness didn't mean she could stop for coffee with him. Not when Jesse was locked up in jail.

"No, really, I've got to run," she said, feeling a tremor of regret that she would never even know this man's name. "Thanks anyway." Without glancing back—it was silly to wish she'd gotten a better look at him—she hurried down the steps and darted across the street toward the police station, noticing from the reflection in the bakery window that he was still watching her.

It was crazy, though, to let her thoughts linger on a man she would never see again. Right now she had her nephew to worry about.

Just when she'd dared to hope he was straightening out, Officer Winslow had called to report that Jesse was in trouble again. He had skipped school a few times before, but this was the first time he'd been caught smoking in the old Reardon mansion, where the worst kids in town hung out. If he was mixing with that crowd again, Sarah knew, she was in for a tough summer.

Checking her reflection in the dust-spotted window of the police station, she squared her shoulders and pushed open the heavy door.

"I'm here to pick up my nephew," she told the young policeman at the front desk. "Jesse Corcoran."

He didn't bat an eyelash. "Yes, ma'am."

All right! Sarah exulted to herself as he disappeared into the back room. She must have impressed him as the very soul of respectability... which, for anyone connected with the notorious Adele Corcoran, was no small feat. Her sister's reputation as the most promiscuous girl in town had been established long before she came home pregnant from a weekend with the mayor's son.

Jesse emerged from the back room with his usual swagger, but his cocky grin looked a little shaky, and she felt her heart twist. He was so dear, so special, this boy who had replaced the children she yearned for and would never have. Her first instinct was to hug him, reassure him, but he would never forgive a greeting like that in front of an audience. Instead, she gave him a comforting smile and stayed on her side of the desk.

"Hi, hon."

He only nodded, but she could read the gratitude in his eyes. *Thanks for not making a fuss.* "Uh, yeah," he said. "Sorry you had to come down here."

"No problem," she said lightly, although the school principal had been outraged by her leaving an hour early. The Gilroy Elementary School library was supposed to stay open until four, even though no student would ever darken its doors a week before summer vacation. "Is there someone here I need to talk to?"

The policeman answered for Jesse. "Not this time, ma'am. We can't charge him when all he's got are the rolling papers."

"Rolling papers?" Sarah repeated blankly. "You don't mean—"

"Marijuana," he confirmed, and she felt her stomach tighten, her skin grow cold. Surely her nephew wasn't getting involved with drugs. But one look at Jesse, scuffing his foot against the worn industrial carpet as he avoided her gaze, told her that his skipping school was the least of their problems.

"If we have to bring him in again, though," the policeman added, "it won't be so easy. You'd better see to it he stays out of trouble."

"Yes, of course," she agreed, wondering how she could keep a promise like that. She would have to worry about it later. For now all that mattered was getting Jesse out of here. "Jess, you ready?"

"Yeah," he said, with a faint quirk of relief in his voice. "Anytime."

"And he admitted it!" Sarah gave up all pretense of scanning the Help Wanted section and threw up her hands. "Skipping school is one thing, but smoking marijuana? I've got to get him away from those kids."

Her friend moved the newspaper out of the way and sat down on the book-repair table. "It's hard in a town like this," Eileen said sympathetically. "Especially when school gets out and there's nothing to do."

"If I could afford it I'd stay home all summer, just to keep an eye on him." She had struggled over her checkbook for three hours last night before giving up on that plan. "But now more than ever I need the money to send him to college this fall. Or at least to junior college. It's like he's right on the edge, and I've got to keep him out of trouble."

"Was he sorry, at least? Maybe all he needed was a scare."

"He was sorry I found out, that's all. 'It's no big deal,' he kept saying. *No big deal!*" The words stung all the more, echoing as they did her husband's constant excuse for spending weeks on end away from home. But she didn't need memories of Phil right now, not when the problem was Jesse. "It just scares me how easily he could turn out to be like Adele."

"You've raised him better than that," the other librarian said comfortingly. "But you're right. Hanging out with that gang isn't the best way to spend a summer. Maybe he could get a job, too."

Sarah grimaced, already envisioning Jesse's idea of a job. "Like going on the road with some photographer he met in jail. Can you believe this guy offered him a job and Jesse wants to take it? I told him he's crazy if he thinks I'd let him drive Route 66 with some convict I don't even know.''

"As opposed to some convict you *do* know, right?" Eileen teased. "Remember, travel is supposed to broaden your horizons. Maybe that's what Jesse needs.''

Maybe it was, but her nephew was not traveling all over the country with a total stranger he'd met in the police station, of all places. Even if this Ryan wasn't a criminal, he still didn't sound like the kind of chaperon Jesse needed. "Can't you just imagine the kind of trouble a teenager could get into on a trip like that?''

Eileen's eyes crinkled. "The kind I would've given a million dollars for, before I got old and sedate. Sarah, where's your sense of adventure?''

Adele had used to say the same thing, back in high school when a shower of pebbles against their bedroom window meant an invitation to some party down by the creek. Adele had gone blithely chasing adventure night after night, month after month, and look where it had gotten her.

"I can't afford a sense of adventure," Sarah objected, before realizing how silly that sounded. A sense of adventure was something you had to be born with, and there was no use regretting that she'd always been the responsible twin. "Jesse's got enough for both of us. What I really need is some way to keep him out of trouble and still hold down a summer job.''

"Well, you could always waitress the night shift at Angelo's," Eileen suggested. "The pay isn't so great, but you might make it up in tips.''

Sarah reached for the Help Wanted section again, already shaking her head. "Anybody who could tip me enough to send Jesse through college wouldn't be eating at Angelo's.''

Before Eileen could answer, the library door swung open. Silhouetted against the sunlight outdoors was the figure of a man, and Sarah blinked. He looked remarkably like the one she had bumped into on the courthouse steps, the stranger whose image was still curiously vivid in her mind.

"Hi, can I help you?" Eileen called.

He advanced a few steps into the room, and Sarah caught her breath.

"Yeah," he said, squinting at a slip of paper as he approached the desk. Then his glance fell on her, and she saw the recognition hit him with the same force that was already rocketing through her veins. "Don't tell me," he said, as the same slow, incredulous smile she remembered from two days ago crossed his face. "*You're* Sarah Corcoran?"

"Speak of adventure, and what walks in the door?" Eileen murmured. Showing a great deal more poise than Sarah would have credited her with, she gathered up a stack of books and moved toward the shelves with a barely noticeable glance of appraisal at the man whose sleeveless shirt and worn jeans seemed completely out of place in the Gilroy Elementary School library.

Sarah stood, feeling suddenly a little too warm. "Yes," she said. "How did you know where to find me?"

He looked at her strangely. "Jesse—I guess he's your nephew?—said you wanted to see *me.*" Before she could protest that she didn't even know him, he prompted, "About the Route 66 shoot."

With a jolt of disbelief, it hit her. This man must be the photographer who had offered Jesse a job. And Jesse, taking a wild gamble, must have reported that his aunt just needed a little reassurance before letting him embark on such a trip.

"I see," Sarah said. Had her nephew seriously thought all she needed before permitting a cross-country journey was to meet the photographer? Or was he planning to go regardless of whether or not she gave permission? "Mr., uh . . ."

"Just Ryan," he said, extending his hand and giving her the same easy, appraising glance she had remembered half-a-dozen times already. "Listen, you want to move someplace else? Get some lunch or something?"

"Well..." She was surprised by how much she liked the idea, even though she'd already taken her lunch break. "I can't just walk out at two o'clock in the afternoon."

"Maybe some other time." He leaned back against the bookshelf beside her desk, looking very much at home. "I would've been here earlier, but Bunker canceled out and I had to go pick up the Winnebago. Jesse said school's over Friday, so I figured we could hit the road Saturday."

"You *what?*" Sarah blurted, and stopped as she saw his incredulous smile.

"Talk about coincidence," he murmured. "I can't believe you're Jesse's aunt."

She could feel herself blushing and hoped the man wouldn't notice. He hadn't come here to see her, anyway; all he wanted was to talk about a job she couldn't possibly let Jesse accept. "Well, I am," she said. "He was my sister's son, so—"

He looked startled. "You mean Adele? She was his mom?"

"That's right." Apparently her sister had never mentioned Jesse to this man...but then, Ryan had said they didn't know each other that well. "And now that I'm responsible for him, I can't send him off to California for the summer."

Ryan looked surprised at her vehemence, but he still didn't back away. "Why not? Is he supposed to spend summers with his dad or something?"

"No, it's not that." Jesse's dad would never know or care what he did with his summers. As soon as Adele had announced that she was pregnant, Tom Bradley had given her a check for five thousand dollars and taken off for Europe, where he had eventually married a Swiss travel agent and had never once written to ask about his son. "It's just that I can't let Jesse go to California with someone we don't even know!"

"Well, that's why I'm here," he said easily, glancing at the crumpled slip of paper in his hand and then back at her.

"I figured you'd probably have some questions...Sarah Corcoran. Anybody ever call you Corky?"

There was no reason to feel so acutely aware of this man, no reason to notice the intriguing warmth of his smile. Her first priority was to look out for Jesse, after all, and Ryan wasn't making it easy. "No."

"They should," he said, leaning back against the bookshelf and eyeing her thoughtfully. "Anyway, Corky, about the trip..."

It shouldn't be this difficult to carry on a simple conversation, Sarah thought, a little rattled by how quickly he seemed to shift gears. All she had to do was explain that she couldn't just send Jesse off to California for the summer. But already she could hear the echo of her nephew's vow: *One way or another, I'm getting out of this town.*

She took a deep breath. Maybe if she approached this right, she could enlist the photographer's help. "Ryan, don't take this the wrong way. It's just that I have a responsibility for Jesse. And I'd really appreciate it if you'd tell him he can't go with you."

He shook his head, his eyes narrowed. "Why would I want to do that?"

Even though his tone hadn't changed, she felt a definite challenge in the air. This man could be a formidable adversary, Sarah realized, and she'd better not admit that Jesse might run off if she refused to let him go. "Well," she explained, forcing herself to look straight at him as she spoke, "because he'll take it better from you than from me. And I can't just let him go off for the summer without anyone to look after him."

"What do you mean, look after him?"

"You know. Make sure he's all right."

Ryan shifted his stance, leaning back against the bookshelf with the same lazy, casual grace she'd noticed the other day. "What are we talking about, here? Has he got some kind of disease or something?"

"No, of course not." Was the man being deliberately stubborn, or did he really not understand the problem? "But Jesse's only seventeen."

There was a pause. "So?"

"So, I can't let him go chasing off to California without someone to keep an eye on him! He's—"

Ryan straightened up. "I'm not bringing along a nanny," he said. "We're gonna be crowded enough as it is, and I've still got to find a researcher."

Eileen picked that exact moment to return to the desk and gave them both a cheerful smile, as if she hadn't heard their raised voices clear across the room. "Sarah's a researcher," she announced brightly.

"Not anymore," Sarah said. Her research career had ended a long time ago, right after she signed the divorce papers and moved back to Gilroy with her nephew. But Ryan was looking intrigued.

"No kidding. I had a guy lined up to research all the sites along the way, but he backed out on me. Can you...I mean, I thought you were a librarian."

"That's right." *A librarian with no sense of adventure,* she could almost hear Adele saying with that mixture of pride and ruefulness. Exasperating as her twin could be, she had still known Sarah better than anyone else. And Adele would probably be amazed if she could see how this man was affecting her.

"But you know how to do research?" His voice was suddenly eager, suddenly intense. "I'm serious, I need someone who can find all those background details the editor likes to see. You know, who built that bridge and where they got the wood. Can you do that kind of thing?"

Of course she could, but it was ridiculous to even think of spending the summer traveling Route 66 in a Winnebago with a man Jesse had met in jail. Wasn't it? "Yes," Sarah said. "But—"

"She's terrific," Eileen interrupted. "The cultural anthropology professor at Northwestern said Sarah was the best he'd ever worked with."

How on earth had Eileen remembered that? It had been five years since she'd left Chicago and brought Jesse back to her hometown...knowing she would never again find such satisfying work, but knowing, too, that family had to come first. Jesse needed a home, and the only place she could afford to give him one was in Gilroy, where her parents had left her their house.

"You couldn't find a better researcher," Eileen concluded, and Ryan smiled at Sarah with new warmth.

"Hey, terrific."

Maybe it would be a pleasure to exercise her skills again, but it would be wildly irresponsible to embark on a trip like this with a man she barely knew. Especially a man who was obviously more her sister's type. "Ryan," she began, but he wasn't finished.

"This is great. Last thing I expected was to find an assistant and a researcher in one stop."

"You haven't," she protested. Adele wouldn't hesitate to spend a summer on the road with a man whose lazy smile made her feel unusually warm, but Adele had never worried about setting the right example for Jesse. "Ryan, I can't do this. I don't even know anything about you."

"I'll give you some references," he said easily. "Besides, I thought you wanted to keep an eye on your nephew. Make sure he doesn't fall off a cliff in the middle of Kansas. Make sure he doesn't get attacked by sharks in the Mohave Desert."

She couldn't help smiling at the dry humor in his voice. But even if it meant being able to keep an eye on Jesse, she couldn't just take off for the summer. Not when she had to come up with the money for college. "I still can't do it. I have to work."

"Don't you get the summer off?"

"Sarah has another job planned," Eileen said sweetly. "The tips alone are going to pay for Jesse's first year of school."

That was a wild exaggeration, Sarah knew, but already Ryan was turning back to her with a gleam in his eye. "You want to get into a bidding war? What kind of money are we talking about here?"

She swallowed. He couldn't possibly pay her enough to get Jesse started in college, could he? Besides, researching Route 66 with a man whose touch could make her skin tingle would be a crazy way to spend the summer.

Wouldn't it?

"Well," she said slowly, "it depends on how much time you're talking about. For three months—"

"More like two. The magazine deadline is the middle of August."

Two months of work. Two months of adventure. Two months on the road with Jesse and a man she couldn't afford to let herself enjoy.

It would be irresponsible. It would be crazy. It would be completely different from anything she had ever done.

It would help her get Jesse into college.

She could feel the silence growing longer, growing louder. She could almost hear Eileen willing her to answer. Sarah closed her eyes, calculating wildly, and wondered if she could possibly spend a summer working with this man. She took a deep breath, opened her eyes and named a figure.

There was a pause. Then, with a quick grin, Ryan reached forward and shook her hand.

"Corky," he said, "you've got yourself a job."

Chapter Two

What had she gotten herself into?

Sarah took an armload of shirts from the closet, threw them onto her bed and started yanking out the hangers.

Two months on the road with a man she felt much too acutely aware of. With a teenager who couldn't wait to get out of town and start testing his boundaries. With a research assignment more challenging than any she had ever tackled before.

She must have been out of her mind.

"Sarah, what happened to my Stryker-concert shirt?" Jesse called from his room. "I had it yesterday!"

"You had it on the floor with a week's worth of laundry," she called back. "Check the dryer."

Jesse, in spite of his cool facade, was ecstatic about the prospect of two months on the road as a photographer's assistant. He had packed and repacked his canvas duffel bag three times already, not at all daunted by having to cram an entire summer's worth of clothes into a single knapsack.

He came bounding upstairs into her room, waving his clean Stryker shirt like a banner. "Ahh-right! Thanks." Then, at the sight of her bed piled high with clothes, he halted. "You think maybe we ought to rent a truck?"

Sarah couldn't help laughing, and as he grinned in response, she reached out and ruffled his hair, enjoying the rare moment of closeness. "I'm not bringing all this," she told him. "I'm just trying to decide."

"Just grab anything," Jesse suggested. "Ryan's gonna be here in twenty minutes."

"I know that!" She had put off packing for too long, but there had been so many other chores to finish. Writing year-end reports to the school board. Arranging for Lillian next door to keep an eye on the house. Briefing Eileen on the calls she was sure to receive from the busybody school principal during Sarah's absence, then biting her tongue when Eileen predicted that this would be the best summer of her life.

"It'll be an adventure! It'll be good for Jesse. *And* it'll be two months with a man who, if you don't mind my saying so, looks like exactly what you need."

The last thing she needed was the kind of man Adele used to bring home, in spite of the flutter she still felt whenever she remembered the teasing warmth of Ryan's smile. "Eileen, come on, don't start planning a summer romance!"

"Did I say one word about a summer romance?"

"You didn't have to." She knew perfectly well what her friend had in mind, and it wasn't going to happen. "For one thing, he's not my type. And besides, Jesse's already seen way too many casual affairs."

"Probably so, but one summer romance doesn't mean you're going to turn into your sister," Eileen said. "You've got more sense than that."

"Adele had sense!" No one had ever understood that, and after so many years, Sarah knew it was a waste of time trying to defend her twin. Maybe Adele hadn't shown much sense when it came to flaunting her series of lovers, but there was more to her than just the town "bad girl" everyone remembered. There was also the sister who could make anything seem like fun, who had wept with Sarah over the loss of her baby and who'd laughed with her over things no one else would understand.

The sister who would applaud her for even considering a summer romance.

Even so, Jesse didn't need to see any more casual affairs happening right before his eyes. Sarah had made a point of telling Ryan at the library that their relationship had to stay strictly business, and she'd felt a ripple of trepidation when he'd simply stared at her without answering.

Then he'd given her the slow, easy smile that made her breath come a little faster. "Right," he'd said. "If that's how you want it."

What had she gotten herself into? Sarah wondered again, grabbing four shirts that would go equally well with her old jeans, plaid walking shorts and khaki divided skirt. Nobody could make it through two months with only three changes of clothes, but she had already decided to save her energy for the arguments that really mattered.

There would probably be a lot of those. Jesse was avidly looking forward to the freedom of the road, and she knew he expected Ryan to side with him in pressing for liberties she would never allow at home. Staying up until all hours, eating nothing but taco chips and probably going for midnight snacks in all the local taverns. Such wide-open spontaneity, according to the photographer, was an integral part of any road trip.

"But if you want to make sure he's tucked in bed by eight o'clock every night," Ryan had concluded, "that's up to you. Just don't expect me to back you up."

Well, she could look after Jesse with no help from anyone. She had done it for six years already—longer than that, if you counted the times Adele used to drop him off for a weekend and return a month later.

It was tempting to blame those occasions for the breakup of her marriage, but Sarah knew her nephew's presence hadn't been the final straw. The final straw had been when Phil, who'd promised to be home for their fourth anniversary "come hell or high water," had phoned to announce that his new client needed a little more hand-holding. She'd realized then that when it came to promises, Phil's were worth no more than her father's had been.

"Sarah, you're not bringing all these groceries, are you?"

Jesse's horrified cry came floating up the stairs, and she halted in front of her makeup drawer.

"Yes, I am," she called back. "There's a kitchen in the Winnebago, and there won't be fast-food franchises everywhere we stop."

"Yeah, but four cans of asparagus?" She could hear him scrabbling through the boxes stacked near the door. "Lemon juice? Stewed tomatoes? Why can't we bring something good, like taco chips?"

"Because we're not eating taco chips every night for the next two months!" She dropped a packet of eye shadow and a mascara wand into her bag, wondering whether she would even need such niceties on the road. "If Ryan wants to eat junk food, that's his business. But I hope he's got better sense than that."

The man had to have sense in order to be employed by *Odyssey Magazine,* she reminded herself as she zipped her canvas carryall. She had seen copies of the glossy travel publication in various libraries and waiting rooms, and the very name spoke of glamour and prestige. Knowing that a magazine like *Odyssey* was buying Ryan's story, she felt safe waiting until they paid him before expecting her check.

Meanwhile, though, it was a relief knowing that as soon as the check arrived she could pay for Jesse's first semester at Gilroy Community College. Financially, at least, she had made the right decision.

She deposited her carryall by the front door, noting that Jesse had already moved the groceries and his duffel bag to the edge of the porch, ready for departure at a moment's notice. It was sweet seeing him so excited about this project, Sarah thought as she gazed at his rapt profile. Maybe the chance to get out of Gilroy, away from all the people who expected the worst from Adele Corcoran's son, was just what Jesse needed.

"Ryan's coming!" His voice was deliberately even, but she could hear the excitement in it. Sarah joined him on the porch, feeling a curious tingle of anticipation as the giant motor home pulled up to the curb.

What had she gotten herself into?

"Morning," Ryan called, slamming the driver's door behind him and striding up the walk. He wore faded jeans and a crumpled shirt under a multipocketed vest, and it was easy to imagine him standing by the freeway with one of those handmade California Or Bust signs. He seemed out of place in a neighborhood like this, Sarah thought, where everyone's lawn was perfectly trimmed and every house sported regimental rows of flowers along the front walk.

But he didn't seem to notice anything amiss. He gave her and Jesse an easy, friendly smile, ran up the steps to the porch and stopped dead at the sight of the boxes.

"You guys get evicted or something?"

Jesse grinned. "Looks that way, doesn't it?"

"There's not that much here," Sarah protested. The Winnebago looked bigger than she had imagined; they should have no problem fitting in a few boxes of groceries. "I'm just not letting us eat fast food every night, that's all."

Ryan squinted into one of the boxes, lifted a can and gazed at her quizzically. "Stewed tomatoes?"

"We don't have to bring it," Jesse volunteered. "It's not like we're gonna starve or anything."

"I don't think there's a can opener, anyway," Ryan said. "A bottle opener, yeah. But I'm not sure if the kitchen even works."

"It has to work," Sarah exclaimed. "Haven't you ever used it?"

"Well, I keep film in the refrigerator. But that's about it." He dropped the can back in the box, then shrugged. Squatting down beside the boxes, he lifted the first load in one smooth, effortless move that made her close her eyes for a moment. "What the hell, it'll be something different. Right?"

Jesse opened his mouth to speak, closed it again and hoisted the next couple of boxes. "Uh, yeah," he said. "Right."

It took them less than five minutes to load all the gear into the motor home, and Sarah used the time to make one last check of the house. When she locked the door behind her, she saw the two of them just closing the last storage compartment on the side.

Jesse turned to greet her with an unmistakable look of pride. "Sarah, you gotta see this. This is great."

Ryan stepped back, allowing him to conduct the tour. "Look, there's a seat by the door where you can watch TV. You can get in the front seat from back here, or you can get in the door like a regular car. There's a tape deck, so we can listen to my Stryker tapes—"

"Sorry, Jess, the tape deck doesn't work," Ryan interrupted, and Sarah gave a silent prayer of thanks. Two months without Jesse's blaring music seemed too good to be true. "But everything else is in good shape."

There was slightly more room than she had expected, and it was a relief to see that they wouldn't be living in each other's laps twenty-four hours a day. "You've got the bedroom back there," Jesse told her, pointing past the kitchen. "Ryan and me are up here. We're gonna trade off—the couch opens into a bed and there's another one over the top. You sure that's big enough?" he asked the photographer.

"No problem," Ryan assured him. "I've slept in doorways smaller than that."

Jesse grinned, but Sarah wondered if he might have been speaking literally. Even though Ryan's references had checked out and an *Odyssey Magazine* secretary had confirmed that only last week he'd been in the editor's office talking about a shoot, there was still an unsettling roughness about the man.

All the more reason not to let this feeling of attraction get out of hand.

"Only one thing you gotta watch out for," he told her as she tried to banish the qualm of doubt. "Don't put anything in your bedroom closet. That's the darkroom."

"We can develop pictures the same day we take 'em," Jesse announced. "If something doesn't turn out right, we'll just shoot it again the next day."

"That won't happen often, though," Ryan reminded him, closing the darkroom door and making her aware again of how fluidly he moved. "I've been doing this long enough that there shouldn't be many retakes."

He sounded less casual when he talked about photography, Sarah noticed. More intense. More sure of himself. Well, he must be good at his work if *Odyssey* had chosen him to shoot their Route 66 story.

"This is really nice," she stated, relieved that her voice sounded normal. The stove and microwave and even the sink looked brand-new, as if no one had ever used them. "Ryan, how long have you had this motor home?"

"It's called a Minnie Winnie," Jesse informed her as Ryan answered.

"My partner and I bought it a few years ago when we were shooting in Alberta. Bunker's been using it lately, but he's kept it up all right."

Bunker must be the researcher whose job she had inherited. She owed him, Sarah thought again. "What's he doing, anyway?"

Ryan snorted as he leaned over the dinette table to open the tip-out window. "He's in Las Vegas, getting married. Fourth time."

From his tone of voice, she gathered Ryan wasn't a big fan of wedded bliss. "You're not married, right?" She already knew he was single; the secretary at *Odyssey* had confirmed it. "Are you divorced?"

He straightened up, looking grim. "No," he said. "Any other questions?"

She knew better than to linger on what was evidently a prickly topic, but Jesse answered for her. "Yeah, how do you hook up the generator?"

"I'll show you when we stop at a campsite," Ryan told him. "We'll work out a list of who does what, and switch around. You know how to drive, don't you?"

"Yeah, sure." Jesse sounded awed. "You mean I can do some of the driving?"

"Count on it. I'll get us out of town, and then you can take over. Unless," Ryan amended with a questioning look at Sarah, "you'd rather start?"

She would rather not drive a monster like this at all, but it wouldn't be fair to refuse. "Go ahead," she said. "I've got to start looking over my notes."

Jesse scrambled forward into the passenger seat, where he busied himself with the window controls and the contents of the glove compartment as Ryan checked the door latches and came around front to the driver's seat. Sarah gathered her file of maps and information on the road and settled into the swivel chair behind Jesse. "Seat belts," she reminded him.

With a disbelieving glance over his shoulder, Ryan fumbled for the buckle of his seat belt and fastened it with a loud click before starting the ignition.

"Okay," he said. "Route 66, here we come."

The streets of Chicago were even more congested than he remembered, and Ryan had to admit Sarah's familiarity with the city came in handy. "You can be the official navigator," he suggested, and she gave him a quick, sparkling smile that made him wonder once again if keeping this relationship strictly business might prove more difficult than he'd guessed.

The lady was hard to figure, Ryan thought as they followed the Kennedy Expressway. She was the spitting image of Adele, but somehow the resemblance didn't extend past the long-legged exterior.

"You want the Jackson Boulevard exit," she announced, interrupting his reverie. "Coming up in about a mile."

He'd had a hard time keeping his eyes on the road since she and Jesse had traded seats. She wore white denim shorts and a neatly tailored blouse, very simple, very plain. But her legs were so sleek, so perfect, so enticing that he was finding it difficult to remember this wasn't Adele sitting next to him. This lady, he was pretty sure, wouldn't be too pleased if he braked by the side of the road and started running his tongue across her smooth, silky thigh.

Adele would have loved it.

Adele, in spite of—or maybe because of—her inability to carry on more than a two-minute conversation, would have been a much easier companion on a trip like this. But then, back when he knew Adele, he wouldn't have been capable of organizing a trip like this. He certainly wouldn't have been able to convince the *Odyssey* editor that of all the photographers ever listed with the magazine, no one could do a better job of shooting Route 66.

Huey hadn't been completely convinced, even after a lengthy explanation of why things would be different this time, but at least he had agreed to look at Ryan's photos. Once he saw them, Ryan's name would be back on the list. Maybe not at the top, but he would be working again. And before long he'd be taking his pick of assignments, the way he had done before he let it all slide downhill.

This story would be his salvation.

"There's the exit," Sarah said, pointing, and he quickly eased into the right lane.

"Yeah. Thanks."

They made their way up Jackson Boulevard, past the Sears Tower rising beyond view, and Jesse craned his neck out the Winnebago window for a glimpse of the top. "Man, that's taller than I remembered. You think we ought to take a picture from up there?"

"We don't want city photos," Ryan explained. "This is really a highway story. All we need here is the beginning of the road."

They reached the edge of Grant Park, where the bronze lions guarded the entrance to the Art Institute of Chicago, and Ryan stopped. "Okay, guys. This is it."

The first photo on any assignment was always a special pleasure, and it was even better when he had the freedom to shoot whatever he liked. The old Route 66 signs had been taken down when the interstate rolled through, but anyone who had traveled the road to paradise would remember that it began at the corner of Adams and Michigan Avenue.

"Go ahead and wander around if you want," he told Sarah and Jesse, relieved that he could turn his attention back to business. "I've got to find my shot."

"Don't you need any help?" Jesse asked. "Seems like if I'm your assistant, I oughta be doing something."

The kid had a point, but for some reason Ryan wanted to keep this shot to himself. The first and the last had a magic of their own, and never more so than on this story. The story that would reestablish him in the field he loved.

"You're right," Ryan acknowledged. "But where I'm really going to need your help is in the printing, and in setting up the lights. Right now I'm just scouting around."

He could see Sarah watching him thoughtfully; then she put her arm around the kid's shoulder and gave him a gentle squeeze. "Jess, let's go look at the Art Institute. We'll check back here in an hour, and every half hour after that until Ryan's finished."

She understood, he realized with amazement. Without any awkward explanations, she knew he wanted to do this alone. "I'll see you later," Ryan promised, and watched her with a curious tug of gratitude as they disappeared up the steps of the gray stone building.

He was on his own.

The pulse of the city was invigorating, and for a while he let it soak into him without making any effort to find a shot. There would be one, Ryan knew. There would likely be half a dozen within the next few minutes. Already he could feel his senses quickening, could feel the intensity of the light and the density of the shadows on the sidewalk around him. He could feel the color of the cars moving past him and the texture of the buildings just ahead. God, he loved this! There was nothing like the joy of hefting his camera and seeing, everywhere he looked, the vivid angles and patterns and wonders of color and light, waiting to be immortalized on film.

He spent the next hour glorying in the sights around him, knowing he was shooting far more than he could ever use but unable to stop, basking in the sheer joy of being behind a camera again. He had shot a few perfunctory assignments during the last couple of months, but this was the first one that proved he hadn't lost the magic, that he could still make a camera sing. The first that promised that, in spite of the past two years, he was on his way back to the life he wanted.

By the time he finished his fourth roll of film, Ryan felt drained. He slowly flexed his shoulders, aware of the world around him sliding back into perspective, and wished he could keep the electric sensation a little longer. It never lasted, though. All he could do when that frenzied passion ebbed was to find himself a cold beer and a warm bed, although without someone in it the bed was never truly warm.... It was then, with a sudden shock, he remembered Sarah and Jesse.

They were waiting outside the Art Institute, exactly as promised, and neither of them seemed disturbed by his having been gone so long. "You get some good pictures?" Jesse asked in greeting.

"Yeah," Ryan said, still trying to get the prospect of a warm bed out of his mind before Sarah could read his thoughts like she'd done before. She wasn't the kind of woman he could frolic with the way Adele had been; he knew that perfectly well. "Tomorrow I'll show you how to use the processing equipment, and we'll get them printed up." Now that he had his magic back, sharing it with an assistant seemed a lot more appealing.

They walked back to the motor home in relaxing harmony, with Ryan still glowing from the wonder of the afternoon. Digging the keys out of his pocket, he tossed them to Sarah and laughed with approval when she caught them one-handed. "Here you go, Corky. You can get us out of Chicago."

She looked at the keys as if he had just handed her a ticking bomb. "You mean, right now?"

"Unless you want to spend another couple of weeks here. Do some shopping, visit the stockyards..." His high spirits didn't seem to be rubbing off on her, Ryan noticed. "You want to wait till tomorrow? We don't have to get to Cicero tonight."

Sarah swallowed. "No, that's okay. I mean, I love being here again, but I know we have to keep going—"

"Can I drive some more?" Jesse interrupted. "Sarah, I'll trade you for tomorrow."

With an almost visible sigh of relief, she handed him the keys. "Sure. Once we're out of town, I'll go ahead and start dinner."

"No stewed tomatoes, okay?" Ryan said as Jesse unlocked the back door. She only smiled at him, settling in the passenger seat and waiting for Jesse to fasten his seat belt.

Ryan let the two of them navigate down Ogden Avenue as he extracted an icy beer from the refrigerator and twisted the cap off, savoring his first sip. Jesse had turned the radio to some jazz piece, and he sank down into the chair behind Sarah to let himself float in the rhythm, still envisioning the shots he had captured this afternoon. That one of the guy with the plastic-tub drums, flailing away to the music only he could hear. The cabdriver with the black arm band, staring morosely at the red traffic light in front of him. The sun reflecting off Orchestra Hall, lighting the floating sparkles of dust that rose like a chorus of music notes into the sky.

God, what a day. He felt at peace with the world right now, better than he had at any time during the past two years. He should have gotten back on track sooner, Ryan knew. He should have listened to Bunker and Huey and everyone else who had tried to tell him to put the past behind him and move on.

He hadn't listened, and now he regretted it. But at least he was starting to move.

By the time they reached their campsite, the summer twilight was fading into dark. Ryan roused himself to show Jesse the trick of connecting the generator, pleased to notice that the kid had a good mechanical sense. They lingered outdoors, enjoying the cool of the evening, the chirp of crickets in the air and the sharp smell of something spicy that drifted out from the kitchen.

Sarah was chopping green peppers to add to the onions sizzling on the stove when Ryan came in for another beer. He sniffed, curious, and she moved closer to the counter so he could squeeze past her.

"Guess the kitchen works, huh?" he observed, looking over her shoulder and trying not to let himself think about the last time a woman had cooked dinner for him. "What's that?"

"You don't care, as long as it's not stewed tomatoes," she reminded him, and he grinned.

"You got me there." Leaning against the refrigerator, he watched her slide the peppers into the frying pan, turn down the heat and measure three handfuls of pasta into a pot of boiling water. "You cook very often?"

"Well, just breakfast and dinner." Sarah stirred the onions again, setting off a sharply sweet aroma, then opened a package of ground beef, which she emptied into another skillet. "If Jesse had a choice, though, he'd live on taco chips. I wouldn't be surprised if you find a couple of bags stashed around the darkroom."

Ryan raised his eyebrows. "They won't last long if I do."

"Don't tell me I'm spending the summer with *two* taco-chip fanatics!" She took a can of corn from the cupboard and emptied it into the pepper-and-onion mixture. "I can see it now—three o'clock in the morning and you guys are closeted in the darkroom, scarfing down junk food."

"You wanna join us? I'll leave the door open."

"You leave the door open and no one in the camp-grounds will sleep through all that crunching."

She stood on tiptoe to reach the saltshaker on the high shelf overhead, and Ryan handed it down to her. "Maybe," he said, "I'd better put you in charge of dealing with irate neighbors."

"Maybe you'd better put me in charge of cleaning out the darkroom."

He laughed. "Whoa. I gotta warn you, you'd be taking your life in your hands."

This was fun, Sarah thought. Ryan was better at lazy conversation than Phil had ever been, and just because they had to keep their relationship strictly business was no reason they couldn't trade easy banter at the end of a work-day. She started tearing a head of lettuce into pieces, and when Ryan reached for a chunk of tomato beside the bowl, she slapped at his hand.

"You stay out of my salad and I'll stay out of your dark-room."

He popped the tomato into his mouth anyway and reached for another. "Okay. It's a deal."

"Some deal. You're already in my salad!"

"All right, how's this for a deal? You take care of the cooking, and Jesse and I'll take care of the driving."

"That'd be great," Sarah told him. Especially since she had expected to take care of the cooking all along. "I was a little shaky about driving something this big."

Ryan smiled at her, and she felt another twinge of pleasure as his eyes lingered on hers. "I thought you might be. This way we all get the best of the deal."

She turned back to the salad, still conscious of his gaze on her. Business, she reminded herself. They were going to keep things strictly business. "You're missing your calling, you know that? You should be negotiating for peace in the Middle East."

"I should be shooting in the Middle East." And as she gave him a startled glance, he lifted an imaginary camera. "Photos."

"You mean you'd actually want to go over there?"

"For a shoot? In a minute."

"But it's full of terrorists."

"It's as safe as staying at home," he said, and his voice was hard. But when she turned to put the salad in the refrigerator, he looked as relaxed as ever. Maybe, Sarah thought, she had just imagined that flash of tension.

"Have you worked overseas before?" she asked, moving back to the stove and covering the pan of ground beef.

"Off and on. Mostly in Asia."

"And you miss it?"

There was a pause. "Yeah," he said. "But I won't be going back."

"That's right, *Odyssey* doesn't do many stories overseas, do they?"

Ryan drained the last of his beer and rested the empty bottle in his hand, looking at her curiously. "I didn't know you read *Odyssey*."

"Well, not every month. But I've seen it."

"In your dentist's waiting room, right?"

"Right," she said, opening the oven door to check the garlic bread. "It's the best part of going to the dentist."

"No, the best part is when he's got your mouth wide open and asks if you've seen any good movies lately."

"You can always start humming the theme from *Rocky*."

Ryan grinned. "I'll keep that in mind. How does it go, anyway?"

They attempted half-a-dozen versions before she gave up to finish the casserole, and Sarah couldn't help laughing as he vowed to request the song from a radio station and dedicate it to her dentist. This man was so easy to talk to!

She drained the ground beef and stirred in the contents of the frying pan, then turned and saw Ryan gazing at her with such curious wonder that she felt an unexpected wave of warmth. For a moment their eyes held, and then he spoke.

"You look so much like Adele," he said, "it knocks me out."

She felt a thud of apprehension in the bottom of her stomach. "I didn't think you knew her that well," she managed to say.

He shrugged, confirming her suspicion. "It was only a couple weeks." Then he glanced toward the door, and for the first time he looked a little uncomfortable. "But Jesse probably... I mean, kids don't want to think about their mothers like... well, you know."

Sarah turned back to the stove, feeling suddenly wooden. She should have guessed. This man had known her sister far better than he would ever know her.

"You're right," she said tightly.

It shouldn't be any surprise. Adele had always been able to take her pick of men, and Ryan obviously liked women with a sense of adventure. It was silly to have imagined that they'd never been lovers, not with Adele's magical ability to draw attention whenever she so much as walked into a room.

Of course she would have drawn this man's attention. Adele had always been the one with all the spirit and fire, and Sarah would always be the quiet, responsible one. That wasn't going to change. And if Ryan hadn't yet figured out the difference between them, it was about time he realized that she had no intention of taking Adele's place.

She drained the noodles and poured the seasoned ground beef over them, transferred the mixture into a serving bowl and set it on the stove top.

"Jesse!" she called out the back door. "Dinner's ready."

Then she turned back to Ryan, who was blocking the refrigerator where the salad waited. Who was slowly caressing the neck of his empty beer bottle. Who, she realized with amazement, was looking with frank admiration at her legs.

"Ryan!" she said sharply. "Listen. I am not Adele."

His eyes swung back to her face, and when he spoke, his voice was troubled.

"I know," he said. "Believe me, Corky, I know."

Chapter Three

You couldn't ask for a better way to spend a summer, Jesse decided as he dug the tripod out of the storage compartment. Getting out of Gilroy was the best part, but even after a single day on the road he could tell that traveling Route 66 was going to be a kick and a half.

He climbed the narrow ladder to the roof of the motor home, then hefted the tripod onto the flat surface, where Ryan stood in the blazing heat, adjusting the lens of his camera.

"This one?" he asked.

Ryan looked up. "Yeah, that oughta do it. Let's see." He deftly unfastened the clamps and settled his camera in position just a few inches above the surface of the roof. Then he squinted into the lens, raised the tripod another inch and beckoned to Jesse. "Look at this. We got it."

Stepping carefully, Jesse squatted down and peered into the lens. The view startled him. The highway, snaking off into the infinite distance, looked so much more vivid through the camera than it did through his own eyes.

"You see?" the photographer said. "Standing up here, you have a sense of where the road goes. But from that angle, it could go on forever."

Jesse nodded. There was a lot more to taking pictures, he was beginning to realize, than just focusing the camera. "This oughta be a good one."

"All we need now is the traffic," Ryan told him. "I want to get one big rig coming over the rise, but it better happen soon. We're coming up on magic hour."

Photographers, Ryan had explained this morning, lived for two periods of time when the light took on a special magic. The first light of sunrise and the last, most intense sunlight of the afternoon turned everything golden for a few shining moments, and any photo taken during that time held a luminous, unmistakable glow.

Magic hour would make this stretch of highway come alive.

They settled down to wait, with Ryan poised by the camera and Jesse near the edge of the roof for a better preview of the approaching traffic. "Station wagon coming up," he reported. "It's not moving very fast."

"No, I need a tractor trailer, a school bus, something like that."

A pickup went by. A motorcycle. Three sedans, shimmering in the heat.

"Damn," Ryan muttered. "We're wasting the light."

"A sports car. Bright red."

"Might be worth a shot." He clicked off a few frames as the car sped toward them. "Nah. Too small."

"What if nothing comes by? We just wasted the whole setup?"

"It won't be the first time." Ryan shifted his weight, trying to ease the tension in his shoulders without losing his view. "We can shoot from the other direction tomorrow morning, but I'd rather get it facing south."

Without comment, Jesse resumed his lookout. "Another station wagon. And a bike right behind it."

The kid was good at this, Ryan thought. No fussing about the endless wait for a perfect shot that might never materialize. No worthless suggestions about hiring a trailer to drive past so they could call it a day. No questions about whether they might get something just as good with a lot less trouble. In fact, Jesse was better company on a shoot like this than Bunker had ever been.

"There's a Jeep coming up. A blue one."

Bunker, though, would've been a lot easier to spend the summer with than Jesse's aunt. There was nothing confusing about Bunker.

Sarah had thrown him for a loop last night. He hadn't been prepared to find himself enjoying such an easy, sparkling, teasing conversation with any woman, much less a woman with whom he'd already agreed that the summer would be strictly business. He'd felt a mixture of regret and relief when she laid down that rule, knowing it would make things a lot simpler if he didn't have to worry about getting involved with his traveling companion.

It would have been a hell of a lot easier, though, traveling with someone like Adele. She had been perfectly safe to enjoy, because they both knew there was no risk of falling in love. Sarah, who had understood so effortlessly that he wanted to shoot his first photo alone, was a different kind of woman altogether.

The kind he could find himself caring about. The kind of woman who could matter.

The kind he had to avoid.

"Something slow... Ahh-right! An oil truck."

Ryan tensed, preparing for the first glimpse of the truck in his viewfinder. When it appeared, he felt his pulse pick up speed. This was exactly what he had envisioned—a lonely giant dwarfed by the mysterious splendor of the road.

"Good...come on...." The light was practically dancing, skimming over the surface of the road, bouncing off the cab of the rig. Two more frames. A tighter focus. One last shot, and the truck moved out of range, leaving Ryan with the familiar rush of adrenaline that marked the end of a successful shoot.

"All right! We got it."

"Yeah?" Jesse sounded as triumphant as he felt. "Want to see if anything else comes along, or is that it?"

"That's it. We've lost the light." He flexed his shoulders, untangled himself from the tripod and shut down the lens of his camera. Moving stiffly, he stood up and twisted his neck in a stretch. At thirty-seven, he was finding it harder to hold an awkward position for half an hour at a time.

They climbed down out of the searing sun, stowed their equipment and headed inside, where Ryan opened the refrigerator and felt the welcome shock of a blast of cold air as he took a bottle of beer for himself and tossed Jesse a soda. "We gotta start running the air-conditioning if this keeps up. Either that or do more shots indoors."

"Yeah, like maybe an ice rink." Popping the top off his soda can, Jesse collapsed onto the couch. "Or a meat locker. Something like that."

"Sounds good." Ryan took a long, cold swallow, touched the icy bottle to his forehead and settled into the swivel chair across from the couch where Jesse sprawled in exhausted comfort. "That oil rig was worth a lot, though. I couldn't have picked a better one."

"Is that gonna be your cover shot?"

"Could be. I don't get to decide, though. The editor does."

"Be great if they used that one," Jesse mused. "I could tell people, 'Look at the cover of *Odyssey Magazine*. I was there.'"

"Yeah. You get kind of a charge out of seeing your stuff on a cover." At least he always had in the past. And he would again, after this shoot restored his reputation. "It won't be out until April, though."

The kid looked incredulous. "How come it takes that long?"

"It always does. That's just the way magazines are."

"April... I'll probably still be in school. At least if Sarah has her way."

"Yeah?" Ryan leaned back a little farther, sliding down so his neck rested on the back of the chair. "You finished with high school?"

"Yeah, I got out a year early because I skipped third grade. So now Sarah's signed me up for college... but I'd rather be *doing* something." He shrugged, dismissing the topic. "Whatever. As long as it's out of Gilroy."

"That shouldn't be too hard. Just about everything is out of Gilroy."

Jesse grinned. "That's for sure. It's, like, nothing but the same stuff, all the time. The same people, the same girls..."

Of course, a kid that age would put girls high on the list, Ryan realized. "That's the trouble with small towns, all right."

There was a pause. Then Jesse spoke again.

"Did you see that girl last night?"

He sounded so carefully nonchalant that Ryan had to fight back a smile. "Guess I missed her."

"She was at the campground. Over by the water."

"Ah." He remembered that feeling vividly, just from hearing the suppressed excitement in Jesse's voice. The tantalizing prickle of awareness, the whisper of possibility, the enticing prospect of a girl who might be more than just a stranger at a campsite. Not that he felt that way about Sarah Corcoran, Ryan assured himself. "Did you get to talk to her?"

"No. She... I don't know, I just noticed her."

"Well, if she's camping on Route 66, we've still got a long way to go."

Jesse set his drink down, gesturing with his hands as he warmed to the topic. "She wasn't really beautiful, exactly.

More like, if you saw her, you'd want to know her. Like you'd keep on seeing her. You know?"

"Sounds pretty intense," Ryan observed.

"I don't know, I only saw her once. It's just, like, I keep seeing her in my mind."

This was none of his business. But Jesse was a good kid, and maybe a word of warning would save him a lot of grief.

"Let me give you some advice," Ryan said slowly. "There's all kinds of women out there, and you'll probably meet a lot of 'em."

Jesse grinned in acknowledgment. "I can handle that."

"And that's fine. I mean, it's fine having somebody you can enjoy, somebody you can have a good time with. There's nothing wrong with that." How could he put this so the kid would understand? Ryan leaned forward, groping for words. "But what you've got to remember is, don't ever let *anyone* mean everything to you."

"You mean, like, getting really serious? I'm not gonna do that. Not for a long time."

"Not ever," Ryan said. "Don't ever let anyone get that close. Because if you lose her—" He broke off, feeling his chest tighten as he forced himself to continue. "Don't let it happen. Don't ever let it happen. Because if you lose her, it'll kill you."

This had been a productive day, Sarah decided as she looked over her notes at the copy machine. Once she had gotten down to work, her research skills seemed to come flooding back. In less than four days, she had found enough material to cover the first two hundred miles of Route 66.

She only hoped Ryan would appreciate it.

But of course it didn't matter whether he did or not, she reminded herself as she headed outside. She wasn't trying to impress Ryan. She was just doing the job she'd been hired to do, and it had nothing to do with impressing a photographer who probably saw her as a pale imitation of Adele.

Not that she cared what he thought. All she cared about was earning the money to start Jesse in college, and the best thing she could say about this trip was that at least her nephew was having a wonderful time.

Jesse seemed to thrive on the photographer's brusque attention. For the past four days he had accompanied Ryan everywhere, whether or not an assistant was needed, and already he had picked up some of Ryan's expressions and gestures. He had even started copying the photographer's walk, which Sarah felt was carrying hero worship a little far.

Still, he was learning more from Ryan than he ever would have learned in Gilroy, and he appeared totally engrossed in their work. "We're gonna get some terrific shots today," he had announced this morning when he and Ryan dropped her off at the library. "First we've gotta do the prints, but then there's this real old truck stop and a place where they make maple syrup."

"Why don't I meet you guys at the syrup place when I finish getting quotes?" Sarah offered. They had been scrupulous about picking her up whenever she completed her work, but surely in this part of the state she could get a ride without much worry.

She did get a ride from a friendly farm wife, who urged her to stop by Funk's Grove, during syrup season, and found the motor home parked in a shady spot. Sarah went inside, blinked as her eyes adjusted to the absence of sun and stopped at the sight of the table piled high with photos.

The very first one caught her eye, and she bent to look at it more closely. Jesse had described this scene a few days ago, she remembered, with the truck nearing the crest of the ridge and the road shimmering beyond it in mysterious, evocative splendor.

Sarah sat down, still staring, and picked it up. "Wow," she said aloud.

This one must be the pick of the crop. There was an unusual strength to it that intrigued her, captivated her, made her feel both the power and the loneliness of the highway.

The light seemed to beckon as well as to threaten, the truck looked both massively solid and strangely fragile, while the road almost hummed with a vast, vibrant energy of its own.

"Wow," she murmured again.

They couldn't all be this good, of course. No one could possibly create art like this five or six times a day. But she had to admit to a new respect for what Ryan and Jesse were doing. Anyone who could make her feel such a tingle of awe must be a better-than-average photographer.

A photographer who wasn't her type, of course, but he certainly had a way with a camera.

The next photo was even better. A cowboy-hatted truck driver waved goodbye to a middle-aged waitress outside a highway diner shaded by the first darkness of twilight. They both looked tired, as if it had been a grueling day, but flickering between them was a faint and tantalizing awareness. *You know what we're both thinking, don't you?*

This was amazing. She turned over the next photo, and the next, and the next, marveling at the clarity, the desolation, the hunger, the joy. She didn't usually respond to pictures with such emotion, with such intensity. But these caught at her heart. They drew her in, they made her shiver, they warmed her and chilled her and touched her with awe.

When Ryan came in, she was surrounded by photos. She looked up at him, feeling almost shy at being caught in such an intimate reverence, and for a long moment neither of them spoke.

Then Sarah murmured, "These are amazing."

He moved slowly toward her, looking over her shoulder at the print she held. It was a shot from downtown Chicago, with dust sparkles dancing like music notes over the lofty Orchestra Hall.

"Ah," he said softly. "Yeah. Well, thank you."

She set down the photo, wondering if there might be still some residue of magic in the air. This man must have depths she'd never dreamed of. "How do you *do* it?"

Ryan smiled. "It's my job," he said, setting his camera on the counter and digging into his vest pocket for a canister of film. "Ever since I got out of the army, I've been shooting this kind of thing. I'm glad you like it."

"I started looking at these, and they just... Ryan, you are so *good!*"

There was a pause, during which their eyes stayed fastened on each other. Then he abruptly turned away and dropped the film by his camera. "I oughta have you call some editors," he said, and flashed her a teasing grin. "Keep talking, though. This is great."

Sarah couldn't help laughing, a little embarrassed. "You must hear it all the time. I just didn't realize you were this good." She pulled the diner photo from underneath a few others and gently laid it on top. "I like the way you got that guy in the last little bit of light. As if once he leaves, it's over."

That might not have been the best one to mention, she realized as soon as she said it. The awareness between the man and woman in the photo felt a little too close to the awareness flickering between her and Ryan. Even though they hadn't spent two minutes alone together since that night he'd mentioned Adele, she could still feel it humming between them... and from the way he watched her, a little on edge, she knew he was feeling it, too.

He leaned back against the counter, a safe distance away from her. "You noticed that, huh? You've got a good eye."

"Oh, well, no."

"No, you do. Jesse must get it from you."

She felt curiously flattered, even though there was no way Jesse could have inherited anything from her. "That's good," she said hastily. "I mean, him learning about photography."

Ryan extracted another roll of film from his pocket and set it on the counter. "He's gotten pretty good at packing up the gear, too." He glanced outside, where Jesse was evidently loading equipment into the storage compartment. "That was our last shot. We're knocking off for the day."

Sarah glanced at her watch. "Shall I start dinner?"

"No rush. We usually kick back for a while, anyway, before we pick you up." He took a beer from the refrigerator and gestured questioningly; she shook her head. "Tell you what you can do if you're feeling ambitious, though, is start writing to some photo editors and tell them to buy more of my stuff."

For a photographer employed by *Odyssey Magazine,* this man didn't seem to have much confidence in his own work. "You've probably got all the jobs you can handle right now," she reminded him. "I mean, it looks to me like you're already up there with Ansel Adams."

"Not even close," he said, closing the refrigerator door. "Nobody's ever hung an N. H. Ryan collection."

"They will someday," she predicted, straightening the prints on the table. "What's the N.H. for?"

"You don't want to know."

"I don't, huh? What's the matter, don't you like your name?"

"I don't mind the Ryan." He took a slow swallow of beer and faced her straight, as if daring her to laugh. "It's the Nathaniel Hawthorne I could live without."

Her eyes widened. "Seriously?"

"Yeah, well, my mom was an English teacher. She named my brothers Herman Melville and Charles Dickens."

Sarah fought back a smile, but she could feel it curving her lips. "That must have been tough, growing up."

"It caused a couple of black eyes," he admitted. "Once I got everyone to stick with Nate, it was all right. But I knew anytime Mom said, 'Nathaniel Hawthorne Ryan,' I was in big trouble."

For some reason it was easy to see him as a boy, quick with his fists and yet still accountable to his mother. There was a trace of that boy in him now, a cocky sureness mingled with an occasional flash of gentleness that warmed her even as it puzzled her. He had shown it the afternoon they met on the courthouse steps, with his genuine sympathy for her loss, and again when he smoothed over her reluctance to drive the Winnebago with such easy, understanding grace.

"Did your mom call you that very often?" she asked, already knowing he must have been a hell-raiser. Adele had never fancied the type of man who came from a strict, conventional family.

Ryan shrugged. "She died when I was twelve. But I wasn't ever the best-behaved kid on the block."

"Somehow I'm not surprised."

He leaned back against the counter, regarding her speculatively. "I bet you were always the best-behaved kid on your block."

"Well," she said dryly, "there wasn't a whole lot of competition."

She could tell when the recognition hit him, because he grinned in acknowledgment. "I guess there wasn't."

The sooner they could move off the subject of Adele, the better. "Who took care of you?" Sarah asked, seizing the first topic that came to mind. "Did your dad remarry?"

Ryan didn't seem at all surprised by the change of subject. "No," he said. "My dad wasn't around. I lived with my brother for a while, until he got drafted, and then I pretty much went my own way."

His voice was matter-of-fact, but she could imagine what his teenage years must have been like. No family. No roots. No real incentive to stay out of trouble.

He sounded too much like Jesse for comfort.

"Were you a... I don't know, a hell-raiser?" Sarah asked.

Before he could answer, the storage compartment slammed shut and Jesse yanked open the door.

"Okay, Ryan, we're all packed up! How about a beer?"

Sarah caught her breath. "What?"

At the sight of her, Jesse stopped short. "Sarah. I didn't know you were back yet."

"We've been looking at the prints," Ryan told him. "You know, the one of—"

"Wait a minute," she interrupted. "Jesse, you're not drinking beer?"

He shifted his feet, looking uncomfortably at the photographer. "I, uh..."

Suddenly she saw, with wrenching clarity, what must have been happening every afternoon when they finished their work. "You haven't been paying attention to *what* he drinks, have you?" she demanded, turning to Ryan.

"Well, no," he said, as if wondering why it mattered.

Jesse glared at them both. "I was just kidding, okay? I'm out of here."

"Jess, wait a minute," she began, but he was already out the door.

Knowing she couldn't possibly catch up with him, Sarah swung back around. "Ryan, he's only seventeen! What on earth do you think you're doing?"

"What do you mean, what am I doing? You expect me to count the bottles every night?"

"He's only seventeen! All this time I've been trusting you to take care of him, and here you're telling him it's okay to come home and get drunk—"

"Hold it," Ryan interrupted. "I never said that."

"But you might as well say it. You don't even notice if he's helping himself, like it doesn't matter *what* he drinks—"

"I never said that, either! Where are you coming up with this?"

She would have to tell him, Sarah realized. "My mother drank," she said, keeping her voice as steady as she could. "Whenever my dad left town, she'd stay up all night with a bottle of vodka. Every night, every week and finally every day until it killed her. And I am *not* letting that happen to Jesse."

"Well, okay." Still looking completely matter-of-fact, as if a mother who drank was nothing to worry about, Ryan took the remaining beer out of the refrigerator and dumped it into the trash. "If that's the way you want it, that's the way we'll play it."

It sounded altogether too simple. Altogether too easy. "Do I have your word?"

He stared at her in disbelief. "You want me to sign in blood? Damn it, yes! You have my word."

"Well, fine," she snapped. "You don't have to swear at me. I just want to make sure Jesse's safe, that's all."

He folded his arms across his chest. "You want me to hold his hand when we cross the street?"

"Ryan—"

"I mean it. There's such a thing as overprotectiveness, and lady, you've got it in spades."

"You mean, just because I don't want my nephew getting corrupted by some...somebody who doesn't believe in following rules?"

"Somebody who thinks that kid can handle a little more freedom than you're giving him, yeah!"

"Oh, and I suppose you'd let him go drinking every night and try every kind of drug he can get his hands on. I suppose you think that's all just fine!"

Where was she coming *up* with this stuff? Ryan wondered. "No, I don't think that's fine. But I damn sure think there's a difference between a kid doing drugs and an adult having a beer after work."

"Jesse's not an adult."

"Not if you have your way," Ryan retorted. "You'll keep him tied to your apron strings for the rest of your life."

Sarah reeled backward, looking as if she'd been slapped. "I—he—" She broke off. Her face was flushed, her voice was choked, and for a moment he wondered if she might be on the verge of tears.

"I'm sorry," Ryan said. God, he had gone too far. He couldn't blame a woman for fighting to protect her child with every ounce of passion she possessed. "Corky, I'm sorry. I shouldn't have said that."

She swallowed hard. "I just don't want him hurt."

"I know. I know." He put his arm around her shoulders, trying to offer both comfort and apology, and when she didn't pull away he drew her a little closer, feeling her tremble against him. "Sarah... I know."

For a long, tremulous moment she stayed sheltered in his embrace, so close he could almost feel the rhythm of her heart against his chest. For a sweet, aching moment he let himself hold her, let himself feel the warmth of her, let himself remember the searing comfort of whispering a woman's name as he held her gently, safely in his arms.

This couldn't last. He knew it couldn't last, even before she drew a shaky breath and straightened up. She took a step back, ran her fingers across her tumbled hair, and finally looked up at him with such bewildered hesitation that he felt his heart turn over.

This couldn't last. But, God, how he wished it could.

Ryan forced a reassuring smile. This had been an apology, a gesture of consolation and nothing more, and she probably knew that better than he did. "You okay?" he asked.

"Oh...yes." She ducked her head and took another step back. "It's just that I've got to keep him safe. And he's already...well...before we left Gilroy he was hanging out with these kids who smoked marijuana."

"He won't be smoking anything on this trip," Ryan assured her. "I wouldn't put up with that. But it probably isn't a big deal to him, anyway."

"That's what he said," she admitted. "I don't know. Just the idea of him drinking beer—"

"Yeah, I'm sorry. I should've made sure he wasn't touching any. I mean, I should've known you'd get upset." That didn't sound quite right, he realized. But maybe she would understand his intention of atonement. "It won't happen again, okay? You have my word."

Sarah smiled, and he thought of a sunrise. "Thank you. I appreciate it."

"Okay, then. No more beer." Ryan poured the last few inches down the sink and dropped the bottle into the trash. "So."

"You didn't have to do that," she protested.

"I was finished anyway." The smart thing to do, he knew, would be to get out of here. Get the lingering feel of her warmth, her softness, her fragrance out of his mind before he started wanting anything more. "I'm gonna look around a little, see, uh...see if there's any syrup running." Bad choice of words, Ryan realized. He had to get out of here.

"I'll have dinner ready in an hour," Sarah told him.

"Right." He opened the door and felt the warm air wash over him like a benediction. Outside was safety. Outside was solitude. "See you later."

One lousy beer. You'd think it was poison or something, the way she acted.

Jesse kicked a rock on the side of the road and watched it skitter across the pavement. If he had his way, he'd stay out here all night. Maybe catch a ride in one of those cross-country rigs heading out West. He could pass for eighteen, no problem, maybe even twenty if he had to. Wind up punching cattle on some ranch where nobody cared if you drank one lousy beer at the end of a workday.

The rock rolled to a halt, and he looked around for another one. A smaller one.

This was stupid, wandering around kicking rocks. What he ought to do, Jesse knew, was stick out his thumb and wait for some driver to offer him a ride. Get out of here altogether, to someplace where he could live on his own. Where no one would have to worry about him. Where he could be free as the Western wind.

He already knew he wasn't going to do it, though. He had a commitment to Ryan, for one thing; he couldn't very well go off and leave the photographer without an assistant. And it wouldn't really be fair to Sarah, taking off without a word when she had worked so hard to give him a family. Not that he needed one now... but it might have been tough to live on his own six years ago, when his mom had died in a car wreck with some guy on their way to Detroit.

No, he would stick around for a while, at least. Finish the Route 66 trip. Finish this journey down the road to paradise, and as long as he was at it, keep an eye out at every campsite for the girl he had seen that first night.

Aurora.

He called her that in his mind, only because it was the right sort of name for a girl like her. Like the girl in the Disney movie he had seen as a child, who had seemed to his five-year-old mind the most beautiful, the most wonderful, the most remarkable princess in the world.

Nobody was really named Aurora, of course. At least nobody he knew. But as long as he kept it to himself, it was kind of nice to think of her that way. And if he saw this Aurora again, Jesse had already resolved, he was going to say something. Not just stand there staring at the princess of his dreams.

Squaring his shoulders, he kicked one last stone clear across the road and turned back toward home.

And there she was.

Running across the field looking so free, so alive, with her dark hair teased by the wind, that he felt for a moment as if he had turned into stone. No, to fire. She was moving toward him, drifting across the grass like a summer breeze, and he could almost hear the echo of her voice beckoning, "Jesse..."

Was he dreaming?

No, he couldn't be. Because she *was* calling out; she was raising her voice.

"Brandon, you get back here this instant!"

A towheaded boy came charging before her, so fast that he almost collided with Jesse.

"Whoa," Jesse said, grabbing the kid.

"Brandon!" She came running up, her hair flying, and almost skidded to a halt at the sight of him and the squirming, wriggling boy who was furiously kicking at Jesse's knees. "Oh, dear."

"I didn't do it!" the kid yelled, and burst into what must be a familiar chant. "Vicki is a poop-face, Vicki is a poop-face!"

Jesse picked up the boy and swung him around sharply, cutting him off in midsong. "Watch your mouth," he said fiercely. "There's a lady here."

They both stared at him.

He set the kid down, noting with a fraction of his attention that Brandon seemed suddenly much more manageable. But Jesse's primary focus was not on the boy. It was breathlessly, heart-poundingly on the girl.

Vicki. Not Aurora. Vicki.

"Uh ... hello," Jesse said.

Oh, great, Jess. Real smooth.

She smiled. Tentatively at first, almost shyly.

"Hi," she said, in a soft, lyrical voice he could listen to for hours on end. "Thanks for catching him."

Beside her, the kid was blessedly silent. Maybe, Jesse thought crazily, Brandon was wondering about the sparks of heat, of light, of vivid awareness that must be glittering between Vicki and himself. Sparks that were careening radiantly, wildly out of control.

"We were over at the syrup place," Vicki said breathlessly, "and Brandon decides he's had enough. And boom, he takes off! And I'm going crazy, wondering if he'd run out on the highway or *what,* and then ... there you were. You really saved my life."

"My pleasure." Had he really told Ryan she wasn't exactly beautiful? He had never been so wrong. "Are you camping around here?"

"Probably someplace. We've been staying at all these little campsites along the highway. You know, traveling Route 66."

"The road to paradise," Jesse said, and Vicki blushed. Then, as Brandon tugged at her hand, she recovered her composure. "Anyway, thanks for helping with B.H., here."

"My name," the kid said loudly, "is *Brandon*. Brandon James Hall."

Vicki nodded, then leaned close enough to Jesse so he could hear her whisper, "I call him the Brat From Hell."

He laughed. He couldn't help it. "You're terrific," he blurted.

She actually covered her face, as if to hide the soft wave of color that crept up her cheeks. Without even thinking, he reached out and moved her hand away, and her blush grew even rosier.

But she didn't withdraw her hand from his.

"I'll walk you back," Jesse offered, and she nodded.

"We're just over that way." She pointed with her free hand, and then smiled at him in sudden amazement. "I don't even know your name."

"Jesse," he managed to say. "Jesse Corcoran."

"Jesse," she repeated, and the sound of his name on her lips was sweet, soaring music. "I'm Vicki Landen."

Landen, he noticed, not Hall. Apparently she wasn't the Brat From Hell's sister. But before he could ask why she was caring for such a kid, she offered a question of her own. "Jesse, are you from around here?"

"No," he said, basking in the pleasure of walking with this girl, with his Aurora, through a sweet-scented field kissed by the first glow of sunset. "I'm doing the same thing you're doing."

She looked startled. "You are?"

"Not baby-sitting," he explained hastily. "Traveling Route 66. This afternoon we did a shoot here at Funk's Grove, and tomorrow we'll be in Springfield."

"A shoot?" she repeated as Brandon caught sight of what must be their motor home and started racing toward it. "You mean like for a video?"

"No, this is for *Odyssey Magazine*. It's a photo essay on Route 66."

"And you're going to have photos in the magazine? That's wonderful." Vicki sounded so impressed, he decided not to mention that the photos were actually Ryan's. Besides, he might still do some shooting before the trip was over.

"Yeah," Jesse said lightly, as though this were a common event. "It won't be out until April, though."

"I'll have to get a copy," she said. "What's it like, being a photographer?"

"It's great," he answered immediately, relieved that at least this much was the truth. "The best part is the freedom. You know—being able to go anywhere and shoot whatever you want. Route 66, a ranch in Montana . . . you name it, there's a photo waiting."

"Vicki!" Brandon came charging back toward them. "Dad says we're leaving in ten minutes."

She shot a glance of irritation over her shoulder at the motor home. "Thank you, Brandon. Tell your dad I'll be there."

Jesse couldn't let her go yet. "Are you traveling with Brandon's family?" he asked.

Vicki nodded, looking a little embarrassed. "They needed somebody to take care of the kids—Brandon and Katie, who's really cute—and I was free for the summer, so it seemed like it'd be a good experience. You know, see the country and all that."

She must be a nanny, he realized, one of those girls who put themselves through college by taking care of rich people's kids. "That's great," Jesse said, trying to sound matter-of-fact about it. She was older than himself, if she was already making her own way in the world. But at least she thought of him as another working adult, rather than as a seventeen-year-old kid escorted by his aunt. "This'll probably be a slow trip. We're stopping at every roadside attraction between here and California."

She ducked her head, and he saw a sparkle of pleasure in her eyes. "So are we."

All right! "Well, then," Jesse said, not even trying to hide the matching pleasure in his own eyes, "looks like we'll be seeing each other again."

"Yes," she whispered, gazing up at him once more and making his breath catch in his throat. The Aurora in the movie had never looked so infinitely appealing, so beautifully enticing, so winsome and fragile and promising as Vicki did right now.

With his eyes still on hers, he reached for her hand and gently touched the tips of her fingers. It was the lightest possible contact, but they both felt the shock. Then, just as the tingle of awareness threatened to explode into something more, Brandon emerged from behind the motor home and began a singsong chant.

"Vicki's got a boyfriend, Vicki's got a boyfriend!"

She blushed.

"Brandon," Jesse said evenly, "I don't want to hear one more word out of you. You got that?" And as the kid subsided into a petulant silence, he turned back to Vicki. "But I'll tell you," he said softly, "I hope it turns out Brandon's right."

She didn't answer. She didn't need to. Her shy, slowly blossoming smile was answer enough.

Chapter Four

Forty-two more days on the road.

All he had to do, Ryan reminded himself grimly, was make it through six more weeks. Sarah was doing her damnedest to keep things strictly business—he had to give her credit for that—yet even so he couldn't get her out of his mind.

It was going to be a long six weeks. But at least he was getting some great photos. And tonight's shot of the Ted Drewes Frozen Custard stand ought to be another winner.

Leaving Sarah to take notes on St. Louis's most popular summer gathering place, he wandered to the edge of the parking lot, trying to guess where the moon would rise—and stopped dead at the sight of another photographer just finishing a shot.

"Marco," Ryan acknowledged, instinctively comparing the other photographer's setup to his own and noticing with a sense of triumph that he'd chosen the better vantage point. "How's it going?"

Marco glanced up from his camera and halted, a look of astonishment creeping over his plump face. "Well, if it isn't the Lost Soul." Recovering his composure, he blew a speck of dust off his camera lens and turned back to Ryan. "I must say, you're looking better than the last time I saw you. Calgary, wasn't it?"

It might have been Calgary. Ryan had no idea where he had spent those first few agonizing months after his life shattered into oblivion. "Yeah," he said, rather than admit he didn't know. He and Marco had crossed paths a few times before, usually while competing for a free-lance assignment, and the other photographer wasn't one to overlook a competitor's weak spots. "You been keeping busy?"

"More than you, anyway, from what I hear." Marco's eyes narrowed as Jesse emerged from the motor home with Ryan's tripod in hand. "You shooting for Huey?"

So they were both after the Route 66 story. "Yep," he said, taking the tripod and nodding at Jesse. It would be too much to hope that Huey hadn't offered the same assignment to any other free-lancer. But if his only competition was from guys like Marco, he had nothing to worry about.

Marco frowned. "I knew he was talking to a couple of people, but I didn't know you were back on the list. Think you'll make it through the shoot this time?"

It was becoming clearer by the minute, Ryan realized, why he had never liked the other photographer. Not just because the guy was a dilettante with more money than skill—it was rumored that he'd won a few assignments by paying off the competition—but because he enjoyed twisting the knife.

Ryan gave him a deliberately casual smile, ignoring Jesse's questioning glance. "Makes it more interesting, doesn't it," he observed, "knowing who you're up against. Anybody else on this story that you know of?"

"Huey said only two. So it's just you and me." Marco zipped his camera into its case and shrugged it onto his shoulder. "I'll tell you, a few years ago it might not have been any contest. But now I feel perfectly safe saying, 'May the best man win.'"

"Well, thanks. I appreciate it," Ryan answered, unable to keep the satisfaction out of his voice as the other photographer turned toward his van. If this was all the competition he had to worry about, the assignment was already won. "Be seein' ya, Marco."

Jesse waited until the guy was out of earshot before firing a question. "Who's that?"

"A so-so photographer who thinks he's better than he is." Ryan positioned his tripod without even waiting to make sure Marco didn't see their setup. Marco wouldn't know a good location if it bit him on the neck. "All he's got going for him is a ton of money, but you can't buy a good eye. We've got this shoot in the bag."

"Does he work for *Odyssey,* too?"

"In his dreams," Ryan answered, locking the camera into place as Sarah came across the parking lot with three "concretes" of chocolate ice cream with candy chunks. "Look where he set up here! This terrific sign, and the moon coming up over the edge, and he's focused on the side of the damn building."

"He shouldn't be much competition," Jesse agreed, turning to Sarah and accepting a paper cup of frozen custard. "Hey, thanks. I gotta go get the film."

They had another few minutes before the light faded to the right level, Ryan knew. They might as well call a break. "Thanks, Corky," he said, taking the ice cream she offered him and feeling a twinge of relief and regret that their hands didn't touch. He had to stop thinking about how she'd felt in his arms, he reminded himself, or this was going to be an awfully long trip. "Good place for research, isn't it?"

She smiled, somehow looking both innocent and inviting as she ran her tongue around the curve of her plastic spoon. "Maybe we should stay here another few weeks and research every flavor they've got," she said, licking the swirl of ice cream with such careless sensuality that he closed his eyes for a moment. "Who won't be much competition?"

He nodded in the direction of Marco's departing van, grateful for the distraction. It seemed to be getting harder by the hour not to notice this woman, who could move so swiftly from insightful sweetness to scathing passion and back again. "Guy trying for the Route 66 story. He hasn't got a chance."

"Well, I should hope not!" Sarah sounded indignant. "It's *your* story."

"That's the spirit." Such wholehearted support, Ryan thought, was sweeter than the rich chunks of chocolate on his tongue. "It won't be much of a contest, that's for sure."

She pulled a stash of paper napkins from her shorts pocket, looked around for Jesse and then handed one to Ryan. "How could it be a contest at all?"

"Well, it isn't much of one." What would happen, he wondered, if he used the napkin to wipe the swirl of chocolate off her lips? Or if he forgot the napkin and used his fingers? But this wasn't Adele, he reminded himself. This was not the kind of lady he could play with and leave.

With an effort, he pulled himself back to the conversation. "You can't really call it a contest when any editor looking at Marco's and my photos would know in a minute whose they're gonna buy."

Sarah gave him a puzzled glance. "But they already hired *you* to do the story, didn't they?"

Oh, Lord. "Well," Ryan said carefully, "not yet. Once they get a look at these pictures, though, it's pretty well guaranteed."

"But—" she began, just as Jesse called across the parking lot.

"Hey, Ryan, you want to shoot a Polaroid first?"

The kid had remarkable timing. "Yeah, bring it. Thanks." Shooting a Polaroid would give him something to do, something to justify brushing aside Sarah's questions. He didn't especially want to get into a discussion of why no editor would trust him with an assignment yet. "This oughta be a good one," he mumbled, glancing in the viewfinder.

"Ryan," she said, raising her voice as he made no move to look up. "Wait a minute. Do you have a job or don't you?"

How had they gotten into this, anyway? "I don't have a contract, no," he said, concentrating on his camera lens. "But it's a pretty sure thing."

Sarah didn't answer, and when he looked up again he saw her heading rapidly toward the lighted building, passing Jesse without a word.

"Sarah!" Ryan called, but she didn't turn around.

Oh, damn.

He had to go after her. Why it mattered so much, he didn't know, but he couldn't let her go storming off this way. Ryan tossed his frozen custard into a trash can, shut down the camera lens and started across the parking lot, leaving Jesse staring after him in astonishment. "Your shot, kid," he called over his shoulder, catching up with Sarah just as she reached the battered wooden stand.

"Corky." Ignoring the curious stares of the people waiting in line, he touched her arm, and she jerked away.

This was going to be worse than he'd thought. But until now, there had never been a reason to talk about his job status. "Corky, look—"

She whirled around to face him, clutching her ice-cream cup so tightly it crumpled in her fist. "I don't want to hear it. Whatever you're going to say, I don't want to hear it."

All this fury over an as-yet-unsold story? It didn't make sense. "Well, you're *going* to hear it," Ryan snapped, guiding her away from the stand and the crowd of gawking kids with a firm hand on her shoulder. "What's going on with you?"

She twisted away from him, her cheeks flushed, and faced him under the uneven glow of a streetlight. "Answer me one question, will you? If we hadn't run into that other photographer, would you have let Jesse and me go the whole summer thinking we had a job?"

Was that all that had her so upset? "You do have a job," Ryan told her.

"How can we? *You* don't even have one!"

But with Marco his only competition, the job was a certainty. "Sarah, come on. There's no way they're gonna buy Marco's photos instead of mine."

"You don't know that. What happens if we get to California and they say, 'Sorry, Ryan, you're out'?"

He winced. That was exactly what they'd said in the past, one editor after another, until he had run out of editors, run out of excuses, run out of hope.

But it wasn't going to happen this time. He was finally on his way back.

"Sarah," he said, raising his voice over the din as a cluster of kids moved past with their ice cream. "Look. I guarantee you, this story is going to sell."

"You guarantee it?" she repeated incredulously. "Oh, now I feel a *whole* lot better."

The sarcasm stung more sharply than her anger, and Ryan made no attempt to hide his annoyance. "Listen here—"

"You know what bothers me?" she continued without even stopping for breath. "You didn't even *tell* me it was up in the air. You let me go right on thinking you had a contract, it was definite, it was guaranteed—"

"*Nothing* is guaranteed!" The raw passion in his voice startled him—this wasn't news; he had known it for two years now—but Sarah didn't seem to notice.

"Well, now's a wonderful time to tell me that!" Her voice was shaking. "You've been lying to me this whole trip."

God, was she serious? "I have never lied to you," Ryan said sharply.

"What do you call letting me think you had a job with *Odyssey Magazine?*"

Taking the line of least resistance, maybe, but he damn sure wouldn't call it lying. "I'm *going* to have a job! I don't know what it'll take to convince you of that, but—"

"If I thought there was any chance of getting hired in Gilroy this late in the summer, I'd be out of here so fast you wouldn't know what hit you."

She meant it, he realized. She would actually walk out on this job just because he hadn't mentioned that the *Odyssey* contract wasn't definite. After all these days on the road, after that moment of recognition when they'd faced each other across the stack of photos, after the dizzying bursts of harmony that still flashed between them even when he tried to pretend there was nothing there... she would actually pack up Jesse and go home?

No, Ryan thought. She wouldn't. And he felt certain enough to say softly, "You wouldn't do that."

She glanced across the parking lot at Jesse, whose enraptured expression showed he was still completely focused on the shoot, and for a moment her shoulders slumped. But she rallied, drawing herself up to her full height, and when she spoke there was barely a quaver in her voice.

"Don't bet on it."

"Sarah—"

"I trusted you!" she cried, and he knew from the anguish in her eyes that they had finally landed at the heart of the matter. "Maybe that was stupid, but I actually thought you had a job with *Odyssey Magazine*. And you weren't going to tell me any different, were you?"

"It never came up!" he protested. Somebody somewhere must have lied to this lady in spades, but that was still no reason for her to blame him. "If you'd asked me, I would've told you."

"And I wouldn't have come. Ryan, I was counting on this trip to pay for Jesse's first year of college."

"Fine," he said, feeling suddenly bleak. If all she cared about was the money, he could safely reassure her on that score. "It will."

She looked up at him, meeting his eyes for the first time, and his heart lurched as she twisted her lower lip between her teeth, fumbling for words. "But—but what if you don't sell your photos?"

Ryan took a long breath, and when he finally spoke, his voice was grim and low. "Then, lady, I will sell my camera if I have to. But I'll tell you something—you stick with this trip and you're damn sure going to get paid."

She should have known better.

Sarah twisted her pillow into shape with a savage yank and slammed it back in place.

She should have known better than to trust one of Adele's old lovers. Especially one who lived for the road.

If she had any sense, she would cut her losses right now. Take Jesse back to Gilroy and try to salvage some kind of a summer job. But it would break her nephew's heart to abandon this journey only two states into Route 66. And unless she could find a well-paid job that would let her keep an eye on Jesse, staying with Ryan was probably the lesser of two evils.

Besides, you'd miss him.

She yanked the pillow over her head and buried her face in the wrinkled sheet. Her bed was as big a mess as her life right now, and it was all due to Nathaniel Hawthorne Ryan. She had known the man for barely two weeks, shared barely a dozen polite "good mornings"—and yet, she would miss him.

It didn't make sense. He was an adventurer, for heaven's sake! A man who'd had an affair with her sister and moved on, the way Adele's lovers always did. And being an adventurer, he'd felt no qualms about drawing Jesse and herself into this trip without any idea of whether his photos would ever sell.

Sarah kicked the sheet out of the way and jerked her pillow into a new position. The man was irresponsible, there

was no way around it. She should have known better than
to trust him.

But the damage was done. She had already committed her
summer to this Route 66 job. And with Jesse so clearly
blossoming under Ryan's influence—he had been elated at
the responsibility of shooting tonight's ice-cream photo—
she might just as well stick with this journey and hope for
the best.

Maybe with that decision out of the way, she could finally get some sleep.

The air felt hot and sticky tonight, making it hard to find
a comfortable position. Jesse and Ryan evidently hadn't
noticed; she didn't hear any tossing and turning up front.
But then, Jesse could fall asleep wherever he laid his head,
and the photographer apparently shared that gift. Anyone
who could take off for the jungles of Asia without so much
as a tent, the way he'd mentioned doing over the years, must
not worry about sleeping comfortably.

Sarah shoved at her pillow one last time and sat up. Her
room wasn't likely to cool off anytime soon, and the longer
she fussed with her sheets, the hotter it felt. But on a night
like this, in the quiet privacy of a reputable campground, she
could easily slip outside for a few minutes of cooler air.

She pulled on a pair of shorts under her loose nightshirt
and slid into her sandals, then tiptoed into the front room,
where Jesse lay curled up on the couch, breathing lightly and
evenly. For a moment she gazed at him, enjoying the moth-
erly pleasure of watching him safe at rest. But with Ryan so
close she didn't linger. Resolutely avoiding any glance at the
sleeping compartment overhead, she opened the door and
stepped outside.

After the close humidity of her room, this was heaven.
She stretched her shoulders, basking in the wide-open feeling of being alone under a full, white moon, and scanned
the grassy courtyard. There was an uneven row of motor
homes, now quiet for the night, a chain-link fence sur-
rounding the play area and a white painted picnic table with

one end butted against a sycamore tree. And sitting on the
far side of the table was a man who leaned back against the
tree trunk, watching her.

Ryan.

She caught her breath.

He looked different in the night. Rougher. More harshly
drawn. In his faded jeans, with his bare chest and shoulders glinting in the uneven moonlight, he looked both
younger and older, both more approachable and slightly
more dangerous.

Now that they'd seen each other, though, she couldn't
very well turn around and go back inside. Sarah took a few
careful steps toward the picnic table. "Hi," she offered.

His voice was distant and detached. "You're the last person I expected to see out here."

You're the last person I *wanted* to see, she almost answered, but that wasn't completely true. "I...couldn't
sleep," she explained.

He only nodded, and for a moment she wondered if they
could pretend they had never seen each other. But she
couldn't just turn away, leaving him alone in the shadows....

"Times like this," he said suddenly, startling her, "I really miss having a cigarette."

Oh, yes.

She was surprised by the surge of recognition that flooded
through her veins. She had given up smoking years ago, but
on a night like this she could easily imagine the pleasure of
lounging in a quiet courtyard and gazing up at the stars with
a cigarette in hand. And the wistfulness in Ryan's voice
echoed the sensation in her memory.

"When did you quit?" she asked him.

"Couple years ago." He shook his head, and then seemed
to realize she was still standing. With a casual crook of his
wrist, he invited her to join him at the table. "I don't miss
it much. Just once in a while."

"I know." She didn't quite want to share his picnic bench—although that was silly, Sarah told herself. It wasn't like she'd never seen a man without a shirt before—but she settled on the opposite side of the table all the same. "I feel the same way."

"You used to smoke?"

"A long time ago." It was hard to believe now that she had ever let Phil talk her into starting. But it was just as hard to believe she was actually sitting here in the summer moonlight, having a conversation with Ryan. Their last words tonight had been cold and abrupt, and it made absolutely no sense to feel any hint of warmth between them now.

"What, you started when you were a kid?" she heard him ask.

"No." She leaned back against the tree trunk, where she could share his view of the distant moon instead of gazing at his muscled shoulders. "I was grown-up. I mean, I was out of school, married and everything.... I quit when I got pregnant."

Oh, dear God. What had she said?

There was a sudden silence, and she could feel his eyes on her. Startled. Curious. Wondering...

Don't ask, she begged silently. *Please, just let it go.* But she couldn't give voice to the words, and the silence grew longer.

"I'll bet," Ryan said slowly, "that's the last thing you want to talk about right now."

Sarah let out her breath. He wasn't going to ask.

"It didn't work out," she said, settling for the simplest explanation of the ectopic pregnancy that had left her unable to bear a child of her own. Eight years later, she still couldn't manage to discuss the anguish of it lightly. But the man across from her didn't seem to expect any discussion at all. He reached across the table and covered her hand with his.

"I'm sorry, Corky."

For a moment she stayed still, afraid to breathe, unable to turn and meet his gaze. But the warmth of his hand on hers was curiously comforting, and she could feel herself drawing in his quiet, solid strength.

"Knowing I couldn't have any more kids...it took a while to get over," she murmured when her voice felt steady, and with a gentle squeeze, he let her go.

"I can see why Jesse's important to you."

"Oh, God, yes. He is." Here was a topic she could feel safe with, a topic they could follow back to an ordinary level of conversation. "He's like...well, like having a son of my own. And when I think how Adele didn't want him, how Tom Bradley never even *saw* him—"

"Is that his dad?"

They were certainly airing their dirty laundry tonight, Sarah thought, but then, it was no secret that Jesse's father had refused to marry Adele. "He left for Europe before Jesse was born, though, and I don't think he's ever been back. Which is just as well."

"How come?" Ryan sounded genuinely curious, which was a relief. He evidently wasn't feeling any leftover sensation from a moment ago. And neither was she, of course. Neither was she.

"Well," she explained, sitting up a little straighter and risking a glance at Ryan, who looked perfectly relaxed, "because if he ever *did* come back, he might try and take Jesse." The possibility seemed slimmer every year, but it still gave her an occasional twinge of worry. "If he did, though, you'd better believe he'd have a fight on his hands."

Ryan nodded in agreement, and she felt a quick flutter of pleasure at how readily he seemed to understand. "I believe it. You're a great mom."

"Oh, I don't know," she murmured, looking away in embarrassment. But before she could recover her composure, he was moving around the table and standing right in front of her, lifting her chin so she had to meet his eyes.

"Sarah. You know you are."

His voice was gentle, and yet she could almost feel a kind of heat radiating from him. An intensity, an energy that confused her even as it beckoned her on a deeper, more primal level. This wasn't happening, Sarah thought. He had been Adele's lover, for heaven's sake! And it made absolutely no sense to feel this current of warmth still flowing between them.

But there it was.

She stood up, trying to come up with a coherent thought. A comment on the weather, something, anything to get them back on an everyday footing. Anything to get them over this sudden, pulsing silence and back to a safely cordial indifference.

She couldn't think of a word.

Ryan cleared his throat.

"So..." he said softly.

Nothing more. She risked a look at him and saw he was standing as carefully, as uneasily as she was. He must be feeling the same bewildering current, Sarah realized, that had her at a loss for words.

But he seemed to recover faster. He shoved his hands in his pockets, squared his shoulders and faced her without quite meeting her eyes.

"So," he repeated. "You staying with this trip or what?"

Was that what he'd been leading up to this whole time?

"Yes," she murmured. "I am."

He let out his breath, closing his eyes for a moment, and she saw his shoulders relax. "I'm glad."

"It means a lot to Jesse," she said hastily, and Ryan gave her a long, slow look of assessment before he spoke again.

"What about you?"

What on earth was happening tonight? There was no reason to feel her heartbeat slowing down, to feel as if this man were touching her as intimately as a lover. He wasn't touching her at all; there was a good two feet of space between them—and yet for some reason she couldn't find her voice.

"Uh..." She faltered. "I..."

Ryan took a step back, as if he felt the same heated awareness she did and knew it was time to retreat. "Never mind," he said. "You don't have to answer that."

"No, it's just—"

"Sarah," he interrupted. "It's okay." His voice was relaxed, and when she dared to look at him again she caught the faint warmth of a smile teasing at his lips. Almost as if he had glimpsed something special and wanted to treasure it on his own. "Listen, don't worry about the money, okay? I mean, even if these photos don't sell, we made a deal."

A deal. Yes, of course. They had made a deal.

"Okay," Sarah said. Maybe she still couldn't quite trust this man, but there was no point discussing that now. "That's fine. And really, Jesse *is* enjoying this."

"I'm enjoying him," Ryan answered easily, leaning against the railing that bordered the picnic site. In the shifting moonlight, he looked completely at ease, as if nothing had ever flickered between them. "He's got a good eye. And it's a great way for a kid to spend the summer."

Well, if all the kid cared about was having adventures. But Sarah didn't say that, and Ryan evidently didn't detect any reserve on her part. He gave her a companionable grin and boosted himself up to sit on the railing, where she found it hard to take her eyes off his hard chest and massive shoulders. "I would've given anything," he said, "to hit the road that way when I was his age. Or, well, maybe a little younger."

Sarah swallowed. She had to keep up her end of the conversation. She couldn't just stand here staring at this man, remembering how warmly, how swiftly, how thoroughly he had gathered her into his arms the other afternoon...and wondering what would happen if he tried it again. "You've spent your whole life on the road, haven't you?" she managed to say.

Ryan shrugged. "Pretty much. It's the only way to go, really. Just pack up and head out whenever the spirit moves you."

That was exactly how Phil had felt, and probably her father, too. And of course Ryan had every right to feel that way if he wanted to. "But . . . if someone has a family—"

"I don't," he said shortly, and in the shadows his face was suddenly hard. "No strings. No commitments."

No strings. No commitments. Not even Phil had put it that bluntly. But then, it was none of her business how Ryan chose to live his life.

"Well," Sarah said hesitantly, "if you're happy that way . . . I mean, if you hate being tied down . . ."

He shrugged, and when he spoke his voice was carefully nonchalant. "I think if I ever had to settle down in one place, I'd drive over a cliff instead."

All right, then. They each had their own standards, and that was that. At least Ryan wasn't abandoning a family every time he took to the road. "For someone who loves traveling," she offered, "you sure picked the right job."

He smiled at her in agreement, and another flash suddenly sparked between them. It was a burst of recognition, a shared understanding too quick and too ancient to be expressed in words. "Yeah, I guess I did," Ryan told her, and for a moment they stood balanced in a shimmering, fragile silence before he spoke again. "I picked the right researcher, too."

There was a pause. They both felt what was happening, Sarah realized. They were both feeling that same curious tug of attraction—and they both knew they couldn't let it grow.

But before she could even muster the strength to squash it down, he seemed to gather himself together. Without even attempting to confirm or deny whatever had just flickered between them, he squared his shoulders, reached for her hand and looked her straight in the eye. "Sarah, I'm glad you're staying."

Such a straightforward statement made it easier to remember that they had nothing in common but an *Odyssey* story. That to pursue anything more, or to expect anything more, would only lead to trouble. The intimacy of the road notwithstanding, the best they could hope for was to be friends.

And Ryan was offering the hand of friendship.

Sarah met his gaze and clasped his hand. "Thank you," she said firmly. "So am I."

They stood still for a moment until, as if with one accord, they let each other go. Without another word, they headed back to the motor home, where he opened the door and stepped back to let her in. With equal politeness, she nodded her thanks and moved past him toward her bedroom. But before closing the door behind her, she turned back to the front room, where she knew with utter certainty he would be waiting.

"Good night, Ryan," she whispered.

His voice was husky, but she could hear a confirming smile in it. "Good night, Corky. Sleep well."

Friends. They were friends.

It was nothing more than friendship, Sarah knew, that had kept her feeling a certain buoyancy over the past week. That kept Ryan scanning the radio stations for old Beatles songs after she mentioned how much she liked them. That kept her waking early each morning so that when he and Jesse returned from a sunrise shoot she could greet them with the fresh-squeezed orange juice he loved.

It was friendship. Nothing more.

"Sarah! Over here!"

She turned to find Jesse waving from the sidewalk, and hurried to meet him at the door of the Joplin library. The three of them planned to visit Fred And Red's tonight, to sample what was supposedly the best chili in southwest Missouri, and she was looking forward to a change from cooking dinner in the motor home.

"Ryan's driving around the block. We couldn't get a parking place," Jesse told her. "Listen, I ran into Vicki this afternoon, and I'm meeting her for dinner, okay?"

"I guess it's okay. Do you want us to pick you up afterward?"

"Nah, Ryan already found the campsite for tonight. There's a pizza place right next to it, and we might go to a movie later."

Jesse seemed almost as skilled as Ryan when it came to making himself at home in a strange town, Sarah reflected. They both had the same easy confidence, the same casual certainty that things would go exactly the way they wanted. But in Ryan, who obviously didn't need anyone worrying over his safety, she had to admit that such carefree competence was considerably more attractive.

She thought the same thing again half an hour later as he guided her to a seat at the counter of Fred And Red's. Customers were crowded around the U-shaped bar, staking claims on seats not yet vacant, but Ryan had managed to land them both in exactly the right place at the right time.

"You're good at finding your way around, you know that?" Sarah told him as he deposited his camera on the counter, and he smiled at her.

"I've had some practice."

"I guess you have." She took a sip of water from the glass that had almost magically appeared as soon as they sat down. With a crowd this size, the service must go awfully fast. "So, where are you off to after the Route 66 shoot?"

Ryan shrugged. "Don't know yet. How about you?"

He must be joking. "Back to Gilroy, remember? School starts the Monday after Labor Day, and Jesse will have to get his books— Oh, darn it. I hope he's got enough money for pizza." She had completely forgotten to ask before they dropped him off.

"He's fine," Ryan promised. "We won twenty bucks last night."

Sarah almost choked on a swallow of water. "You did *what?*"

The waitress chose that moment to ask for their order, and when she left, Ryan grimaced.

"I should've known this was coming. You don't want your nephew shooting pool, either, am I right?"

Dear God, he sounded as though all she ever did was bicker about Jesse. "No, it's just... I don't think the subject ever came up," she said slowly. "What were you guys doing, anyway?"

He shrugged, turning his attention to his coffee. "We did that shoot at the tavern, remember? Went inside and shot a better game than the guys who challenged us. That's all."

"Oh." That didn't sound as though he'd been encouraging Jesse to bet. "You're not turning him into a pool hustler or anything, are you?"

Ryan closed his eyes for a moment and then turned to face her straight on. "Corky... no. I'm not."

She felt a pang of remorse slice through her. "I don't even need to say it, do I," she mumbled. "You must be sick of hearing me tell you what to do with him."

He squinted at her curiously. And then a glimmer of a smile crinkled his face. "Only five more weeks to go. I can stand it for that long."

"It's just that it'd be so easy for Jesse to start thinking he'd rather be like you than—well, than the way I've tried to raise him," she continued, wishing he could really be as lighthearted about this as he looked. "Not that there's anything wrong with being a photographer—I don't mean that. But we don't exactly have the same values."

Ryan stared at her for a moment longer and then shook his head. But before he looked away, she caught the teasing sparkle in his eyes. "You got that right." He pulled his white ceramic coffee mug toward him and took a sip. "Not if you think he shouldn't know how to beat the hustlers at their own game."

It was obvious they would never agree on the best way to raise a seventeen-year-old boy. But he didn't seem to realize what a fine edge Jesse was walking. "He's still a teenager," Sarah explained. "I have to be careful."

"Corky," Ryan said gently, "if you don't mind my saying so, you worry too much."

He had said as much before, but for the first time she felt that he wasn't just dismissing her worries. That he was willing to put up with the difference between their views...even though he would never truly understand her concern.

"I've got to make sure Jesse turns out all right," she repeated. "And there's not that much time left. He's going to be starting college this fall, maybe living in a dorm at the university next year—"

"Does he know that?" Ryan interrupted.

"Well, of course. You don't think I'd send him off to college without telling him, do you?"

There was a pause, and she could see him hesitating, choosing his words carefully.

"The way I see it, if this were my kid...I don't know that I'd automatically send him off to college in the first place."

He probably wouldn't. But Ryan lived by a completely different set of standards from her own. "I can see it now," she agreed, only half joking. "You would've had him out hustling pool the minute he finished high school."

He grinned at that, but his eyes were serious. "Only if that's what he wanted to do."

Oh, she could imagine all too well what life would be like for a seventeen-year-old living with Ryan. "Then," Sarah said lightly, "it's a good thing he's not your kid, isn't it?"

There was another silence, and then Ryan gave a short laugh. "Okay. Point taken." He took another swallow of coffee and turned to face her again. "So. No more pool, is that what you're saying?"

Darn it, why did she always have to be the bad guy? Why, after only a few days of easy friendship, did she have to push him away again?

*Because Jesse is your family, and there's nothing more
important than that!*

She nodded, relieved to see the waitress approaching with
their chili. "If you don't mind. I mean, it's only for five
more weeks."

This time Ryan surprised her with a laugh of genuine
amusement. "Corky, you're something else." After the
waitress deposited their order, he spoke again in a softer,
more reflective tone. "Five weeks, huh? You know, I'm
gonna miss you."

He couldn't be serious. Not when all she did was argue
with him about Jesse. "I think," she blurted before she
caught herself, "you're confusing me with Adele."

Ryan stopped in the middle of crumbling a handful of
crackers into his bowl and stared at her. "You think I don't
know the difference between you and Adele?"

"Uh, well—"

"I mean," he interrupted, turning back to his chili,
"nothing against your sister, but she wasn't the kind of
person you'd stay in touch with. We spent some time together, yeah, but we weren't ever really friends. Not like you
and I are."

Sarah swallowed. But before she could find the right
words, he went on, still without looking at her.

"You've got more... I mean, the way you look out for
people. You're in there pulling for Jesse, every day of your
life. You're even looking out for me! And if you think I
could ever get you confused with Adele... all I can say is,
Corky, you don't know much about yourself."

For the first time in years, she felt an ancient emptiness
in her beginning to fill with warmth. With hope. "Thank
you," she murmured, but he still wasn't finished.

"Or me, either, for that matter." Ryan stopped when he
saw her blink back an unexpected rush of tears and gave her
the same slow, compelling smile she had loved from the day
they met. "But what the hell. We've still got five more
weeks."

Chapter Five

He was asking for trouble.

He knew it, and for some reason he couldn't seem to stop.

"Ready!" Jesse called from the edge of the field, and Ryan waved in acknowledgment. If they could get two of those big red cows lined up against the vivid green horizon, this would be a hell of a shot.

Focus on the shot, Ryan. Come on.

He adjusted his lens, letting the white fence blur into the background, and settled in to wait.

If he really wanted to stay out of trouble, all he had to do was keep away from Sarah. That ought to be easy enough. All he had to do was spend more time with Jesse, skip the early-morning orange juice, skip the easy conversation while she did the dinner dishes and keep out of the motor home whenever the kid wasn't around to provide a distraction. No problem. He could do that with one hand tied behind his back.

"Light's shifting," Jesse called, and Ryan squinted at the sun before tightening his focus.

It would be simple enough to stay away from her.

He just didn't want to.

But of course, there was nothing to worry about. They were friends, sure, but nothing more. In five weeks they'd both head off in different directions, Sarah back to Gilroy and himself to whatever assignment he could scare up. He could certainly make it through five more weeks without getting in over his head. Without forgetting what could happen when a woman started to matter.

"Right," he muttered to himself, and then caught his breath as the second cow moved into focus. Here came his shot.

Ryan clicked off two, three, four frames of the vivid Santa Gertrudis cattle against the verdant backdrop of the pasture, and shook his head in wonder. The light was dazzling, the colors were vibrantly intense and the entire setup had taken less than ten minutes. Some days you just got lucky.

Of course, other days you just couldn't get a woman out of your mind.

Impatient with himself, he clicked off a few more frames and straightened up. "I'm gonna try another angle," he called to Jesse, who nodded and collapsed the white reflector that he'd used to direct the sunlight. If he stood on the fence, Ryan figured, the higher vantage point would give him a nice contrast.

He tried a range of shots from various positions before the light lost its luminous beauty.

"Sun's too high," Jesse observed. "You want to come back here around five?"

"Nah, we've got enough," Ryan answered, before realizing the kid had pinpointed exactly the right time to catch the sun dancing off the barn. "Good call, though. We're gonna turn you into a photographer yet."

Jesse looked pleased. "I feel like I'm getting the hang of it. I want Vicki to think... Well, anyway, it's getting easier."

"You're doing good." Ryan rewound his film and fished for the canister in his pocket. "Another couple years and you could make a living at this."

Jesse stopped in his tracks, almost dropping the reflector. "You mean, for real? I could really do it?"

"Sure, if you wanted. You've got most of the basics already. You'd just need some more practice. Be easy enough."

The kid looked as if someone had just offered him a Ferrari and then swallowed the keys. "How am I gonna get any practice in Gilroy?"

"Well, there's got to be photographers in Gilroy." A town that size ought to have two or three who offered apprentice training. "You start out as an apprentice—you know, an assistant, same kind of thing you're doing for me—and pretty soon you're doing more and more assignments until finally you're out on your own."

"You think anybody would hire me?"

It was a fair question, Ryan admitted as he dropped the film into its canister. He had seen aspiring photographers sign on with the pros and last no more than a week. But Jesse had a good eye to begin with, and he was picking up a solid base of skill. "By the end of this summer," Ryan told him, "I guarantee you, kid, anybody who looks at your work would be glad to take you on."

There was a moment of silence. Then Jesse swallowed. "What about you?"

Ryan halted. It had never occurred to him to hire an assistant, but the boy *was* being a big help this summer. And while there were no assignments lined up for this fall, there would be once Huey saw the Route 66 photos. Ryan wouldn't mind keeping Jesse on board.

Except...

"Your aunt probably wouldn't take it too well if I suggested you forget about college and work for me."

Jesse shrugged, acknowledging the point and dismissing it just as quickly. "Thing is, I'd learn a lot more working for you than I would going to school."

He probably would, Ryan knew. But Sarah wouldn't likely see it that way, and he couldn't imagine convincing her that a photographer needed hands-on experience more than a college degree. No, if he had to take sides between Jesse and his aunt, he'd rather skip the whole business.

"I mean," Jesse continued as he folded the reflector back into its battered case, "all I'd be learning in college is stuff like trigonometry. Where am I ever gonna use trigonometry, anyway?"

"Tell you what," Ryan said, trying to come up with a safe response. He couldn't think of any reason to turn the kid down, other than not wanting to hurt Sarah, but that was reason enough. Still, he didn't want Jesse blaming her for anything. "Let me think on it," he hedged. At least that would buy him some time. "Don't mention it to your aunt, though, okay? She's got enough to worry about, finding us a Fourth of July picnic."

"Yeah, okay." Jesse unlocked the compartment where they stored the equipment and shoved the reflector inside. "I hope she comes up with something good."

For the past few hundred miles, nearly every town had sported fliers about the local Independence Day festivities, and Ryan had decided that the right small-town picnic would be a terrific subject. But finding a setting that could pass for everyone's American dream was no easy matter. It required phoning around for descriptions of every picnic site in northeastern Oklahoma, and Ryan was only too glad to turn that mission over to Sarah. She had a remarkable talent for gathering information, and that was one more reason he enjoyed having her along.

But of course, he reminded himself as the field of cattle disappeared in the rearview mirror, just because the woman had a talent he admired didn't mean he was getting in over his head. No matter how much he enjoyed having her around, there was nothing between them but friendship.

And friendship was safe.

Friendship was fine.

It was particularly fine on a day like today, Ryan decided the next morning, as they navigated toward the chosen picnic in an out-of-the-way pasture. There was a holiday feeling in the air, and he could tell that Sarah and Jesse were looking forward to a full day of celebration as much as he was. Lately it seemed they had spent every waking hour on the move, so the Fourth of July would be almost a vacation.

"You might as well take the day off," he had told Jesse at breakfast. "I'm just gonna grab whatever comes up, so you don't need to stick around." He knew the kid had arranged to meet Vicki at the chosen picnic, and a shoot like this wouldn't require an assistant. Especially one whose attention was somewhere else.

Jesse had jumped at the offer, and now he was practically twitching with impatience as Sarah consulted a slip of paper for directions. "We're supposed to turn at the bridge," she told Ryan. "But I don't see any bridge."

"No problem," he assured her. "We can build one."

She looked up at him, startled, and then broke into the smile he loved. It was a shy smile, almost innocent, but with a sparkle in her eyes that spoke of familiarity, fascination and fun. A hell of a combination, Ryan thought whenever he saw that look. It was getting so he found himself thinking of teasing remarks, in hopes of seeing it again.

Still smiling, Sarah swatted at him with her paper. "Take time to build a bridge and you'll miss the fireworks."

"Yeah, *then* I'll be sorry. Jesse, you see any bridges around here?"

"Uh, not unless . . . yeah! Up ahead there, see?"

"Way to go, kid. We'll make it to the fireworks with nine hours to spare."

But nine hours would be barely enough time to capture the wonder of this day on film, Ryan realized when they arrived at the picnic. This was the kind of scene any photographer loved, and the sheer all-American glory of it would make these photos the centerpiece of his Route 66 shoot.

"This is incredible," he told Sarah. "Corky, you couldn't have picked a better setup." The wide-open pasture, the weathered barn in the background, the long trestle tables filled with food from the church ladies auxiliary—it was as picturesque a setting as anyone could possibly ask for, right down to the clusters of wildflowers dotting the field where three redheaded children chased after their puppy. Ryan could feel his senses quickening, feel his heartbeat picking up speed, and he knew the next few hours would be filled with the soaring, passionate joy that danced through his most successful shoots.

But this time there was an added sweetness. This time Sarah was with him.

He didn't know how it happened, exactly, but it seemed like every time he looked up from a scene that enchanted his eye, Sarah was a part of it. She never interfered with his setups; she never got in his way, but whenever he finished a shot, he could count on finding her beside him, explaining about *Odyssey Magazine*'s Route 66 feature and jotting down everyone's name.

"You're doing a great job, you know that?" he told her as she completed the circuit of a twelve-person table, recording names and exchanging bright, lighthearted comments with everyone she passed. She made it look easy, but he knew from the few times he'd done his own captions that it was a demanding job.

But she surprised him with a radiant smile. "I'm enjoying it, really. I've never seen you in action before."

Come to think of it, she probably hadn't. Not like this, anyway, not on a day where everywhere he looked there was a perfect photo clamoring for his attention, and where he could hardly find a wrong angle no matter which way he aimed. Days like this were a rare and wonderful gift, Ryan knew, and he felt oddly pleased that she was here to share it with him.

"If you want to take a break, though," he offered, "I'll just get scenics for a while. You know, shots that don't need any captions."

"No, I'm fine. Really, shoot whatever you want. I like watching you work."

"Okay, then. You got it." He liked having her watch, for some reason, although he couldn't say why. Nobody older than Jesse should care whether a lady was impressed with his photographic skill.

But it added to the festive sparkle of the day, knowing she shared the pleasure of turning faces and gestures and visions into a lasting record of this celebration. A record that would touch his heart with sweet nostalgia whenever he caught sight of these photos in the years to come.

The twins sharing a hamburger, their faces splotched with mustard. The woman laughing with her daughter as they tried to straighten a lopsided flag. The farmers gathered in conversation near the wooden barn, completely ignoring the line of sunshine and shade that cut their group in half.

The band that took over the makeshift stage halfway through the afternoon, alternating between songs that brought first teenagers and then grandparents onto the dance floor. The elderly man giving his wife a courtly bow as she blushed like a girl of sixteen. The kids daring their friend to approach a young lady with a pink ruffled skirt and an air of eager superiority. The blue jays quarreling raucously atop an empty picnic table.

And Sarah laughing as she covered her ears at the sound of the birds. Sarah kneeling down to chat with a toddler at eye level as she examined his purple-spotted toy dog. Sarah smiling as she refused an invitation to dance with a man in a cowboy shirt, looking a little embarrassed when Ryan caught up to her.

"I, uh, told him I'm with you," she explained, and he was surprised at the sense of rich satisfaction that filled him.

"You are, Corky. You are."

Having Sarah with him made a difference, somehow. Normally on a day like this he would keep going as long as he could shoot, finally collapsing in exhaustion while the world around him slowly retreated back to its usual colors, its regular intensity, its ordinary patterns of light. But today, when he reached for another roll of film with shaking fingers and realized it was well past time to stop, she appeared beside him with two cups of lemonade, as if she knew already that he'd captured every possible shot.

"You can take a break for a while, can't you?" she suggested, handing him one.

Ryan drank it down in four gulps, feeling a little dazed. "Yeah, I guess that's enough. Thanks, Corky." He wiped his face with his sleeve and felt the familiar ache of a five-hour shoot beginning to settle into his shoulders. "Let's get out of here."

She handed him the other cup, glancing around. "Jesse's off with Vicki, but I'm not sure where."

He took another swallow of the tart, icy lemonade before realizing she had given him her own, but when he tried to hand it back, she waved him off. "You need it more than I do. Let me go find Jesse, and we can leave."

"No, don't do that." He didn't want to spoil the kid's afternoon; all he wanted was to get away from the crowd while his senses recovered from the overload of the past few hours. "Let's just walk around somewhere, okay? Anywhere."

She smiled in agreement. "Sure."

Stopping only long enough to lock his camera in the motor home and return for a refill on the lemonade, they wandered through the pasture toward the creek lined with cottonwoods. The music followed them, but beside the gently rippling water it seemed to fade into a distant blur, and the quiet was curiously relaxing. Sarah didn't seem to feel any need to chatter, Ryan realized, and her easy companionship was far more soothing than the solitude he usually craved after a shoot like this one.

The meadowlarks, though, didn't care about silence. Their sporadic song trilled through the sunlit trees, covering the distant sounds of the picnic and effectively sealing the creek off from the rest of the world. That was fine with him, Ryan thought as they settled down in a grassy clearing with the water meandering past. For the moment, all he wanted or needed in the world was right here beside him.

The afternoon was pleasantly warm, and in the shade of the cottonwoods time seemed to drift as lazily as the water in the creek. The birds kept up their music, but the world seemed bathed in a sea of leisure, as if they could stay here for hours and never notice the time. He had no idea how long they sat there, basking in tranquil silence and trading only an occasional easy remark, until Sarah picked up a stone from the creek bank and sent it skipping across the water.

Five bounces. Six. Seven, Ryan counted with amazement. "Damn, you're good at that!"

She laughed, brushing a wisp of hair off her forehead. "And you thought all I could do was research."

He sat up slowly, stretching the last few kinks from his shoulders. There was a hell of a lot more to this woman than research, and they both knew it. "I'll tell you, anybody who can skip rocks the way you do is destined for greater things."

That smile again. "Well, everybody has a hidden talent."

"Not me."

"I'll bet you do."

If this conversation were taking place anywhere else, Ryan mused, they would be talking faster. But here by the creek, it didn't seem to matter how long a sentence took...or how long a pause before the response.

"Well," he offered, leaning back on one elbow, "I know how to hot-wire a car."

Another pause.

"I don't think that counts."

"Sure it does."

"No, because you might *need* to know that. I mean, if you were escaping from the bad guys or something and you had to steal a car..."

"Yeah? What if you were stranded on a desert island and the only way you could summon help was by skipping rocks?"

Sarah laughed. "Maybe I ought to get some more practice, just in case. You think?"

"Couldn't hurt," Ryan agreed, and suddenly the air was split with a sizzling crash of thunder. "Good Lord."

"It's not coming this way, is it?" Sarah asked in alarm, but he was already jumping to his feet, reaching to give her a hand up.

"Come on, Corky. We don't want to be out in this."

A creek surrounded by towering trees was the worst possible place to wait out a summer thunderstorm, Ryan knew. It was hard to believe they hadn't even noticed it approaching, but the important thing now was to find shelter as close as possible.

"We passed that shed on the way down here, remember? Come on."

The rain started falling in big, splattering drops as they scrambled up the rise, and by the time they reached the field with the small, ramshackle shed, it was hard to see through the pelting raindrops. As they hurried toward the shed, Ryan gritted his teeth, hoping they could get inside. The building was probably an old storage facility, but what if the owner kept it locked?

Fortunately, the door swung open easily at his touch. People out here didn't seem to worry about trespassers, which was all to the good. And a quick glance inside showed there was plenty of room to wait out the storm.

"It's okay, Corky. Come on in."

Gasping for breath, she accepted his hand and followed him into the darkening shed, just as another crash of thunder exploded in their ears and made her jump. Then a bolt of lightning split the sky, and in the flash of light, he could see her staring out the cracked window at the torrent they had just escaped. Her face was flushed, her hair tumbling loose and wet, and she was beginning to tremble, but she didn't seem to notice. "We made it!" she exclaimed, and flashed him a dazzling smile of triumph.

"We sure did." They were soaked to the skin and still tingling from the run, but this haven of safety made their exhilaration all the sweeter. In a burst of exuberance, Ryan grabbed Sarah by the shoulders and gave her a resounding kiss.

She was drenched with rain and her lips were cool, but the sudden heat that leapt between them startled them both. It was supposed to be a simple kiss between friends, a moment of shared celebration and nothing more, but in the space of a moment it had already flared into something more than triumph, more than celebration.

More than friendship, Ryan knew, and a ghost of warning fluttered at the edge of his mind. But as she gave him that same enticing smile, the warning was lost in a heated pulse of recognition, of instinct, of sheer elation. *God, she belonged in his arms!*

He buried his hands in her hair, pulling her closer to him, and she almost melted into his embrace. It happened so swiftly, so completely that there was no time for hesitation, for caution, no time for anything but the wealth of sensation that engulfed them both. The feel of his fingers on her cheek. The warmth of her silky skin against his. The roughness of his shirt as she dug her hands into his shoulders, wordlessly demanding more of him.

And he was giving her more, Sarah knew with a surge of joy. He opened her lips with his tongue, and she gasped at the heady sweetness of the invasion, so ruthless, so hungry, so very intense that she felt as if she might drown in this man's arms and never know she was lost. It made no sense, but somehow sense didn't matter. They had gone beyond sense, beyond reason, and all that mattered now was his kiss.

She would drown and never care; she would gladly follow anywhere he led; she would willingly take him in deeper, savoring the taste of his mouth, the scent of his skin, the feel of his body against hers. The pressure of his hips. Setting off a searing heat inside her, so primal and so sweet that she pushed herself even closer to him, running her hands down his spine and pulling him nearer.

She heard the harsh sound of his breathing, or maybe it was hers. A deep gasp of pleasure, of yearning, of need. A shuddering sigh of acquiescence, of invitation, of longing for more and knowing it was coming even as he pulled away from her, staring in wonder, and slowly reached to caress her cheek.

"Sarah..." he murmured, and she lifted her face to his, trembling with anticipation as he traced the curve of her cheek, lightly, lingeringly. "I never thought this would happen."

She gloried in the softness of his lips kissing her everywhere, moving from her mouth to her neck, to her cheek, to her earlobe. And then she felt a sudden jolt of surprise as he returned to her mouth and caught her lower lip between his teeth, gently twisting, teasing, nibbling until she thought she would die if she didn't have him inside her again.

She arched her back, groping for his waist, trying to coax his tongue back into her mouth, and he met her demand with a thrust of his hips that set her reeling, shivering, throbbing with desire. Only then did he return to the kiss, plunging into her, devouring her with such heated passion that she wondered if they might explode into a fountain of flame.

For a moment it almost seemed as if they had; she could see the orange flames of fire in the distance. But surely that wasn't real, that hazy vision of orange and yellow and red. It had to be a fantasy engendered by his touch.

She closed her eyes, willing the fantasy to consume them both in a swirl of radiant heat, but when she opened her eyes the flames were still visible through the window. And now the sky seemed clouded with smoke.

"Ryan," she murmured when they pulled apart for another breath. "Do you see anything out there?"

He followed her gaze to the window, and suddenly she could feel his muscles tighten. "Yeah," he said, in a voice she barely recognized. "It must be the barn."

His face was white, and at first she couldn't understand why. Then it registered. "You mean, in the pasture by the picnic?"

He nodded, still holding her. "All that lightning."

Oh, dear God. Her nephew was out there right now.

"Ryan," she whispered, jerking out of his embrace, "we've got to find Jesse!"

"He'll be all right." But Ryan's voice was hollow, and he abruptly headed for the door. "We'll just make sure."

In spite of the languorous daze still clinging to them, it took far less time to race back to the pasture than it had taken to reach the shed. Partly because the rain had slowed to a drizzle, with no sign of the lightning except the flames darting from the wooden-roofed barn, but also because they were moving faster, fueled by a fear neither one wanted to voice.

The barn was surrounded by neighbors from the volunteer fire department, which Sarah found reassuring. If someone who knew about fires was here, Jesse was more likely to be safe. Still, when she finally saw him sauntering across the field toward them with his familiar cocky grin, she felt a rush of relief so strong it almost made her dizzy.

"Jesse! Are you all right?"

"Yeah, sure. You guys see what happened? The barn got struck by lightning, and there's all this hay inside. They've got the whole fire department, but I don't know how long it'll take to put it out.''

Ryan glanced at the fire, and she saw that his face was still white. "Let's get out of here."

"Don't you want any photos?" Jesse protested. "This'd be a heck of a shot."

"No," Ryan said, sounding so harsh that Sarah gave him a questioning look. They were safe now; Jesse was safe. What could he possibly be upset about? Unless it was the interruption of the fire.

What would they be doing now if it hadn't interrupted? she wondered breathlessly as the three of them hurried back to the motor home with Jesse chattering excitedly and Ryan mostly silent. The very thought of what they might be doing sent a spasm of warmth spreading through her, and she struggled to keep herself from sinking back into a haze of fantasy. This was not the time or place to explore what had started during the thunderstorm.

This wasn't even the kind of thing she expected from herself. It was more like what Adele might have done. And for the first time, she could understand what her sister must have felt with all those men. Not that she would ever be like her twin, who had the radiance to attract any man in the world with just a promising glance. But Ryan already knew she wasn't Adele—from the very beginning, he had whispered Sarah's name—and that alone was enough to send her heart spinning. For once she could enjoy the feeling of being wanted for herself.

Had it surprised him the way it had her? A surprise that was all the sweeter for not being completely unexpected. Had he felt the same thrill of recognition, of joyful certainty, before losing all conscious thought in that wild, sustaining heat? Had he let himself wonder during that first moment, the way she had, whether they'd somehow known all along there would be more between them than friendship? Or had he meant it literally when he whispered, "I never thought this would happen"?

Oh, if only she could ask him now! But he was focused on backing the motor home out of its space between two pickup trucks, and he still wore the same remote expression that had clouded his face ever since they left the shelter of the shed. It was a look of solitary endurance, of deliberately shutting himself off from any feeling at all. If it weren't for the aching smile of reassurance he gave her as they reached their nearby campsite and he opened the motor-home door for her, she might have thought he regretted the entire afternoon.

But that wasn't possible. No one could share a kiss like that and five minutes later wish it had never happened. No, all she needed to do was be patient, go through the motions of fixing a light dinner, wait for them to finish shooting the campsite fireworks coloring the summer sky, listen to Jesse's exuberant report of how he and Vicki had confiscated Brandon's cherry bombs...then wish them both good-night, retreat to her bedroom and wait for Jesse to fall asleep.

It seemed to take forever. She found herself nodding off as the voices out front continued exchanging occasional remarks, but surely he would be asleep soon. Meanwhile, she might as well get comfortable. Just stretch out on the bed for a minute while she waited, and let herself remember the pleasures of the day.

The joy of watching Ryan at work, and knowing she was part of it. The lazy, relaxing quiet by the creek. The frantic dash through the rain. The sudden rush of electricity when he grabbed her, both of them soaking wet, and they felt the spark of heat charging through their lips, their skin, their souls.

The way he touched her cheek, so very gently. Then the way he kissed her a few minutes later, with such fierce and savage passion she felt her knees growing weak. The way he whispered her name. The way it felt when he teased her, slowly, leisurely, all the while promising with his eyes that there was more to come, that this was only the beginning—

"Annie! No!"

The anguished cry shattered her reverie like a crash in the night, cutting through the silence and the memory with equally horrifying intensity. Sarah jerked awake and hurried for the door, completely at a loss. What on earth? That couldn't be Jesse or Ryan, but it had sounded so close.

"Oh, God—Lia—no!"

She flung open the door and saw Jesse still asleep in the overhead compartment. On the couch, Ryan was thrashing as wildly and desperately as if he were being ripped apart by invisible hands.

What on earth? She grabbed his shoulder, which was hot to the touch, and tried to shake him awake. "Ryan. Ryan! It's all right. You're having a nightmare."

He gave another convulsive sob and shook himself away from her hand, but he seemed to be quieting down. "Ryan," she repeated in the same soothing voice she had used for Jesse when he used to see monsters under the bed. "Wake up. You're okay, sweetheart. It's all right."

With a long, shuddering gasp, he slowly opened his eyes and stared at her in blank confusion for a moment. "Sarah?"

"Yes." He looked exactly the way Jesse used to look when she woke him from a bad dream, stunned at the revelation of a safe new world. "Everything's okay. You were just having a nightmare."

"Oh, God." He ran a hand over his forehead, across his face and down onto his chest, and for a shameful moment she found herself wishing he would just keep on going, throw his sheet to the floor and invite her to join him. "I haven't done that in a long time."

"You're okay now. Everything's fine." The same soothing phrases she had used for her nephew seemed to work equally well for this hard-muscled man; already he looked a little calmer. Maybe now, if she could just get him to talk about it, the nightmare would fade into darkness and he could drift back to sleep. "It sounded like you were calling for someone."

Without speaking, he slowly moved to sit up, and it looked as if his body ached with some bone-deep hurt. He stared straight ahead for a minute, never meeting her eyes, and when he finally spoke his voice was rough with pain.

"Yeah. It happens."

Whatever *it* was, it seemed to have him tied up in knots. His hands were cold, his breathing tight and shallow. Jesse had been the same way, Sarah remembered, in the days of the monsters, but it had been a long time since she'd had to coax someone into revealing what had horrified him so badly.

"Ryan, do you want to tell me about it?"

He was silent for so long that she finally sat down beside him on the couch. Already her muscles were beginning to ache with the tension of waiting for him to speak, but it probably couldn't compare to what he was enduring: such stillness spoke of an anguish beyond words. And yet he was making no move to shrug the pain off; it seemed as though he was trapped under its weight. Oh, if he could only talk about it!

"Ryan," she asked gently, "who's Annie? Or Lia?"

He drew a long, shaky breath, and for the first time she saw that his hands were clenched into white-knuckled fists. But then, in a voice unlike any she'd heard, he answered.

"My daughter," he said softly, without ever meeting her eyes. "And my wife."

Chapter Six

"Your wife," Sarah whispered. "Oh, dear God."

"I came home from an assignment in Monterey," he went on, his voice still raw. "I was gone two weeks, and then the day I got back... If I'd come back a day earlier, it never would've happened. Or if it had, at least I would've been there."

I don't want to hear this! But she couldn't say that, not in the face of such pain.

"It's all right," Sarah murmured, groping for words of comfort. Although why she should try to comfort a man who had never once mentioned his wife was hard to explain. And at the memory of this afternoon—had that been only a quick diversion, like what he'd enjoyed with Adele?—she felt her heart constrict even more tightly. What on earth had she done?

"It was the electrical system," Ryan continued, still without meeting her eyes. For a moment she wondered if he even knew she was there, he sounded so alone. "A spark or something, I don't know, started the house on fire. There was so much smoke that Lia never even woke up. But Annie—for the next three days, I kept hoping . . ."

Sarah felt a chill of dread inside her. This sounded worse than anything she could have imagined.

"But . . . she didn't make it," he mumbled. "The doctor told me later that she'd inhaled so much smoke they'd never thought she had a chance. But I'd kept hoping—" His voice broke, but he swallowed and went on. "Sometimes it's like I still see them—Annie and Lia—in my dreams. Before the fire ever happened. But the whole time I know it's coming, and I can't ever make it stop—"

"Oh, Ryan." With a swift, instinctive gesture she gathered him into her arms, feeling his body shudder against her as the wave of misery crested and broke. "Ryan, I'm so sorry."

He didn't speak, but there was nothing more to say. For a long, silent moment she held him close, offering what little comfort she could, and finally he drew a long, shaky breath and pulled away.

"I'm sorry, Corky. I didn't mean to get into that."

"Oh, no, it's okay." She felt ashamed that he would think it necessary to apologize—surely he couldn't have sensed the dismay behind her sympathy. "Really, it's okay."

He ran a hand through his rumpled hair, leaving it just as disordered as before, and for the first time he seemed a little embarrassed. "Look, let's just forget about it, okay?"

Forget about what? she wondered in a rush of confusion, wishing she could read his face in the shadows. The nightmare? The loss of his family? The surprising passion that had flared between them this afternoon?

"I mean, it's been two years now, and I'm pretty much over it," he explained, still looking at a point just beyond her. "Or at least I'm working again. The nightmares don't happen much anymore. It was just, you know, the fire and everything."

It was more than just the fire, Sarah felt sure. What made her so certain, she couldn't say, but somehow she knew this afternoon's passionate encounter hadn't been just a quick diversion for him, any more than it had for her. If he was going to have nightmares about it, though, she couldn't very well expect any repeats.

Dear God, if only she had known he was married! Or not exactly married, but still dreaming about his wife. Why on earth had he never mentioned it until tonight?

Because today you got too close, that's why. And he can't let it happen again.

She closed her eyes for a moment, almost frightened by the depth of her understanding. He had been hurt too intensely to want to risk such closeness with anyone else. As much as she hated to admit it, his reluctance made sense. But where did that leave her?

Wishing the rainstorm had never happened, that's where.

Sarah straightened her shoulders and gave him a carefully constructed smile. "Sure," she said lightly. "No problem. You okay now?"

"Yes," he said, and as she turned away he reached for her hand. "Thanks, Sarah." For a moment he held her hand to his chest, clasping it so tightly she felt her skin growing warm. Then, as if he felt the same warmth and recognized its danger, he abruptly let her go. "I'm sorry I woke you up."

So am I, she almost said, but she knew he was apologizing for disturbing her sleep. He had no idea that this afternoon had woken something in her she would rather had never come to life.

"No problem," she said again, keeping her voice light as she escaped to the seclusion of her room. "After all, that's what friends are for."

"Aw, come on," Jesse teased Vicki. "What are friends for, anyway?"

"Are you sure? You really don't mind?"

"Hey, if the only way I can see you is with Brandon and Katie along, I'm not gonna pass up the chance."

Taking a couple of kids to Tulsa's child-size amusement park wouldn't have been his first choice for a way to spend the afternoon with Vicki. But when Ryan had suggested that they postpone their photo of the oil-driller statue until evening, Jesse didn't stick around to ask questions. He had raced to find a trucker with a CB radio who could contact the Halls, and two hours later he found himself at Bell's Amusement Park, feeling the same vivid pleasure that always swept through him at the sight of her.

She looked terrific, as always, even with her red shirt and white shorts bearing the marks of chocolaty fingers. "I told the kids they could pick their own ice-cream flavor while we waited for you," she explained. "Then Brandon decided Katie's looked better than his, and things got kind of crazy. You're sure you don't mind hanging out with them?"

"Really, I don't mind." Jesse swung Katie onto his shoulders for a piggyback ride and grabbed Brandon before he could tip over a nearby stroller. "Okay, gang, let's ride."

They hit every ride in the park, and even with the kids along, Jesse knew he wouldn't trade this afternoon for anything. To be with Vicki, to laugh with her and argue with her and watch her face light up as they followed the wooden roller coaster along its rattling course...nothing in the world could be more satisfying. More enchanting. More fun.

And Vicki seemed to feel the same way. "I didn't think," she told him as they waited for the kids to finish their final ride on the merry-go-round, "this would be any fun at all, taking them to the park. But with you here, it's a whole different kind of day. Did your friend mind covering for you?"

"Ryan? Nah, he'll be fine. He was gonna drop Sarah off at the library and do some prints."

"Sarah," Vicki repeated cautiously. "Who's that?"

Oh, Lord, he hadn't planned to mention his chaperon. "Uh, she's, uh, Ryan's girlfriend," Jesse said. "She just came along for the ride.'' Sarah would be horrified to hear that, but what else could he say? And besides, Vicki seemed relieved that his female companion was already spoken for. She gave him an apologetic smile and returned to the subject at hand.

"I'm glad you didn't have to take pictures."

"I figure Route 66 will still be here tomorrow," Jesse told her. "But who knows where you'll be?"

She waved at Katie, who clung to a pink pony as if her life depended on it. "Oh, well, actually we're staying here in Tulsa for a few days. My... uh, the kids' cousins live here, so we're visiting them."

"Get off the road for a while, huh?" he answered, watching Brandon kick an alligator with gleeful determination. "I hope we don't get too far ahead of you."

Vicki blushed. "I was thinking the same thing. Maybe if Brandon gets too obnoxious, they'll throw us out and we'll have to move on."

It sounded well within the realm of possibilities to Jesse. "You think you might encourage him a little?"

"I wish I could! Except it'd look kind of strange if all of a sudden I start letting him run wild."

"Yeah, I guess it would." She did a terrific job with the kids, he knew, and the Halls probably had no idea how lucky they were to have Vicki as their nanny. "Are you gonna stay with them after the summer? Or—no, you're going back to college."

She ducked her head, looking embarrassed. "It's just my mom's got this thing about education. If she had her way I'd stay in school until I got a doctorate or something."

"My aunt's the same way," Jesse said, and then caught himself. He had mentioned being raised by his aunt, but always kept it in the past tense. "I mean, she's a librarian, so of course she thinks everybody ought to go to college."

"Was she really disappointed when you didn't?"

It was a simple question, but he wasn't prepared for it. He should have been; Vicki had a way of asking questions that made him talk about himself. And with anyone else he would have been flattered that she found him so interesting. It was just that with Vicki he needed to keep up the facade of being a working photographer. Someone old enough to interest a college girl.

"You know how it is," he hedged. "She probably still hasn't given up hope. But the way I see it, there's a lot more I can learn on the road than I could in school."

Vicki nodded, keeping one eye on Katie as the carousel slowed down. "What road will you be on after Route 66?"

He shrugged, wishing he'd thought to ask Ryan where his next shoot would be. "Depends on the assignment. California, maybe. Montana. Whatever comes up."

"You'll have to send me a postcard," she said, and blushed again. "I mean, if you get the time."

"I'll make the time," Jesse promised, before realizing that a postcard from Gilroy Community College or even the state university wouldn't quite fit the bill. He *had* to stay with Ryan when the summer ended. "You'll start getting postcards from all over."

"I'd love it. Then if you stay anyplace for a while, I could write you back."

He would talk to Sarah tonight, Jesse decided. Explain that working for Ryan would be a lot smarter than going to college. It was only common sense; she would have to agree. "It's a deal," he told Vicki. "I bet you're a terrific letter writer."

Her answering smile left him tingling with pleasure even as the kids came charging toward them from the merry-go-round. "Vicki, we're supposed to meet Dad out front!" Brandon announced. "How come you're still here?"

With a lift of her eyebrows at Jesse, she took both children by the hand. "Because I'm not leaving without you and Katie, that's how come. Does anyone need to stop by the bathroom before we meet your dad?"

Katie nodded, her thumb in her mouth, and Brandon refused with disdain. "I'm not going in any bathroom full of *girls!* I wanna go find Daddy."

This sounded like a man's job, Jesse decided. "Why don't I take Brandon out front? We'll find his dad and wait for you there."

"Well, if you don't mind..."

She didn't seem to realize, he thought, that he would gladly walk through fire or slay a dragon for her. And while keeping an eye on the Brat From Hell might not fall into quite the same category, it ought to be pretty close.

But Brandon was surprisingly well behaved, and when his father arrived, he only yelled, "Katie and Vicki are in the bathroom, let's ditch 'em!" before hopping into the car and squashing a wad of bubble gum against the back window.

"Hi, you must be Jesse. Dave Hall."

The guy shook hands with him as if they were both adults, Jesse noticed with relief. Maybe he shook hands with everyone that way—Vicki had mentioned him being an insurance salesman—but at least there were no awkward questions about what a seventeen-year-old kid was doing with their nanny.

And although with the Halls nearby he couldn't say goodbye to Vicki in private, at least he had her phone number in Tulsa. This had been a terrific afternoon, Jesse thought again as he glanced around for the street leading back to the fairgrounds. Now if he could just convince his aunt that college would be a waste of time for a photographer...

He stopped at the sight of a photographer setting up a shot directly ahead of him.

This guy looked familiar, Jesse decided, even as he noticed the angle of the lens focused on the park entrance. *Be a better shot if he waited another hour, let the sun get farther down.* It must be the same guy, he realized, who had been at the ice-cream place in St. Louis. Marco, Ryan had called him. The one who had a ton of money but a lousy eye.

He was looking at Jesse with thinly veiled curiosity, and the recognition seemed to hit him at the same time. "Aren't you the kid who was shooting with Ryan?"

"Uh, yeah. Jesse Corcoran."

Neither one of them made any move to shake hands. They were sizing each other up, Jesse knew, the way you'd size up anyone who might threaten your turf. Not that either of them would throw a punch or pull a knife in a setting like this, but still there was a sense of measurement, of evaluation.

"So," Marco said, flicking his lens shut. "You still with him, or did he wash out?"

You wish, Jesse almost answered. Instead he said, "You should see what we got yesterday. He's shooting photos any editor would kill for."

"That right?" Marco sounded annoyed. "I didn't figure he'd make it this far. For a while he was blowing every assignment he got."

"Not this one," Jesse said, giving the other photographer's setup a dismissive look. "You might as well save your film."

But as he started toward the exit, he felt a new twist of sympathy for Ryan. If he *had* been blowing assignments, it could only have happened after his family was killed.

It must be pretty awful, having your house burn down and your wife and daughter die, all at once. Sarah had given him a brief account of Ryan's tragedy this morning, and he'd felt a guilty sense of relief at having slept through the whole incident. Still, when they were setting up their shot of the Boston Avenue Church, Jesse had attempted an awkward expression of sympathy.

"Thanks, kid." Ryan had sounded embarrassed. "I don't talk much about it."

There was a silence as they raised the angle of the tripod, and then Ryan let out a sharp sigh.

"I kind of unloaded on your aunt last night, though." He fastened the camera on the tripod and slowly twisted it into place. "She's probably wishing she never came on this trip."

"Aw, no," Jesse said, relieved to be able to offer some kind of reassurance. "Sarah's really good about stuff like that. I mean, like when I used to have nightmares or something, she always wanted to help."

"I guess." Ryan didn't look all that comforted. "Hand me the other lens, will you?"

It might take a day or two, Jesse thought now as he headed toward the fairgrounds, where they were going to shoot the statue of an oil driller. But Ryan would soon realize Sarah never minded offering a sympathetic ear.

He only wished he could be equally certain she wouldn't mind letting him forget about college.

His plan made so much more sense! It was the only way he could learn the business from a professional photographer, get himself out of Gilroy and turn the fantasy he had spun for Vicki into the truth. Not that Sarah needed to know about that last part... but even so, she would have to admit there was no reason to stay in school when he could get started on a real career.

No reason at all, Jesse repeated to himself. If he explained it that way, Sarah would have to agree.

"You want to do *what?*"

"I want to keep working for Ryan when we finish this trip," Jesse repeated. "You know, like what I'm doing now. Learn more about photography."

Sarah shook the dishwater off her hands and turned to face her nephew at the table. She had guessed, from the way he lingered over dinner until Ryan left to set up the camera on the motor-home roof, that Jesse wanted some time alone with her. But she had never imagined a request like this one.

"Jess," she said, fumbling for the right answer, "I think it's great that you want to keep on learning. But even if Ryan spends the next six months shooting around Gilroy, you'll have an awful lot of homework your first semester."

He shifted uncomfortably in his seat, and she felt an ominous clutch in her stomach even before he answered.

"See, the thing is, if I was working for Ryan . . . I could learn a lot more on the road than I would going to college."

Oh, she could just imagine what her nephew might learn from Ryan. Drinking beer, shooting pool . . . "No," Sarah said. "Absolutely not."

"But—"

"If you want to work weekends for a photographer in Gilroy, okay, maybe. But I'm not letting you go traipsing all over the country with Ryan. I don't even want you suggesting it to him!"

There was a silence. Then, with deliberate slowness, Jesse picked up his empty glass from the table and moved past her to set it in the sink before facing her again.

"Well," he said, "actually, we already talked about it. He's thinking it over."

She felt a sickening sense of betrayal stab through her, although whether it was due to Jesse or Ryan, she wasn't sure. At least Jesse had mentioned the subject now. With Ryan, she probably wouldn't have heard anything until the first day of class, when he arrived to whisk her nephew off to Alaska.

"If you think about it," Jesse continued, "you'll see it makes sense. I mean, if I'm gonna be a photographer anyway, why do I need to study trigonometry?"

"Because if you don't have a college degree, you'll never get any kind of a job worth having! You remember how it was with your mom and her jobs, right? I am *not* letting that happen to you."

He started to protest, but just then Ryan stuck his head in the door. "Hey, kid, you want to shoot this one? The sun's just about down."

"Yeah, fine." With a dark glance that told Sarah this wasn't ended yet, he headed outside. And knowing it had to be ended, she hurried after them both.

"Ryan," she said as the photographer started up the ladder after Jesse, "can I talk to you for a minute?"

He turned, looking first surprised and then wary. "Take it, kid," he called, then came back down the ladder.

Now that they were standing face-to-face, she wasn't quite sure how to begin. But she couldn't let this man drag Jesse out of school! "We've got a problem," she announced.

Ryan only looked at her, his expression as unreadable as it had been all day. "You want to talk about it here?"

Not with Jesse so close. If she hadn't been so rattled, she would have realized that herself. "Let's go inside," she said tightly.

He gestured for her to precede him back into the motor home, with the sink still full of dishes. Before either one of them could get comfortable, she took her stand across the room and turned to face him.

"Ryan, I am not letting Jesse skip college."

She could see the reaction hit him; an uncomfortable mixture of irritation and guilt crossed his face. "I asked him not to mention it to you."

"Oh, I believe it! I keep getting hit with these bombshells, and you keep—"

"Bombshells?"

"Things it never occurred to you to mention!" Could he really have no idea what she meant? "Things like letting Jesse drink beer. Like suggesting he forget about school." And those were only the beginning of the list. "Like spending your nights hustling pool. Like not having a contract with *Odyssey*. Things like—like—"

"Like being married," Ryan said.

He might just as well have knocked her sideways, she was so startled by his quiet interruption. Catching her breath in a gulp of surprise, she stared at him.

"Corky, I am really sorry about that," he said. "I probably should've mentioned it. It's just that I never thought it would matter—"

"It *doesn't* matter!" she forced herself to say. Dear God, at least she had her pride. But Ryan only gazed at her for a long, silent moment, as if reading the struggle inside her, and then he spoke quietly.

"Yes, it does."

How he knew, she couldn't imagine. But apparently she hadn't hidden her shameful resentment or guilty confusion well enough, because he was expressing the very thoughts that had tangled inside her all day.

She stared down at the floor, avoiding his eyes, and swallowed hard. "I just never had any idea." Maybe that admission would be enough, and they could let the entire matter drop. "I mean, if I'd known you were still in love with your wife—"

"No," he interrupted, moving a step closer as if to cut off that idea altogether. "It's not that. I mean, yes, I loved her, it's just..." He halted, almost visibly frustrated as he searched for the right words. "It's just—damn it—I wasn't ever going to..."

She knew what he was going to say, probably even before he knew it himself. The memory of his whispered words, *"I never thought this would happen,"* made more sense now that she knew what he'd lost, and why he dreaded letting anyone else get too close. "Yesterday scared you," she acknowledged.

He opened his mouth to speak, closed it again and twisted a fist into the palm of his hand. "All summer long," he growled, "I've been telling myself, hey, it's okay, you're just friends, there's nothing to worry about. And then yesterday it all blew up in my face." He threw up his hands, then let out his breath in a rush. "Yeah. I was scared."

She couldn't fault him for his honesty. But then, he obviously hadn't thought this thing through. He hadn't yet realized, the way she had, that yesterday couldn't have meant anything more than a one-time celebration. "What I figured out," Sarah offered, "is that there's nothing to be scared of. Because it won't ever happen again. It was a fluke, that's all."

The edge of a smile flickered across his face, making him look suddenly younger. But when his gaze rested on her a moment later, his eyes were serious again. "I don't think that's quite all," he said.

Oh, dear, this wasn't part of the script. They were supposed to agree that it had been a one-time occurrence—because really, it couldn't be anything more! "Ryan," she protested, "we're not the same kind of people." He must know that already. "You like to travel, and I—" *I have no sense of adventure,* whispered a mocking voice, but she hurried on "—I like things to be organized."

Ryan looked at her blankly, as if waiting for her to finish. "So?" he asked.

"So, what I mean is, we could never really be any good together."

Another pause. Again the faint smile in his eyes as he stood looking at her. "I thought we were damn good together."

"Well, yesterday..." There was no denying that. "But that was a holiday. It wasn't like real life."

For a moment he was quiet, staring at her with stark disbelief on his face. But she could see him come to the realization that arguing would be foolish, because he suddenly shook his head. "All right," he said. "We going to leave it at that?"

"It's only logical." If they were going to make it through five more weeks together, they both needed to remember how very different they were. Because they *were* different in every way that mattered...which brought her back to the original problem. "Anyway," Sarah told him, "we got off the subject. What's important here is that I don't want you encouraging Jesse to drop out of college before he even starts."

"Yeah, well," Ryan muttered, running his hands through his hair as if he needed time to regroup, "we'll come back to that. What matters is your knowing that I'm sorry about yesterday. I never meant to hurt you."

You didn't, she almost assured him, but she knew neither of them would believe it.

"And I hope," he added, still not moving from his side of the room, but watching her with such intensity she could feel her skin growing warmer, "that you and I are still friends."

Oh, but that was asking the impossible. "Ryan," she blurted, "friends are people you can trust. I can't trust you."

He looked genuinely startled. "Sure you can."

Hadn't he heard a word she said? "Every time I do," she reminded him, "I get hit with another bombshell."

For the first time, he appeared to recognize that she had a real grievance; she could see him frowning over the memory of her list. "Okay," he said slowly, "I see your point. But, Corky, believe me, there aren't gonna be any more bombshells."

That was easy enough to say. "Are you sure?"

He seemed to take the question seriously; she could see him considering and coming to a decision. Then he deliberately moved forward and reached for her hand, cradling it between his. "I give you my word."

She felt a quiver of relief ripple through her. "Well, then. Okay."

Still holding her hand, he gave her the first genuine smile she'd seen from him all day. "Okay."

"Okay," Sarah repeated, and then was struck by the absurdity of it—the two of them standing here holding hands and saying "okay" over and over again. Before she could explain to Ryan what had her on the verge of giggling, the door banged open and Jesse burst in.

"This is the greatest shot! You won't believe it, it looks so great!"

"Yeah?" Ryan said, turning away from Sarah so naturally that she wasn't quite certain when the warmth of his hand disappeared. "Let's take a look."

"Naw, the light's gone. I'm gonna develop this first thing in the morning, okay?"

"Sure. We'll probably hit the road early. Sarah, you need to do any more research in Tulsa?"

"No, I'm fine." She *was* fine, at least for the moment. Even though she would have to watch her step around Ryan until they both remembered they didn't belong together, at least now they recognized the differences between them. Raw physical attraction notwithstanding, they could never be more than friends. "I'm fine," she repeated, and Ryan smiled at her.

"All right, then," he said, and she felt another wave of warmth as his eyes lingered on hers. But just then Jesse grabbed a soda out of the refrigerator, flipped the top with a loud snap and turned back to them both.

"Let's finish this," he said bluntly. "Ryan, will you please explain to Sarah why I'm spending next semester with you?"

Chapter Seven

The kid might just as well have flipped the top off a live grenade, Ryan thought. Sarah was staring at him with such horror that he wished he could grab Jesse and drag him out of there.

But the damage was already done. The startled anger on her face proved she would never believe he hadn't yet offered Jesse a job.

"Tell you what," Ryan suggested, hoping to buy some more time—although what good that would do him, he wasn't sure. Damn it, why were the two people he liked best right now so completely unyielding and so completely opposed? "Why don't we all get some sleep and talk about it in the morning?"

"That's fine," Sarah said evenly. "As long as we all understand right now that Jesse is definitely going to college."

The kid reacted exactly the way Ryan would have at that age: he slammed his soda can down so hard that liquid splashed all over the counter. "I'm telling you, it's a waste of time!"

"Jesse," Ryan interjected, "let me handle this, will you?"

"There's nothing to handle," Sarah protested, but Jesse gave them both a measuring look and then nodded once.

"Okay."

"Okay," Ryan said, feeling like a negotiator caught between dangerously armed opponents. "Sarah, is that all right with you? Can we talk about this in the morning?"

"As long as you understand that I am *not*—"

"Yeah, right," Ryan interrupted. "We'll talk about it tomorrow. Now, if you guys don't mind, I'm going to hit the sack."

With almost identical reluctance, they agreed. Sarah left for her room without even attempting to wish anyone goodnight, and Jesse silently climbed into the overhead compartment as Ryan made up his bed on the couch and hoped no one would hear him gnashing his teeth.

Lord, what was he going to do? He should have put a stop to the idea of Jesse working for him when the kid first suggested it. But he hadn't done that, and now both Sarah and Jesse hated his guts. Or would tomorrow, when he couldn't think of a satisfactory solution.

There *was* no solution. Not when they were so vehemently at odds. He himself would vote with Jesse—the kid could always pick up some classes later on, same as Ryan had done—but he knew Sarah would never stand for that. And if he recommended that Jesse stick with Gilroy Community College and find a photographer in town to teach him, he would miss out on the chance to train a kid who had come to mean a lot over the past few weeks. A kid for whom the right mentor could make a world of difference.

But just try explaining that to Sarah. He'd hurt her once already, crying out for Lia that way, and he sure as hell didn't want to make things any worse. If only she would understand that he didn't mean to denigrate her values, but photography classes couldn't compare with firsthand experience.

She would never see that. She didn't see much of anything the way he did, and they both knew it. "We're not the same kind of people," she'd explained an hour ago, with that faint flush of pink creeping up her cheeks, until he'd had to shove his hands in his pockets to keep from touching her.

She was right, too, although that very difference was what he liked most about her. But she had followed that statement with a conclusion that bothered him more than he cared to admit: "We could never really be any good together."

He should have been relieved, not disappointed. She had seen right through his fear, and she was offering him an easy way out. All he had to do was agree that they were completely different people and that the kiss they'd shared had been a moment of insanity, and then Sarah would drop out of his heart.

But damn it, he didn't want that!

He should want that, Ryan knew. He should know better than to let anyone matter the way Lia had mattered, the way Annie had mattered. He should know by now that another loss would finish him, that he had handled the first one so badly it must never be allowed to happen again.

And yet here he was, gnashing his teeth over Sarah and Jesse as if the prospect of hurting either one of them was more than he could stomach.

Well, there was no way around it. They were all going to come out of this hurting. Because no matter whether he sided with Sarah, who was making him feel things he'd sworn never to feel again, or with Jesse, who reminded him so much of himself at that age, he was going to wind up hurting along with someone he cared for.

"Ryan?"

Jesse spoke so softly that he almost missed it, but there was a thin edge in his voice that Ryan knew was meant to cover a fear no one must see.

Remembering that fear from his own years with nowhere to go, he kept his voice equally low. "Yes?"

There was a silence, as if Jesse were searching for the right words. "I didn't mean to..." He stopped. "I mean, about working for you..." Another hesitation, and then the words came out in a rush. "I thought you wanted me."

Oh, God, he knew that feeling! "I do," Ryan said swiftly. "Jesse, I do. You're a terrific kid, and you're gonna be a terrific photographer, and I want to be around to watch it happen. It's just..." He caught himself. Sarah was acting out of love, however misguided, and she didn't deserve to be blamed for any of this. "Whatever happens," he finished, "don't think it's because I didn't want you. You got that?"

Jesse swallowed; Ryan could almost hear him gathering himself together. "Yeah," he answered, and the edge of bravado couldn't hide the relief in his voice. "Good night."

Everything was supposed to look better after a good night's sleep, Sarah knew. So far, though, it didn't seem to be working out that way.

She'd felt a moment of hope when Jesse left right after breakfast to set up another shot, thinking maybe he and Ryan had agreed to forget the entire business. But instead Ryan must have convinced him to let the adults argue it out alone, because as soon as Jesse left and she started rinsing out the coffee cups, he came up behind her and lightly touched her shoulder.

How on earth could his touch still affect her this strongly?

"Corky," he said, "you don't need to face off against both me and Jesse. We all know you're the one who's got to make this decision, and I don't want to make it tough on you. Could you maybe just think about it for a couple of days?"

But there was nothing to be gained by that, except keeping Jesse's hopes up a little longer and disappointing him even more when she refused. "A couple of days won't make any difference," she said, turning to face him with a wet coffee cup still in hand. "I'm not letting him give up college."

"I know that's important to you. But photographers learn by doing. If he worked with me, he could have all the experience he needs to get started in the business."

"I'm sure he could," she agreed, and saw Ryan's eyes widen in surprise. He probably expected her to be completely unreasonable about this entire business. But she knew how much it would mean to Jesse, staying with his mentor, and during the night she had racked her brain for a satisfactory compromise. "Ryan, how about this? If you want to spend the next six months shooting in Gilroy—"

His jaw dropped.

"—I'd be willing to let him go to community college and work for you after school." It would be hard, watching her nephew pick up even more of the photographer's attitude toward life, but she couldn't keep Jesse safe at home forever. And this was the only solution she could think of.

Clearly, though, it was one that had never occurred to Ryan. He stared at her in amazement, his face aghast.

"Corky," he protested, "I couldn't spend six months shooting in Gilroy. Or anywhere else, for that matter. My God, I haven't spent *two* months in the same place since I got out of the army."

He looked so appalled that she felt an unexpected surge of compassion. "You don't have to, you know." This man lived for the road, after all, and he had never made any secret of it. But she couldn't help asking, "Didn't you stay in one place while you were married?"

"Not even then. I had a home base, sure, but I still kept moving around. I have to. I can't just stay put and wait for assignments to come to me."

Even if he could, she suspected, he wouldn't want to live that way. "Well, never mind," she said, turning back to the sink. "It was just a suggestion." A suggestion she was almost relieved he wouldn't accept.

"But you'd be willing to let Jesse work for me in Gilroy," he said slowly. "So why don't you at least think about letting him come on the road? I guarantee you, it'd be a good experience for him."

"Maybe it would, but I can't—I *won't*—let him do it." She took the dishwashing liquid from the shelf, holding it like a shield, and turned back to face him. "When I first started taking care of Jesse, I made myself a promise. I would do everything I could to give him what he needs in his life. And I am not going to break that promise. As long as I'm responsible for him, Jesse is going to college, and that's that."

He must have recognized the determination in her eyes, because she could see his last argument die before it ever reached his lips. "Okay," he said finally. "I hear you." He hesitated only a moment, then took a step back. "I'll go tell Jesse—at least for now—that we talked it over, and the decision is he'll need to find someone to work with in Gilroy."

"That makes it sound like we're both responsible," she cautioned. Ryan shouldn't have to take the blame for her decision. But he shrugged.

"Yeah, well, I'm the one who gave him the idea in the first place. I don't want him thinking you're the bad guy in all this."

The sincerity in his voice warmed her; she hadn't expected such thoughtfulness. "Thank you."

He looked at her with surprise. "Come on, Corky. I don't agree with what you're doing, but I know damn well you're doing it because you love him." He started outside, then turned back to give her a smile of reassurance. "You're not the bad guy."

She swallowed hard, but it didn't ease the sudden lump in her throat. No one had ever understood her as clearly, as generously as this man did. Whatever else, she would always treasure that.

"Ryan," she blurted, before he could get out the door, "I'm glad we're friends."

He stopped in his tracks, then turned around. She could see the surprise on his face give way to a slowly deepening pleasure.

"Hold that thought," he said.

And went outside.

It was easy to hold that thought. In fact, it was all she *could* hold on to while Jesse raged about worthless classes and wasted opportunities until she wanted to lock herself in the bathroom and scream.

But she wasn't going to do that. She was going to weather this storm the way she had weathered half a dozen others since her nephew came to live with her. At least this time she had a friend on her side.

For that matter, so did Jesse.

Ryan cared for them both, Sarah knew. Otherwise he would never have made such an effort, when Jesse sulked his way through dinner, to guide the conversation toward subjects they could all enjoy. And he would never have done such a thoughtful job over the next few days, as they drifted across the plains of Oklahoma, of avoiding any argument about her decision. No, he somehow knew that she and Jesse would never reach an accord ... and yet, even so, he valued them both.

The way he valued Jesse was obvious in their rough, masculine harmony as they worked side by side through the heat of the day. They still rose before dawn most mornings to capture a sunrise shot of the oil derricks, the boarded-up gas stations or the delicate wildflowers along the highway. They still traded easy remarks about tomorrow's setup, or about their competitor Marco's reputation for buying whatever he couldn't shoot, or about the gusty winds that made it hard to keep a lighting filter in place. Watching the two of them, Sarah could see a friendship based equally on hero worship and gruff affection.

But between Ryan and herself, the friendship was harder to define. It was certainly nothing more than friendship, she had to keep reminding herself. Except for the almost-constant awareness that still flickered between them, they had absolutely nothing in common. But it was hard to remember that fact when the afternoon of the thunderstorm kept replaying itself in her dreams at night...and sometimes even by day.

It wasn't Ryan's fault, of course. He probably had no idea that the sight of his rough, callused fingers deftly loading a camera with film could make her shiver with the memory of his hands gently exploring her back. That the sound of him murmuring a countdown in the darkroom could make her yearn to hear him whisper her name in that low, husky voice. That when he looked up from a page of her notes and gave her that slow, compelling smile, she had to clench her fingernails into her palms to keep from showing what felt like a nuclear meltdown inside her.

No, he couldn't have any idea what his presence did to her or he would never spend so much time sharing lazy conversation. Asking her opinion of the day's photos. Laughing over her description of the newspaper file clerk in Oklahoma City. Tossing out teasing remarks as he had during a conversation between them yesterday, as if the two of them had been friends for a lifetime.

"You really think if you tried driving a motor home, the road would collapse right in front of you?"

"I never said that. I just said I can't stand to do it."

"What if you were stranded on this desert island and the only way off was driving a van?"

"I'm already prepared, remember? That's when I start skipping rocks."

"Oh, right. I forgot the lady has a hidden talent."

He probably assumed it was nothing but friendship that kept her outdoors with him late at night even after Jesse had gone inside, watching the stars grow brighter and talking about whatever had happened during the day. Exchanging pieces of information so precious and yet so trivial it was hard to explain why she remembered each one in the stillness of her bedroom while waiting to fall asleep. Trading memories with increasingly effortless intimacy, as if in the darkness they could afford to let down their guard.

It was on one of those starry evenings that he first spoke about his daughter—so easily, so naturally that she wondered if he realized what a barrier he had just crossed by mentioning Annie's name. He had mentioned Lia before, describing how he had been in Thailand looking for a story and had found a wife along the way. But talking about Annie seemed to come harder for him. When he slowly recounted the simple story about a four-year-old trying to look through a camera lens, there was such loving amusement in his voice that she felt her heart expand. This man was revealing a side of himself she had never seen before.

"I bet," Sarah teased gently, "you started dreaming about turning her into a photographer."

He grinned in acknowledgment. "You're right. It might've taken a couple of years, though."

"Maybe a couple of cameras, too."

"Ouch. It probably would've."

But she noticed he talked about Annie and Lia more readily after that, as though their memories no longer hurt him so deeply. And when she dared to mention the fact, he looked at her for a long moment and then said simply, "You're easy to talk to."

So he feels it, too.

The quiver of certainty whispered through her as softly, as naturally as a breath of air. She didn't need to examine it. She didn't need to mention it. It was simply there, a faint awareness that something was coming into bloom.

And Ryan felt it, too.

She knew, from his quick glance at her when Jesse struck up a conversation with a rancher's son at a general store and accepted his invitation to supper, that they both shared the same curious anticipation at the prospect of an evening alone. They would have work to do—Ryan had decided to camp in a deserted field because it offered such a clear view of a lighted oil derrick. "But you don't need to stick around," he'd told Jesse. "Sarah and I can hold down the fort."

Holding down the fort proved more challenging than she'd expected. Even though there was no sign of civilization for miles around, Ryan wanted three sources of light in this photo: the glittering derrick in the distance, the intermittent flashing of a jetliner among the stars overhead and the glow of a campfire in the foreground.

"We can't start a fire, not with all this dry grass around," she reminded him, and he shook his head.

"We don't have to. I'll show you a trade secret."

The trade secret turned out to be burning a sheet of newspaper in a glass baking dish. "Anyone who sees this photo will swear we had a campfire," Ryan promised. "All we need is the light at the bottom of the frame."

She didn't voice her skepticism, but he must have seen it on her face, because he gave her a teasing grin. "You wait, Corky. I know what I'm doing."

He put her in charge of the fire, and she was astonished at how much preparation a photo setup involved. But when the right airplane finally crossed the sky and he beckoned her to look through the viewfinder, she had to admit it was a strangely fascinating picture. "You've got the ancient kinds of light and the modern ones all mingled together," Sarah said in awe. "It's like a piece of art, isn't it?"

"We'll see what the editor says. But I'm glad you like it." He extracted the film, slung the camera around his neck and collapsed the tripod. "Too bad we don't have a real campfire. We could stay out here and roast marshmallows."

That sounded like a much better way to spend the evening than staying indoors, where she knew the electricity between them would crackle too intensely for comfort. Still, they wouldn't necessarily need a campfire to stay out here. Taking the baking dish back inside the motor home, she found a bag of taco chips and a picnic blanket and hurried out to join Ryan.

"Would you settle for taco chips instead of marshmallows?"

He finished snapping the locks on his camera case and straightened up with a quick smile. "Sure would. Nice idea."

She spread out the picnic blanket while he returned his equipment to the storage compartment, then joined her on the grass and reached for a handful of chips. "Jesse's going to be sorry he missed this," Ryan observed.

"I'll bet he's having a good time, though, talking to someone his own age. Although I'm sure he'd rather it was Vicki."

"Probably."

A budding romance wasn't exactly the ideal topic of conversation, Sarah thought, for people who were still so acutely aware of one another. Seizing the first distraction that came to mind, she blurted, "I hope the *Odyssey* editor likes this picture."

"He will," Ryan predicted. "Even if he doesn't, it might work as a stock shot."

Phil's brother, who worked for an advertising agency, used to talk about buying stock photography. "You mean you could sell it to someone who needs this kind of photo?"

"Well, if I ever get my files together."

Getting files together didn't sound like too big a challenge. Still, talking about business was a safe way to pass the time. "All you'd need is a list, right? A description of everything you've ever shot?"

He grinned. "That's like saying all you'd need to be an inventor is a better mousetrap. If you're going to sell stock

photos, you also need the usage contracts and format cata-
logs and price sheets and somebody to manage the orders."

Somehow she couldn't imagine Ryan sailing smoothly
through a task like that. "You ought to get a business manager," Sarah told him, reaching for the taco chips.

"Maybe after another couple of shoots." He passed her
the bag, looking a little embarrassed. "I don't think anyone would want to represent me just yet."

That was unexpected. "Why not?"

Shifting uncomfortably, he pulled a handful of grass from
the dirt beside him and twisted it tightly in his fingers. "I
was, uh, kind of out of the business for a while. That's what
this shoot is for, to prove I can still do the job."

"But anyone who sees your pictures would know that,"
she told him, and he gave her a reluctant smile.

"Thanks. After Lia and Annie died, though, I . . . I don't
know, I kind of fell apart."

But that was perfectly understandable. "You were grieving," Sarah said gently.

He crumpled the grass and reached for another handful.
"I didn't handle the whole situation very well, though.
People kept telling me to take it easy, to give myself time to
get over it. But I didn't listen. And instead . . ." His eyes
stayed fixed on the torn pieces of grass hitting the ground
one by one. "I started blowing assignments. It's like I was
living on the edge for a while, I wasn't really all there. If
somebody hired me for a shoot, I might do the job or I
might not . . . and in this business, reputation means a lot. It
doesn't take very long for word to get around about being
unreliable."

"That's why this *Odyssey* story matters so much, isn't
it?"

"If I can't deliver this one, nobody's ever gonna take a
chance on me again. I've lost way too many shoots."

"But you're making up for it now."

"Yeah." The second handful of grass followed the first
as he turned to face her. "Sarah, I don't know if it matters

to you, but that whole time when I was dragging around...I'm not real proud of the way I lived then, the way I was. But I can promise you that I never did drugs.''

That seemed like a strange thing to tell her. But obviously it mattered to him. ''Well,'' she said hesitantly, ''thank you for letting me know.''

''I mean, if you were still worried about me being a bad influence on your nephew...''

Suddenly it made sense. And it was sweet to think he wanted to reassure her, especially in view of the fact that Jesse undoubtedly preferred Ryan's influence to her own. ''I know you care about him,'' Sarah offered. ''Watching you together, anybody could tell. You're always so easy with each other.''

''Well, he's easy to be with. I guess he kind of reminds me of myself back then.''

Jesse probably sensed the same thing, which might explain why he liked the photographer so much. It was sweet, in a way, seeing how eagerly he copied Ryan's phrases and opinions and even his gestures, but at the same time it was disturbing to know that he'd rather spend the next few years with Ryan than with her. ''Sometimes,'' she admitted, surprising herself, ''I kind of envy how well you two get along.''

He stared at her in amazement. ''You do?''

Oh, dear, had she really said something that petty? ''I— I didn't mean that,'' Sarah stammered. ''I mean, I'm glad you're friends.'' He was still watching her with a curious look of compassion, and she hurried on, struggling for an explanation. ''It's just that he's growing up. And...we used to be so close.''

Without speaking, Ryan moved nearer to her and gently rested his hand on her shoulder. ''You know,'' he said softly, ''you still mean a lot to him. He was telling me the other day how you're really good at listening when he has a problem.''

''Oh, well...''

"And there aren't many seventeen-year-olds who could say that about their mom." He released her shoulder with a final squeeze, and she felt a faint sense of loss. "Maybe he doesn't realize it yet, but he's lucky to have you."

"I'm lucky to have him," she answered automatically, the way she did whenever anyone commented on her taking in Adele's son. But Ryan nodded as if he recognized the truth of her words.

"Sometimes," he said slowly, "I envy *you*. I mean, having this kid, watching him grow up... Sometimes I think about Annie—" He broke off and took a sharp breath before saying simply, "I'd give anything in the world to have her back."

Her heart twisted with sympathy. If only he could have watched his daughter grow up. To lose a child you loved would hurt even more than never having one of your own, and she already knew how painful that could be. But at least Ryan still had a choice. "Have you ever thought about having another child?" she asked.

He stretched his hands behind his back as if to release an ache in his shoulders and then sighed. "No. To tell you the truth, I don't think I could stick with it long enough to do a good job." Moving abruptly, he reached for the bag of taco chips and took another handful before turning back to face her, his expression a mixture of defiance and apology. "I'm not ever settling down again. And that wouldn't be fair to a kid."

He was right about that. "I wish my father had thought that way," she told him, taking a chip for herself and realizing it was probably just as well they had no campfire; they were talking too intently to bother with marshmallows. "No matter what Adele and I had going on—our birthday party, the school play, the father-daughter picnic—he was always on the road."

"That's why family means a lot to you, huh," Ryan guessed, and she nodded.

"It does. I always wanted to give my child—or at least to give Jesse—the kind of security I missed as a kid." It had been an uphill battle, though, especially during the years when Adele used to drop him off for the night and return a week later with only a casual hello for her son. "I guess, more than anything, I wanted him to realize he matters. That he wasn't just an inconvenience, like Adele used to say."

Ryan shook his head in disbelief as he crunched into a taco chip. "Sounds like you're a better mom than she ever was."

But that wasn't really fair to Adele. "The problem was," Sarah explained, "she was just so young. I mean, she wasn't really equipped to take care of herself, much less a baby." And Adele had insisted on moving into her own apartment, where money had been a constant struggle. "That's one reason it matters so much to me that Jesse goes to college. Adele never did, and she could never get any kind of a decent job."

Ryan nodded in agreement. "I remember when I knew her she'd just started working at the doughnut shop."

"That was a long time ago." Adele had worked at Dizzy's Doughnuts for years, but if she'd just started there, Ryan was talking about ancient history. He obviously hadn't been married at the time... not that her sister would have cared. "She started working there the summer after our junior year."

He opened his mouth and closed it again, looking both astonished and chagrined. "She was still in *high school?*"

Adele would naturally have avoided any such revelation back then, especially if someone might be reluctant to date a high school girl. "She probably didn't mention that," Sarah guessed, and Ryan shook his head.

"My God. That whole summer, we were..."

"Well, at least you had no idea." It was a relief to know Ryan hadn't been the type of man who deliberately went around seducing high school girls. But that knowledge still couldn't keep the tinge of bitterness from her voice when she remembered the mayor's son, who had had no such scruples. "Tom Bradley knew perfectly well she was only seventeen, but that didn't stop him from inviting her for a weekend at the air show."

"The air show?"

"It was a big deal that summer. Over in Afton they had all these planes and stunt pilots and hot-air balloons...."

"I remember it."

Of course. He had been in Gilroy that summer. "Adele went off with Tom Bradley and she came home pregnant. I mean, she didn't know it at the time. But later she said that was when it happened."

Ryan reached for the taco chips. "What did Tom Bradley say?"

Even though it was eighteen years ago, she still remembered it vividly. And in a way it was comforting to share the story with someone who would never discuss it on the streets of Gilroy. "He said he'd pay for her to either have the baby or get rid of it, but he wouldn't marry her. He went off to Europe around Christmastime, and Jesse was born in April."

"April," Ryan repeated.

"That's why Adele never even finished high school. Our mom offered to take care of Jesse if Adele wanted to go back, but she never did." It was amazing, Sarah thought, how the story could still make her squirm with embarrassment at the memory of the small-town gossip that had followed the family around that whole year.

Ryan didn't seem any more anxious to go on with it than she was. He was gazing at his hands, looking as if they might contain the secrets of the universe, if only he could concentrate hard enough. But when he glanced up and saw her watching him, he made a visible effort to return his attention to the conversation. "What were you doing all that time?"

The question caught her by surprise; no one had ever asked it before. "Working at the library after school," she answered, trying to keep her voice light. This wasn't her tragedy, after all; it was Adele's. "Mostly just trying to stay out of the way."

He nodded slowly. "It must've been rough on you."

"I don't think anyone knew I was there." She meant it as a dismissal, but Ryan evidently saw more to it than that. He looked at her closely for a moment, and when he finally spoke, his voice was soft with understanding.

"Adele got all the fuss, huh?"

"Well," she explained hastily, "it just worked out that way." It was ridiculous to feel sorry for herself all these years later, especially when their roles had been determined so long ago. "She was always the adventurous one, and I was always the responsible one. It's how things worked out. She probably felt cheated sometimes, too."

Ryan nodded, as if he recognized that fact. "Because she never got to be responsible, right?" Before she could answer, he went on. "Have you ever felt cheated about not getting to be adventurous?"

"Never," she managed to say. But his words seemed to echo with vivid resonance, and as she met his gaze, she realized he already knew the answer. "I know it's silly," she admitted, and winced as she heard the tremor in her voice. "I have a good life and a good job and Jesse to take care of...."

"But every once in a while," he said gently, as if her secret was nothing to be ashamed of, "you'd like something more."

She swallowed. There was nothing she could say. But Ryan didn't seem to expect any answer. He simply put his arm around her shoulders, lightly, easily, and let the comforting silence wash over them.

For a moment she let herself relax in the warmth of his sheltering embrace, let herself close her eyes and give way to a slow welling of relief. It was sweet beyond words to feel him against her, to hear the soft sound of his breathing, to know he would hold her as long as she needed a friend.

Yet it was also unnerving. Because if all he intended was a gesture of friendship, she really shouldn't be feeling so acutely aware of his nearness. She really shouldn't feel her heart thudding so intensely, or her skin responding to the touch of his fingers, or this gradually increasing warmth spreading through her body. And she definitely shouldn't be wishing he would never let her go.

This had to stop.

Sarah drew a quick breath and blurted out the first remark she could think of. "It's kind of an adventure, anyway, being on this trip."

Ryan looked down at her and smiled, still without drawing back. "It's a start," he said.

Did the man have any idea what he could do to her with a smile like that? "Well, I mean, really, it's been a lot of fun," she stammered desperately, glancing down at the blanket as an excuse for avoiding his gaze. "You know, seeing the country and everything...."

"I've been enjoying it, too," he said, but his voice sounded huskier than before. Could he possibly be feeling that same electric awareness, or was it only her imagination running wild?

There was another silence, during which she tried to keep from breathing too deeply, from pressing too close, from feeling too much. Then Ryan slowly, deliberately slid his arm from around her shoulders and took both her hands in his.

Without a word, he ran his thumb along the palm of her left hand, moving up to her ring finger where he spent a moment circling his thumb over the empty space, and then up to the tips of her fingers.

She caught her breath, but she didn't—couldn't—move away. Her breathing seemed to have stopped; her blood seemed to be moving faster than ever; her entire being seemed to be centered on Ryan's hands as he went on lightly, silently caressing her fingers. A lingering squeeze. A teasing flick of his thumb. A series of soft, gentle strokes that moved from her wrist to her palm and hesitated until she felt a dizzying current of warmth beginning to swirl inside her. "I'm enjoying it right now," Ryan murmured.

Oh, dear God. "So am I," she whispered.

His slow smile seemed to light up his face from the inside, but she could see him searching for words as he stopped exploring her hands and looked directly into her eyes. "Sarah," he said, "I have to tell you. This whole last week—hell, even before that—I mean, I don't know about you, but this feels to me like more than just friends."

The recognition that flashed through her was so swift and so intense that she couldn't speak. She could barely nod. But he must have read the agreement on her face, because he stared at her for a long, breathless moment . . . and then he pulled her to him in a soaring, shivering kiss.

Chapter Eight

Oh, please.

Oh, yes!

She still couldn't whisper the words, not with Ryan's mouth devouring hers so completely. But even so he seemed to know just what she wanted. The salty taste of his lips, so much hotter and more intense than she remembered from the day of the picnic. The urgent pressure of his hand behind her head, drawing her closer, as if any space between them was too much. The rasp of his whiskers against her cheek, scratchier than before but so welcome that she almost rejoiced at the burning sensation.

This was exactly what she wanted, and somehow he knew it; he was meeting her with such sizzling passion that the intensity was nearly too much to bear. But she wanted to immerse herself in the heat, wanted to drown in the fire between them, and as he slid his hands through her hair, she heard herself moan—a low, animal sound of joyous surrender—and knew that tonight there would be no turning back.

"Sarah," he whispered, raising her face to his. For a moment he simply gazed at her, as if fixing her image forever in his mind, and when he finally spoke, his voice was tinged with wonder. "We aren't really so different, are we?"

It was both a plea and a promise, and she responded more to the sound of his voice than to the question itself, lacing her fingers around his neck and pulling him down to meet her in another, more-urgent kiss. Because right now their differences didn't matter. The only differences that mattered were those they could feel, those they could celebrate as their lips fused together, searching, demanding, inviting, accepting. The differences that mattered were in their skin, rough against smooth, in their bodies, hard against soft. In their breathing, though even that was the same now—the same harsh gasps of desire, of demand, of raw and ancient need.

His hands roamed down her back, exploring, caressing, and she shivered with anticipation as he found the clasp of her bra, hesitating for a long moment before moving up to her shoulders again. No, he couldn't leave it fastened, she wanted to protest, and he must have heard her make some sound because he only shook his head, a smile dancing in his eyes, and murmured, "You wait, Corky. I know what I'm doing."

Did he know he was driving her crazy? She wanted him now, right *now,* and in some distant part of her mind she realized this wasn't like her at all. But Ryan was touching something in her that no longer cared about responsibility, about steering clear of adventure, and with every prolonged caress he was sending her soaring, sending her higher, setting her free.

She arched her back, yearning for more of him, and he pulled her closer, so close she could feel his rapid heartbeat pulsing against her own. Good heavens, he was as hot as she was! How could he stand this? And just as she thought it, he let out his breath in a rush and drew her with him onto the blanketed ground.

Oh, please don't stop.

But she knew perfectly well he wasn't going to stop, he wasn't about to let her go. Not now, not when his own searing desire was the very mirror of hers. Not when the joyous anticipation in his eyes matched the burst of happiness in her heart.

They belonged together.

Maybe not forever, but all that mattered was now. Now, with her hands exploring his hair—so thick, so rough, such a pleasure to touch. Now, with her blouse tangled in his fingers until it finally slid over her head and onto the grass. Now, with his arms wrapped around her, cushioning her from the ground as if he wanted her floating on air. She was already floating, already spinning into a whirlwind of sensation, and she knew from the promise in his eyes that there was more to come.

Very slowly, very gently, he lifted her up and unfastened the hook on her bra.

She closed her eyes and reached for him, pulling him back on top of her. "Ryan," she murmured, just for the pleasure of saying his name, and he answered with a series of kisses that started on her throat and moved down, farther, lower, until she felt a burst of warmth building inside her and grabbed his shoulders so suddenly that he shuddered in response.

"Ah, Sarah..."

She couldn't let go, couldn't move away, but he raised himself on one elbow and stared down at her, his eyes dark with passion. "Sarah," he murmured, "I want to do this right."

It can't get any more right than this, she wanted to tell him, but somehow her voice had gotten lost in the whirlwind along with her customary caution. And right now it didn't matter; she didn't need either one to help her reach for Ryan's shirt and slowly unfasten the bottom button.

He caught his breath.

She sat up and moved on to the next one.

He clenched his teeth.

She kept unbuttoning, and he grabbed her wrist.

"If I don't tell you now—ah, Corky—how much you matter to me—"

But he had told her already, with every touch of his fingers, and the words would make no difference at all. She only smiled, brushing her thumb against his lips, and moved on to the next button.

"I mean it," Ryan blurted. "Sarah, I wasn't ever going to let this happen, but—"

It was happening now, and there was nothing to do but glory in it. She ran her hands up his chest and felt the pulse of his heart leap against her fingers as he finished in a rush.

"—There's no one I'd rather be with than you."

She was startled by the surge of elation that raced through her at his words. It shouldn't be a surprise, not after the way he'd whispered her name, but hearing him say it out loud meant more than she would have guessed. And he seemed equally struck by his own words: he stared at her for a moment, his eyes filled with wonder, and then swept her into his arms.

"Yes," she managed to whisper, but there was no need for it, because he was already kissing her again, and this time there was no holding back. Had she ever in her life wanted anyone as much as she wanted this man? Exploring her mouth with his tongue, melting her heart with his touch, claiming her body with his own...

He must have sensed the throbbing need inside her, because he swiftly lowered her to the blanket and knelt astride, gazing at her with such hunger that she felt her blood running hotter and faster than ever. Then he rocked back on his heels and deftly slipped his hands beneath the hem of her shorts, teasing, caressing and finally sliding everything off her in one smooth, fluid move.

For a moment there was a hush as he devoured her with his eyes, but she couldn't wait to feel him against her, inside her, and she thrust her hips toward him. He responded immediately, covering her with a shower of kisses as she fumbled at the waistband of his jeans, and then, as she struggled with the top button, he suddenly tensed.

"Oh, no. I didn't bring—"

"It's all right!"

"No. I mean, you're probably safe, and I know I am, but—" He broke off, and she could see on his face a mixture of relief and embarrassment as he realized there was no need to worry about birth control.

"It's all right," she repeated, touched by the flicker of apology in his eyes. Phil had seen not having to worry as a fine convenience, and for Ryan to see beyond the convenience, however fleetingly, made this moment all the more special. All the more sweet. "Please, don't stop."

The smile that flashed across his face was so warm and so intense she felt as if she had been bathed in sunlight. "I won't ever stop," he whispered, and leaned forward to kiss her again. Then, as she finally worked the stubborn button loose, he reached under her shoulders and lifted her up, holding her tightly for a moment before they toppled back onto the blanket.

There was a crunch, and Ryan jerked back upright. Then, with a muffled laugh, he held up the flattened bag of taco chips and tossed it aside. "Jesse's not gonna be too happy about—"

There was a sudden silence as the realization hit them both.

They had completely forgotten about Jesse.

Oh, good heavens. Why now?

Ryan looked as stricken as she felt. He glanced off into the distance, as if calculating the odds of Jesse reappearing within the next half hour, and shook his head. "Damn it. I never even thought."

"I didn't, either," she whispered. And there was no excuse for it; Jesse was her responsibility. But even so, it took every ounce of strength she possessed to sit up and keep her hands off Ryan. "You don't suppose . . ."

She could see the struggle between hope and reason playing across his face, the same struggle that warred within her. Maybe they still had time, maybe they would have all the time and privacy they needed. Surely that wasn't asking too much. Not on a night like this; not when the planes of the earth had suddenly shifted under them and brought them together in such glorious, searing need.

But if Jesse should return . . .

Even before Ryan sighed, she could see the answer on his face. And as much as it hurt to realize this was over, she couldn't help feeling a twinge of admiration for his choosing the path of responsibility.

Without speaking, he reached for her hand and pressed it to his lips. Then he swallowed. "You know, if it was anybody else, I'd say the hell with it, let's keep going."

She almost wished it *was* anybody else, the need inside her was so painful and so deep. But Ryan was probably aching as much as she was—one glance at the strained buttons of his jeans confirmed it—and if he could endure such frustration, so could she.

"If Jesse showed up at the wrong time," he said hoarsely, "you'd never forgive yourself. And I don't think I could live with that."

How could he know her so well? He was right, but that didn't make it any easier to deny the throbbing desire still crackling between them. To realize she would never feel his body against hers so completely, so intensely—

Before she could even finish the thought, there came a piercing beam of headlights in the distance.

"Tell you what," Ryan growled, reaching for his shirt. "If you want—I mean, we don't have to—but if you want to, we could stay in Amarillo tomorrow night."

Amarillo? What did Amarillo have to do with anything? Then, as she fumbled for her clothes on the grass, she realized what he meant.

A night away from the motor home. A night to themselves. A night to celebrate, to savor, to cherish one another in perfect privacy.

It sounded like heaven.

"Yes!" Sarah said, and she threw herself at him for one last, sustaining kiss.

He held her tightly for a moment, and then, as the headlights came closer, he gave her a slow, teasing smile of relinquishment. "Hold that thought," he said.

And let her go.

What a woman.

What a hell of a woman.

Sarah was such an amazing combination of fire and steel, softness and strength, propriety and passion that she had him tied up in knots. Watching her spread a neat stack of toast with perfect spoonfuls of marmalade, all the while remembering how sensually she had writhed in his arms last night, made it an effort to stay seated at the breakfast table and listen to Jesse describe the workings of a ranch.

It had taken Ryan most of the night to fall asleep, tormented as he was by visions of her shaking loose that silky swirl of hair, which slid over his fingers like satin. Smiling with such promising pleasure as she slowly undid the buttons of his shirt. Yielding to his touch with that soft, shivering moan of desire...

And now she was handing him a plate of toast with cordial precision, a flush of excitement barely visible on her cheeks.

This was one hell of a woman.

"So they keep it going year-round," Jesse was saying. "Even in the winter, there's all kinds of stuff going on."

Had Ryan told her how he treasured her last night? He must have, somewhere in that giddy rush of discovery, because in spite of her thirst for adventure, she wasn't the kind of lady to accept a quick tumble on the grass without knowing it meant something more. And he liked that about her, too—the way she had trusted him enough to let him show her there *was* something more.

"They've got fifty head of cattle in each section," Jesse continued. "Remember those red ones we shot last week? They're the same kind."

Ryan would keep on showing her, too, until she saw how very much more there was. Because they still had the rest of the summer together. The adventure was only beginning.

And yet he already knew it was more than just an adventure. By now, the idea of parting ways when they got to California was no longer an option. He wanted her in his life.

"So what's next?" Jesse asked as Sarah set down her coffee cup and joined them at the table. Ryan swallowed before he realized the kid was asking about their plans for today. Well, that was a question he could answer.

"We've gotten enough of the plains and the oil derricks. I figure we'll head into Amarillo and shoot the Cadillac Ranch."

"Oh, yeah, all those Cadillacs sticking out of the ground? Sarah was telling me about that."

"Sarah's a hell of a researcher," Ryan said, feeling another rush of pleasure as she smiled at them both. Was there nothing this woman couldn't do? Watching her raise the coffee cup to her lips and desperately forcing his thoughts back to practicalities, he went on. "Long as we're in town, we might as well take a break. Stock up the motor home, spend the night someplace else for a change."

Her fingers trembled slightly, and she lifted her eyes to his. "That sounds nice," she said, with only the faintest breathlessness in her voice.

He felt a quick and almost shameful sense of satisfaction, knowing she was as keenly aware of him as he was of her. What did he expect, anyway—that she had gone right to sleep last night? No, she must have lain awake as fever-ishly as he had, remembering how well they had fit to-gether and how very close they had come, and imagining what would happen when they finally closed the door be-hind them tonight....

Tonight he would love her the way she deserved to be loved. Slowly. Thoroughly. Lingering over each stroke. Teasing her with his fingers and his tongue, making those quick swirls that left her gasping for more. Lifting her with him, soaring, cresting, until they exploded in a burst of—

Get hold of yourself, Ryan!

He cleared his throat and saw Jesse looking at him strangely. "You okay?"

"Uh, yeah. Coffee went down the wrong way," he mut-tered, not realizing until he saw Sarah blush that he wasn't even holding a coffee cup.

But Jesse didn't seem to notice. "I was saying, I called Vicki from the house last night. They're leaving Tulsa to-morrow, so we'll probably see them in a couple days."

"Uh-huh," Ryan replied. He'd better stop looking at Sarah, better stop thinking about her if he wanted to make it through this day in one piece. In fact, it would make things a lot easier if they never wound up in the front seat together.

Sarah evidently felt the same way. She announced after breakfast that she had a lot of notes to organize, and set-tled down in the back seat with a stack of files as Ryan drove across the field toward the highway. It wasn't until they reached the main road that he realized how very rattled the lady must be. For the first time all summer, she hadn't re-minded Jesse to fasten his seat belt.

He felt a smile of amusement creeping across his face. She couldn't have shown her state of mind more clearly if she'd hired a skywriter to inscribe Corky + Ryan in the clouds. Which, come to think of it, wasn't a bad idea. He wouldn't mind seeing their names together in the sky.

Good Lord, what had gotten into him? He sounded like a lovesick teenager, and even Jesse had never talked about carving Vicki's and his names in a tree someplace. Yet here he was, a thirty-seven-year-old man with a marriage behind him, getting all sentimental over a woman for the first time in his life. Of course, he had felt downright sappy about Annie, but for some reason Lia had never made his heart race the way it was racing now.

"How'd it go last night?" Jesse asked, and Ryan jerked himself back to the present with a start.

"Pretty good. We, uh, we shot an oil derrick that might work as a stock photo."

"Like those Fourth of July shots—" The kid broke off, looking amazed. "Sarah was in on those, too."

Ryan didn't even want to think about what that meant. "You were in on some others, though," he told Jesse hastily. "That one of the oil rig. And the farmyard, and the kids with the fire hydrant back in Joplin. Those are all good for stock, if I ever get my files organized."

"You should have Sarah help. She could do it in no time flat."

"Well, it'd be more of an ongoing job," Ryan explained. Was every topic of conversation destined to lead him back to Sarah? "But you're right, that's the kind of thing she's good at."

She was good at other things, too, but none were the kind he dared think about right now. Not when they still had the whole day to get through. Not when the road to Amarillo stretched so impossibly long ahead. What, another fifty miles? And even then they would have to navigate through the city and shoot the field of Cadillacs on the other side before settling down for the night.

As the miles inched by, he let himself consider the practicalities. Not the pleasures, not while he had to keep them safely on the road, but it wouldn't hurt to think about where to stay. Sarah deserved the best he could give her, rooms filled with roses and crystal and buckets of champagne—

always assuming the lady wouldn't object to champagne—but until he sold these photos, it would have to stay a fantasy. And again he regretted all the high-paying assignments he had lost over the past two years.

But then, she hadn't batted an eye when he'd told her about those wasted jobs. She probably didn't care about money the way she cared about other things; she had been perfectly happy with a picnic blanket and a bag of taco chips. No, Sarah wasn't the kind of woman you had to buy. She was the kind of woman you wanted to treasure.

The kind you'd do anything for, just to see her eyes light up with that shy, sparkling smile.

The kind you could never get tired of, not with her baffling way of making you see things differently than you ever had before.

The kind who could make you forget you weren't ever going to let a woman matter again.

He could feel himself smiling, feel himself almost laughing with pleasure as the road curved gently before him and he sailed into the turn with sheer joy bubbling in his veins. And then he saw a cow in the road, directly in his path.

"What the—"

Ryan slammed on the brakes, not even hearing Sarah's cry of alarm or Jesse's startled gasp. The motor home skidded past the cow, but now they were sliding too far and too fast.

He jerked the steering wheel to the left, trying to maneuver them back onto the narrow road, but the wheel only spun in his hands. And as the motor home plunged over the edge of the road and down into the drainage ditch, he felt the seat belt slam against his chest and saw Jesse crash straight into the windshield.

The glass cracked into a web, and Jesse fell back. For a moment there was nothing but silence—even the motor had shut down—and Ryan felt himself reel in shock as he heard Sarah scream.

Then he saw the blood.

Jesse's forehead was streaked by a thousand tiny cuts, and the sight galvanized him into action. Unbuckling his seat belt, he grabbed the kid's shoulders, pulled Jesse toward him and lowered the boy to the floor behind the seats.

The kid seemed dazed, and Ryan realized he was dizzy with shock. He turned to see Sarah watching them with a look of horror on her face.

"Jesse, are you all right?"

The kid didn't answer. Ryan squatted so Jesse could sit braced against his knee. Already his scalp was welling blood, and Ryan felt a wave of panic.

What the hell was he supposed to do?

"Oh, no," he heard Sarah say.

Jesse slowly raised a hand to his forehead, and the gesture brought Ryan back to his senses. They had to stop the blood, of course, before anything else. "Get a towel," he told her softly, shifting his weight to give the kid a little more support.

She ran to the bathroom and came back with a folded towel, which she gently laid across Jesse's scalp. "It's okay, hon. You're gonna be all right."

That soothing voice was strangely familiar, and it took Ryan a moment to remember when he'd heard it. It must have been the night after the picnic, when he'd dreamed about Annie and Lia and had cried out in his sleep as if he still couldn't believe they were gone. Funny how it seemed so much easier lately to think of them without that automatic surge of pain.

"Everything's all right," he heard Sarah telling Jesse, sounding perfectly calm as she refolded the towel and applied it again. But Ryan saw the alarm on her face and realized the towel was already wet with blood.

"Tell you what," he said, easing Jesse's head onto her lap and trying to keep his voice as relaxed as hers. No sense worrying the kid if they didn't have to. "There's probably a hospital not too far away from here. I'll get us back on the road." He gave her what he hoped was a reassuring smile and felt a burst of pride at how gamely she returned it. This was one hell of a woman.

It took him three tries to get the motor home out of the ditch, wondering how fast they could make it to Amarillo once they started. Half an hour, maybe, if he floored it. And there would have to be a hospital near the edge of town. Damn it, why hadn't he said anything when he noticed the kid's unfastened seat belt?

But there was no point in kicking himself now, not when he had to get them moving. He winced when he glanced over his shoulder and saw that the towel had turned almost completely red. A cut scalp, he remembered hearing in the army, bled more fiercely than anyone would expect. "Corky, let's get him to the bed in back," he said, turning off the engine and slipping out of his seat. "Come on, kid, I'm gonna give you a hand. Here we go."

Jesse made a clumsy attempt at standing up, but his legs gave way beneath him, and with a muffled grunt of pain, he collapsed back into Sarah's lap.

"It's okay, hon," she murmured. "You're still a little shaky, that's all. But you can do it. Ryan, if you can get under his shoulders..."

"Yeah, here. Jesse, you ready? It's just a few steps."

It would have been simpler for Ryan to carry him like a sack of potatoes, Sarah knew, but then there'd be even more blood rushing to his head. She tried raising his shoulders, as if the momentum might get him started, but Jesse only moaned. "Nah, jus' stay here."

He sounded so dazed, she felt the quiver of fear inside her flickering higher. "Come on, Jess. Once you're back there you can lie down and be comfortable. We'll help you. You can do it."

"Just a few steps, kid. Come on."

There was a long silence, and finally he murmured, "No...later..."

But the blood was still welling from his scalp; they *had* to get him to a doctor, and they weren't driving anyplace without Jesse safely lying down. "Jesse, listen," she said desperately. "If you can stand up, I'll give you any reward you want. Anything. Remember, like if you got an A in math?"

For the first time he smiled slightly, but it took him awhile to answer. "Uh . . . uh-huh."

"And remember, you got to choose anything you wanted? You can do that again, hon. Anything you want, except quitting school. All you need to do is get up. You can do it."

It worked. Jesse slowly, unsteadily climbed to his feet, while she clenched her fists and silently prayed. Ryan knelt beside him and grabbed his waist, rising along with him, then looped Jesse's arm across his shoulders. "Okay, kid. Good job. Sarah?"

Still holding the cloth against his forehead, she moved to let Jesse lean on her shoulders as well, and with him between them they moved to the back of the motor home, where Ryan maneuvered him onto the bed.

"All right, kid, you're doing good. We're gonna get you to the hospital in just a few minutes, so for now you can just take it easy."

Jesse's eyes were already closed, and when she shifted the towel on his scalp, he didn't move. She fought back a tremor of fear and gently shook his shoulder. "Jesse?"

"If he's asleep," Ryan said from the sink, where he was rapidly wringing out the blood-soaked towel, "don't try and wake him up. No sense letting him hurt all the way to Amarillo." He handed her another towel, and she held her breath as she lifted the one she had.

Please don't let there be any fresh blood.

Miraculously, there wasn't much. She stared for a moment, afraid to let herself hope, and then turned to Ryan. "Does it look to you like the bleeding is stopping?"

Ryan gazed at Jesse's head for what felt like an age, then sighed deeply and gave her a smile of relief. "This is one tough kid, you know that?" Squaring his shoulders, he moved forward to the driver's seat. "Anyway, we'll be at a hospital in about half an hour, maybe sooner if there's one on the way into town. Check the map, will you?"

Her first instinct was to stay beside Jesse, but common sense argued that there was nothing she could do for him now. Besides, Ryan could find a hospital faster if he had a navigator. Reluctantly taking her eyes off Jesse, she moved to the front seat and reached in the glove compartment for the map.

"Okay. In about ten miles—" She broke off as she saw the web of cracks in the windshield. "Oh, good heavens!"

Ryan glanced at her, startled, and then winced. "Corky, I'm sorry. I'd give anything to start this day over."

"You couldn't help there being a cow on the the road," she reminded him. He shouldn't have to take the blame for a disaster that was entirely her fault. "*I'm* the one who didn't remind Jesse to wear his seat belt."

There was a silence, and when he spoke, his voice was ragged. "Yeah, but...I saw it. And I didn't say a damn thing." He clenched his hands on the steering wheel and swallowed hard. "I don't think I'll ever forgive myself."

He meant it, she realized. And his stark remorse was so obvious that it blunted any anger she might have felt. "If it helps any," she told him, "I couldn't have gotten through this without you." From the moment they skidded off the road she had been aware of his presence, his strength, his concern, and it was enormously reassuring to have him beside her. She took a long, sustaining breath and concluded, "I'm really glad you're here."

He must have heard the sincerity in her words, because he gave her a shaky smile. "Thanks. You know, all I could think while we were getting him to the back was *Sarah's never gonna trust me again.*"

What a strange thing to worry about. But then, maybe he didn't realize how much she'd trusted him since his promise of no more bombshells. Maybe he didn't realize that with his confession about Jesse's seat belt, he'd shown how seriously he took that promise. Still, whether he realized it or not, this was a man she could count on.

"I trust you," she said simply.

Ryan turned to look at her and then shook his head in wonder. "You don't know how much it means, hearing you say that," he told her. "You're a hell of a woman, you know that?"

"Oh, well..."

"No, you are. I've been thinking that all day. The way you..." For a moment he looked suddenly abashed, as if censoring some private memory, and then he went on. "Like the way you got Jesse on his feet. That was great."

That wasn't what he'd been thinking of, she felt certain, but they'd probably better keep the conversation to safe topics. "Normally I don't believe in bribes," she admitted. "But when he was flunking math I told him he could have anything he wanted if he got an A. And it worked."

Ryan nodded, and she could see a smile flickering on his lips. "Yeah, I can imagine," he said slowly. "It'd work on me."

Their eyes met, and she could feel a blush stealing up her cheeks. Oh, what this man could do to her with just his smile. And for the first time since Jesse had hit the windshield she let herself think about tonight. To be alone with Ryan, to have all the time in the world, to share a leisurely night of teasing and touching and slow, sweet—

Stop it! Sarah told herself. But her heart kept up its faster pace as she plunged into a safer line of talk. "Last time I promised him anything, he drove the car to school for a week," she reported breathlessly. "But he was so careful, I'd feel safe letting him do it again."

"You could get in trouble, though, letting him pick whatever he wants," Ryan observed. "What if he said he wanted to keep shooting with me?"

She felt a jolt of disbelief. "I thought you'd forgotten all about that!"

"Well..."

He didn't sound at all apologetic, and she shook her head in amazement. "You're just like Jesse. When he wants something, he never lets go."

Ryan shrugged. "Works for me."

"Anyway," she reminded him, "I said anything he wants except quitting school. So that takes care of that."

He gave her a quick grin. "You got me there. Where do we turn at this road coming up?"

Apparently he wasn't going to pursue the matter. Which was just as well, because not even for a dozen nights like last night would she consider letting him have her nephew. "Stay to the left," Sarah told him. The important thing, after all, was to get Jesse some help. "The hospital ought to be another few blocks ahead."

"Okay. Keep an eye out."

She hurried back to glance at Jesse, who showed no sign of moving, and then returned to the front seat, where she saw that the traffic seemed heavier as they drew closer to Amarillo. "What do you suppose they'll do there?"

"Where, at the hospital?" Ryan, too, seemed more focused on the road. "Clean up his head, I guess. Take some stitches. Probably give him some blood."

She knew it was likely, he'd lost so much, but the prospect worried her. "I hope he won't need any. I know he has this really weird type. Like only one percent of all people—" She broke off. "I never thought—they might not even have it!"

Apparently Ryan had already considered that possibility. His entire body seemed charged with tension, and his face was white. When he finally spoke, his voice was strained.

"They'll have it."

He didn't sound too reassuring, but she had to take comfort wherever she could. "I guess in a city this size..." she murmured, relieved to see the hospital just ahead. At least Jesse would be in the hands of experts. "I hope they'll take my insurance card."

Ryan pulled up to the emergency room entrance and reached across her to open the door. "Why don't you start the paperwork, and I'll get him inside."

She would rather stay with Jesse, but it made more sense to divide the labor, especially with two medics already approaching the motor home. "Okay," she agreed. "I'll meet you back here."

It took nearly half an hour to process the forms, and when she returned to the emergency room, she learned that Jesse had already been transferred upstairs, where the nurse reported that everything was going just fine. She hovered in his room for a while, watching him sleep and giving heartfelt thanks, before it occurred to her that Ryan must still be downstairs.

"Straight through there," the desk clerk directed her, and she followed the hallway into what looked like a blood-donation center. There were five reclining tables separated by screens, and from behind another screen she could hear Ryan's voice.

"I'm okay, Doc. I just didn't think it'd knock me out like that."

"It hit you a little harder than most people," another voice answered. "I'd guess you've never given blood before."

"Yeah, well, the idea of sticking a needle right in my vein . . ." He sounded a little uneasy and at the same time embarrassed by his own discomfort. "I mean, I'll do it again if he needs it . . . but I sure hope he won't."

"He'll be fine," Sarah heard the doctor promise as she started across the room toward them. "Good thing you had the right type. If you don't like giving blood, though, why'd you do it?"

There was a sudden hush.

"Because," said Ryan, "he's my son."

Chapter Nine

The coffee was growing colder every minute, and she still couldn't bring herself to take a sip.

It didn't matter, though. Nobody in a hospital cafeteria cared whether you drank your coffee or not.

How long had she been here? Twenty minutes? An hour and a half? She had fled without even looking at a clock, but there was still no sign of the lunch rush slowing down. Which meant Jesse must still be sleeping, and Ryan...

She closed her eyes against a wave of sickness.

Ryan must still be waiting for her.

Chatting with the doctor. Drinking his orange juice. Glancing at the clock, maybe, wondering where she was. Sitting on the biggest bombshell of them all.

He's my son.

Why had she never noticed how much alike they were? Why had she always assumed that the only reason her nephew walked and stood and even gestured like Ryan was because he admired the photographer? Why had she ever let this man become part of Jesse's life?

And why, *why* had she let him into her heart?

The memories hurtled through her like a series of explosions, each one crashing with more horrifying impact. "What if he said he wanted to work for me?" "We all know you're the one who's got to make this decision." "This feels to me like more than just friends." "If you want, we could stay in Amarillo tomorrow night."

She could feel the angry tears burning her throat, but she wasn't going to let them spill. Sarah hastily grabbed the lukewarm coffee and took a gulp, finding it so bitter it left her shuddering.

He couldn't have been following a plan. Could he?

"I thought we were damn good together." "There's no one I'd rather be with than you." "Sometimes I envy you having this kid, watching him grow up...." "There aren't gonna be any more bombshells. I give you my word."

No. It wasn't possible.

She swallowed two more gulps of coffee and closed her eyes, desperately trying to reassure herself. Maybe he had no intention of claiming Jesse as his son. *His and Adele's.* Maybe he had been as stunned by the revelation as she was. Maybe he was waiting to share the news as soon as she returned to the emergency room.

Maybe she'd better get back there. Sarah opened her eyes and felt her heart slam against her ribs.

Ryan was coming toward her.

He still looked so good! So intriguing, so familiar, with that slow, compelling smile lighting his eyes. Surely he hadn't been deliberately keeping the truth from her. She couldn't feel this attracted to a man who would hide such secrets.

"So this is where you've been," he said in greeting, dropping into the chair across the table. "I just checked upstairs, and they said you'd been and gone."

He sounded so normal. So completely at ease. "Did you see Jesse?" she managed to ask.

"I peeked in, but he was still sleeping. He looked a lot better, though. Probably won't be any scars, the doctor said."

She was the one who should be worrying about scars. "I know," Sarah said tightly. "He told me."

He leaned his elbows on the table, looking at her with a flicker of concern on his face. "You doing all right, Corky? It's been kind of a rough day."

"No, I'm fine." As if to prove it, she took another sip of cold coffee and felt her stomach contract. "How about you?"

Ryan shrugged. "I don't like hospitals much. But at least they got Jesse fixed up." He glanced at the crowd of people waiting in the cafeteria line, then at her coffee. "You mind if I have some of that?"

"It's cold," she warned, but he only grinned as though she must be teasing and picked up the cup. Then, at the first swallow, his eyes widened. "Good Lord. How long have you been drinking this?"

"I don't know." This was feeling more and more like a bad movie, sitting here with her teeth clenched, making inane conversation and waiting for the ax to fall. "What have you been doing, anyway?"

He turned his gaze back from the coffee counter. "Waiting for you. I stuck around the emergency room for a while, gave some blood—turns out Jesse and I have the same type—and finally figured you must be finished with the paperwork. So I started looking around."

Now, she thought dizzily, right now would be the ideal time for him to reveal his news. Explain how some sharp-eyed technician had spotted the resemblance between his and Jesse's blood type, and reassure her that it wouldn't change a thing.

But instead he was gazing at the line of people waiting for coffee. "You know, I was thinking I ought to get that windshield fixed before we hit the road. It shouldn't take more than a few hours."

"Oh."

"And I figured," Ryan continued, pushing his chair back, "you'd probably rather wait here for when Jesse wakes up. You want some real coffee before I go?"

"Uh, no." The coffee in her stomach was already turning to acid as the realization rattled in her brain.

He wasn't going to say a thing.

"Okay, then. I should be back in a couple hours." He stood and gave her a quick smile before he started toward the exit. "See you, Corky."

Sarah stood up, too, feeling her knees go numb. "Wait!" she cried.

He turned around.

Even as she faced him across the table, she couldn't help remembering how wonderfully they had fit together last night. But there was no going back now, no hoping this was all a mistake. She drew a long, steadying breath and said, "I heard you talking to the doctor."

He froze. From the look on his face, she could tell he knew what she'd overheard. But she had to say it out loud, to hear the words fill the sudden chasm between them.

"Why didn't you tell me he's your son?"

Ryan took two steps toward her, and stopped. "I . . ." he began. "I, uh . . ."

"You've known it the whole time, haven't you," Sarah whispered. He'd known all along, and he hadn't said a word. "What did you do, set up this whole trip just so you could get to know him?"

"No, of course not!" But he sounded too defensive, too quick to deny it. "I had no idea until last night—"

Last night, when she'd felt as if earth had shifted under them. When he'd asked if she'd ever wanted to have an adventure and had swept her into a fever of passion so intense that she couldn't have remembered her own name.

Oh, dear God.

"—And even then, I wasn't sure," Ryan was saying. "I didn't want to mention it when all I knew was—"

"So when *were* you planning to mention it?" she blurted, already dreading the answer. Already knowing what he must have planned. "Tonight?"

"No! Sarah, come on—"

"Did you think all you'd have to do was give me an 'adventure' and I'd let you have him?"

He stared at her in horror. "Damn it, that's not what—"

"But you want him, don't you!" she cried. "All this time you've been criticizing the way I raised him."

"No, you've done a great job."

Was this the same man who'd told her she worried too much, that she couldn't keep Jesse tied to her apron strings for the rest of his life? That her nephew would learn more in six months on the road than he would by going to college?

Suddenly she knew what was coming.

"If you think," she said desperately, "that after seventeen years you can waltz back into his life, show him a couple of tricks and yank him out of school..." She stopped, appalled by the guilty awareness that flashed across his face. "That's why you weren't going to tell me, isn't it?"

"Wait a minute," he protested. "This is all news to me, too."

But she could see it already—the two of them taking off for Alaska with a blithe "So long, Sarah," leaving all her dreams for Jesse shattered in the dust. The vision hit her with such force that she swayed against the edge of the table, and Ryan caught her arm.

"You all right?"

She jerked herself away. "You know what's really funny? All these years I've worried about Tom Bradley trying to come back and take over. When all this time it was you!"

"Sarah—"

"I *believed* you," she persisted, not even hearing the edge of hysteria in her voice, "when you said no more bombshells! And it never even occurred to me—"

"Look," he interrupted, grabbing both her wrists and holding them up so she could see how her hands were trembling. "Look here. This is why I didn't say anything. I didn't want you to worry."

"And that's supposed to make it all right?"

His grip tightened. "Sarah, listen."

With a sudden wrench, she twisted her hands free and took a step back. "What were you trying to do, anyway—see if he met your standards for a son? Is that why you invited him on this trip?"

His jaw dropped. "You don't think I'd really—"

"I don't know *what* you're capable of!" she cried, and with that the wave of anger broke free. "You promise no more bombshells and then you come up with this. But yes, if you want to know, I can *see* you setting up to meet him, inviting him on this trip, and when I wouldn't let him go, you offered me a job." And a romp in the grass for good measure. "My God, Ryan."

He winced, but made no move to touch her. Instead he only fixed his eyes on hers and said slowly, deliberately, "I don't like what you're thinking. It isn't true."

Of course he knew just what she wanted to hear. And part of her wished she could believe him, wished he could prove this was a coincidence and nothing more.

Well, all she could do was ask. Straight out. "Can you honestly tell me," Sarah demanded, watching his eyes as she spoke, "that until we walked into this hospital you had no idea you might be Jesse's father?"

His gaze shifted and he hesitated. "Uh—"

Oh, she had been foolish to expect anything else! "Never mind. There's nothing left to talk about. Go ahead and get the motor home fixed. Do whatever you have to. As soon as the doctor says it's okay, Jesse and I are out of here."

He stared at her in disbelief. "No way."

If he thought she'd stick around for another month or even another day, he was dead wrong. Even if it meant losing a summer's pay, this was the only solution. She couldn't spend another hour with this man, and there would surely be flights out of Amarillo.

"Ryan, there's no use even talking about it. You are *not* getting your hands on him." Or on her, either, but she couldn't bear to think about that now. She picked up her coffee cup and pushed past him, just as he reached out and grabbed her shoulder.

"Sarah..."

She jerked away. "Don't touch me!"

He stopped, looking as if the possibility of her leaving was only beginning to sink in. She could see the awareness flickering on his face as he protested, "You can't just walk out."

Two hours ago she would have said the same thing. But two hours ago no one could threaten to take Jesse away from her. "Watch me," Sarah told him, and she started for the door.

His answer halted her in her tracks. "I know where to find you."

She hadn't thought of that. Still holding the crumpled coffee cup, she swung back around to face him.

"Ryan, please." There was a tremor in her voice, and she made an effort to swallow it. She couldn't let him see how close to the edge she was. "Please. Just forget you ever met us."

He shook his head, as if she was asking the impossible, and when he spoke his voice was as raw and husky as it had been last night on the grass. "I'm not letting you go," he said simply. There was a pause, and then he went on. "Or Jesse, either."

The very idea sent a wave of apprehension crashing through her. "You're not going to tell Jesse about this!" she gasped.

"Of course I am! Sarah, he's my son."

But Jesse couldn't be confronted with information like that. It would prove, for one thing, that Adele and Ryan had... She didn't even want to think about it. Besides, Ryan himself had admitted he would never stay in one place long enough to be much of a father. And for Jesse to skip college and wind up abandoned in Alaska...

It was out of the question, Sarah decided, and the nauseating blaze of anger she felt surged even higher. Ryan had no right to such a claim.

"You can't prove it," she told him, hoping it was true. But her heart sank as he looked away from her, down at the floor.

"I already had them do the blood tests."

This was beyond belief. "We played right into your hands, didn't we?" she said bitterly. "You could have just asked! But no, you had to throw Jesse through a windshield...."

A flash of anger crossed his face, and for the first time she realized he was no calmer about this than she was. "What the hell do you think I *am?*" he demanded. "Damn it, the last thing I want is to see him hurt."

"Oh, sure, that's easy to say. But if he knows you're his father, there's no way he won't—"

"I'm not going to hurt him!" Ryan insisted, his voice so loud that a handful of people turned to look at them. Which evidently made an impression, because he took a long breath before continuing more softly. "Look, I don't want him to get hurt any more than you do."

"Well, fine! Why don't you just forget he's your son and leave us alone?"

Ryan gripped the back of the chair before him so tightly that she heard it scrape the floor. "I'm not going to do that, Sarah. I'm willing to make him start college if you want, but I am *not* going to ignore that he's my son."

"You've *got* to do it." She had nothing to threaten him with, only the heartfelt certainty that she couldn't give Jesse up. "I mean it, Ryan! Jesse doesn't need you messing up his life—"

"I'm not *going* to mess up his life!" he almost yelled, and for a moment she felt a cautious flutter of hope.

"So," she prodded, "you'll forget all this?"

He stared at her in amazement. "No, I won't forget all this. But I'm not going to hurt him!"

"Oh, sure," she said scathingly, no longer caring if anyone overheard them. There was no way to settle this, not if Ryan intended to push his way into Jesse's life and ruin any sense of security she'd managed to give him over the years. "He's already had two parents walk out on him, and now you're going to tell him, 'By the way, you're my son, but I've never cared about you before—'" she could hear a new tremor in her voice, but she fought it back as she hurried on "'—and I just thought it'd be fun to see what you're like, teach you a few tricks. But as soon as you go back to school I'm out of your life again.'"

There was silence. Then Ryan spoke softly. "Maybe I won't be."

It was too big a "maybe" to be believed. "Aren't you the one who said you'd rather drive over a cliff than settle down in one place?"

He stiffened, and she went on. "Aren't you the one who said you'd never have another kid because you couldn't stick with it long enough to do a good job?"

"Sarah, he's my son!"

Instinctively, she looked around to see who might have heard him before realizing Jesse was the only one who mattered. But how could she keep Ryan from going to him with such a claim? "You don't know that for sure," she challenged, wishing her voice would stop shaking.

"I will when the blood tests come back."

He would. Oh, he would, and there was nothing she could do to stop him. "You're so sure of yourself," Sarah accused, swallowing the burning in her throat. "At least . . . please, don't tell him anything yet."

His eyes stayed fixed on hers. "I know it's true," he said simply. "And you know it's true."

The hell of it was that she did know. While Adele had identified the most convenient possibility as the father of her baby—after all, the mayor's son was still in town when she learned she was pregnant—anyone who looked at Jesse alongside Tom Bradley and Ryan would know who his father was.

"Please!" she repeated.

Ryan closed his eyes for a moment, as if wishing he were anywhere else. But then he looked at her again, drew a long breath and shook his head.

"One way or another, he's gonna find out. I don't mind waiting until we see the paternity test, if that'll make you feel better. But once we check in at *Odyssey Magazine*—I told them to mail the results there—I'm not keeping it a secret."

By now the anger inside her was growing colder, heavier, and she felt as if she were speaking through a fog. Still, she had to get the words out; she had to make him understand. "Ryan, I'm warning you. If you start playing with him, the way you did with me—"

He started to interrupt, and she hurried on. "I won't put up with it. I'm serious. Before I let you start messing up his life, I'll take him out of Gilroy." The thought of such a radical move made her feel sick, but she concluded in a rush. "And you'll never, ever find us."

When Ryan finally spoke, his voice was taut. "You'd really do that?"

"In a minute."

He stared at her for a long moment, as if wondering whether she was serious. But he must have read the determination in her eyes, because she could see a grim shadow slowly settle on his face. "You really don't trust me, do you?"

She had wanted so badly to trust him! To love him, to let him into her life the way she had come so close to doing last night....

She had to swallow a knot of tears before she could whisper the answer. "No."

It seemed an age before he dropped his gaze, and she wondered if the pain in his eyes was any reflection of her own. "All right, I'll make you a deal," he said abruptly, squaring his shoulders and taking a step toward her. "You forget about leaving Gilroy, and I won't say anything until this trip is over."

But that was barely a month away. "I'll make *you* a deal," Sarah countered, hoping her voice would stay steady. "Wait until September. Then if you want to come to Gilroy and tell him, at least he'll be home with me."

Ryan looked so wretched that for a moment she thought he would head straight for the elevator and Jesse's room. But he must have used the pause to gather his wits together, because he only shoved his hands in his pockets and faced her again.

"All right, it's a deal...as long as you and Jesse will stick with this trip."

Unnerved as she was by the prospect of staying with him, she knew it was the best offer she was likely to get. With any luck at all, Ryan would be ready to move on to new adventures by the time they reached the end of Route 66 and would never bother to visit Gilroy. She wouldn't have to worry about him dragging her nephew—*his son, his and Adele's son*—all over creation, then forgetting him when another job offer came along. And Jesse would never have to know he'd been abandoned by yet another father.

It was the best available option...if she could just make it through four more weeks with this man.

Sarah took a shaky breath. "Okay," she said.

Four more weeks. If he could just make it through four more weeks without losing control, without grabbing her by the shoulders and shaking some sense into her, he ought to get some kind of a medal.

And if he could keep from remembering the warmth of her skin against his, the shy sparkle of her smile after a kiss, the feel of her gasping beneath him as he—

Get off it, Ryan!

No, there was no chance of a medal there. He'd be lucky to make it through four more weeks without wearing out the cold water faucet in the shower.

"How about this one?" he heard Jesse ask, and he hastily turned his attention back to the road.

"Yeah. That looks good."

They had started scouting highway signs that morning, and the Club Cafe billboard with a genial, satisfied-looking fat man seemed like a winner. It might even be the best shot they'd get today, if he could just keep his mind off Sarah. But right now that was proving to be damn near impossible.

"Thought so," Jesse said, adjusting the baseball cap that covered his bandaged scalp and turning to address his aunt as Ryan pulled off to the side of the road. "One more stop, okay?"

"Sure," she agreed, with only the slightest edge of tension in her voice. "You feeling all right, hon?"

"Fine." Jesse jumped out as soon as they stopped and had the side compartment open by the time Ryan moved silently past Sarah and joined him outside. "Once we've shot this, we can head into Santa Rosa. We're making good time."

Ryan lifted the camera from its case, forcing himself to concentrate solely on the job at hand. This photo shouldn't take more than two minutes; the sun was almost perfect and the angle straightforward. "I told you, don't worry about the schedule. We've got time."

"Yeah, but it was my fault we lost a whole day in Amarillo." Jesse reached for the tripod, moving it swiftly into position. "And Vicki's gonna be in Santa Rosa tonight. I was kind of hoping to spend some time with her."

At least one of them had a lady to spend some time with, Ryan thought as he locked the camera in place. Then he realized what Jesse had just said. "Hey, kid, hold on. You're not thinking it was your fault I drove off the road, are you?"

The boy shrugged, scuffing his foot against the ground. "You didn't go breaking any windshields, though. Okay if I take this one?"

Ryan stepped back to let him finish the roll of film, wondering how he could have spent all day shooting with the kid and never once realize that Jesse blamed himself for the disaster. "You know the whole thing was my fault." Too late he realized that explaining why he hadn't mentioned Jesse's unfastened seat belt would reveal more than he cared to explain. But he couldn't let the boy—his son—take the blame. "I'd already noticed you didn't have your seat belt fastened, and I never said anything. I was just too damn busy thinking about...other stuff."

Jesse gave him a curious look, but didn't press for details. "Well," he said, "don't worry about it, okay?" He rewound the film and dropped it into the canister. "If we need any more shots, I'll load another roll."

"Nah, let's wrap it up," Ryan told him, feeling his chest tighten with affection at how easily Jesse slid over the question of blame. His son was one hell of a kid.

Not that Ryan could take any credit for it. No, the credit belonged to Sarah, who had raised him; Sarah who had taught him; Sarah, who had loved him all his life.

Sarah, who would pull up roots and whisk him out of Gilroy before she'd let Ryan get within ten feet of her nephew.

Damn it! How could he resent her so fiercely on the one hand, and at the same time ache with compassion for what she must be feeling? If he had only raised a question when she'd mentioned Adele getting pregnant at the air show, she never would have reacted with such horror when his suspicion was confirmed as fact. But how could he make her see that when he'd heard about Jesse's blood type, he'd been as stunned by the revelation as she was? How could he convince her that wanting his son had nothing to do with wanting her?

And how could he still care this much for a woman who didn't trust him at all?

"Another two minutes and Sarah'll be out here with the aspirin again," Jesse observed, sliding the tripod into its case. "You'd think nobody ever survived a cut scalp."

"She's still worried about you," Ryan explained. It was probably just as well she couldn't keep her anxious eyes off Jesse's face. At least that provided an explanation for the uneasy atmosphere in the motor home.

Because ever since they'd left Amarillo yesterday morning, it felt as if a lightning storm might descend whenever he and Sarah came within five feet of one another. And if Jesse was going to notice the electric tension between them, better he should attribute it to concern for his health.

But the kid obviously had his own ideas about being fussed over. He refused Sarah's next three offers of aspirin with increasingly shorter replies, and by the time they finished dinner at their campsite, Ryan could see the seventeen-year-old was about ready to snap with frustration.

"Vicki's been here two hours already," Jesse announced, rinsing the remainder of his iron-rich spinach and liver into the sink and setting down the plate none too gently. "I'll be back later."

"You're not too tired, are you?" Sarah asked. "You did a lot of shooting today."

"I'm fine," he insisted, but already she was standing up.

"Well, if you're sure. Let me look at your scalp one more time before—"

He turned away, heading for the door. "Damn it, why can't you just shut up and leave me alone?"

Ryan shoved back his chair, grabbed Jesse by the shoulder and spun him around. "Hold it. You're not going anywhere until you've apologized to your aunt."

There was a stunned silence, and Ryan heard Sarah catch her breath. But he kept his eyes fixed on Jesse, who looked both startled and furious until, after a thundering pause, he finally dropped his gaze, swallowed and turned back to Sarah.

"Uh . . . he's right. I'm sorry."

"It's okay, hon," she whispered, and Ryan wondered if that crack in her voice could be caused by tears. "See you later."

Without a word, Jesse went outside and quietly closed the door behind him. Sarah sank back into her seat at the table and buried her face in her hands.

Was she crying?

"Hey," Ryan said softly, and when she didn't look up, he moved behind her and gently rested his hands on her shoulders. "Come on, Sarah. It's okay."

She drew a long, shuddering breath, and when she spoke her voice was shaky. "No, it's not."

But the kid had apologized, hadn't he? He had resisted at first but had finally complied, which was more than he would have done—

Ah, hell.

Which was more than he would have done for Sarah.

Ryan felt a sudden stab of sympathy, viewing it from her perspective. But there was no use pointing out now that he hadn't deliberately tried to show her up, that in fact he'd been on her side. Because the lady would never believe him.

No, he thought, she wouldn't listen to his words. But maybe he could tell her with his hands. Slowly, soothingly, he gradually increased the pressure of his fingers against her tight shoulders and felt her muscles soften in response. Silently, he continued the steady stroking. Then, as she began to relax, he gave her shoulders a gentle squeeze and brushed his fingers across the back of her neck.

"Don't touch me!"

Her body was suddenly rigid; her abrupt command was like a slap across the face. Ryan lifted his hands and she immediately slid away from him, leaving him aghast.

"You hate me that much?" he managed to ask.

He didn't really want an answer—didn't even expect one—but somehow he couldn't quite move away. And apparently Sarah couldn't, either. She stayed at the other end of the table, not meeting his eyes but not making any move to leave, and when she finally spoke her voice was low with shame.

"No. I *want* you that much."

He felt an unexpected surge of hope—Sarah would never give her body where she hadn't already given her heart—but then she raised her face, and he saw the misery in her eyes as she resolutely went on. "But I can't—"

"Sarah, listen." If only he could make her see how he cared for her! If only he could show her how Jesse had nothing to do with this fierce, protective yearning to keep her by his side. "We can work this out."

She shook her head, and when he reached for her, she backed away. "Ryan, please!" Her voice was shaking, and he could see the glint of tears as she turned and headed for her room. "Don't make this any harder than it is."

How long he stood staring at her closed door, he didn't know. But as he replayed her words in his mind, he couldn't help feeling a cautious sense of hope. If this was as hard for her as it was for him, she hadn't yet managed to put him out of her heart.

All he needed was the chance to show her this could work. That just because he moved around a lot didn't mean he couldn't take care of a son...or of the woman who mattered more than his wife ever had. Wanting Jesse and wanting Sarah were two sides of the same coin, and he wasn't going to settle for one without the other.

All he needed was enough time to convince her. And while four weeks might not be much, at least it would give him a start. Five or six weeks would be even better, if only he could get an extension on his *Odyssey* deadline.

Well, hell, why not try? First thing in the morning, Ryan decided, he would give Huey a call. Because with a few more weeks, he could regain this lady's trust and everything that went with it.

He could win Sarah back.

All he needed was a little more time.

Chapter Ten

"You need it *when*?"

Ryan's incredulous cry echoed across the parking lot, and Jesse shot a startled glance at the pay phone. The photographer sounded ready to kick somebody.

"No way, Huey. We're not even halfway into New Mexico! You can't get a thousand miles of road in two weeks' worth of pictures."

No way, Jesse agreed, waiting to start the gas pump while Sarah paid the attendant. It had taken them a month to make it this far, and the best part of the road was still ahead. No wonder Ryan was practically twisting the phone off its stand.

"Sure, of course Marco thinks he can do it! No photographer worth his spit can shoot a thousand miles in thirteen days."

If they had to finish their trip in thirteen days, Jesse realized, they'd be traveling right alongside Vicki. She had told him last night that the Halls planned to reach Los Angeles in two weeks, and at the time he'd wished he could keep pace with her. But thirteen days from here to L.A. was ridiculous, and Ryan obviously thought so, too.

"Well, too damn bad about the deadline. Why can't you move up some other story instead?"

The gas-pump meter cranked back to zero and Jesse slowly squeezed the lever, keeping an eye on Ryan as he responded to the editor.

"All right, I know. Yeah, if we have to. But I'm telling you, Huey, it's a waste of the best photos you'd ever want to see."

So Ryan was giving in? That stunk, Jesse thought. They were going to miss out on a ton of great photos, not to mention having to cut the trip short. But at least they'd be keeping pace with the Halls.

He wished the prospect didn't leave him with such mixed feelings.

If only he had told Vicki the truth from the very beginning! It was too late to change his story now, but the astonishing pleasure of seeing her last night had made him realize how much he wanted to stay in touch with her.

If he didn't have to maintain the role of a globe-trotting photographer, they at least could see each other on weekends. He wouldn't mind driving into Chicago, or even taking the bus if he had to. Not if it meant he could spend some time with her, see the "really ordinary" place where she lived, meet the friends she got together with "every Saturday afternoon since junior high."

But to phone her at college with some questionable story about shooting in Gilroy seemed worse than letting the relationship die a natural death. And confessing the truth was the worst option of all. She might not care that he was younger than she—from her trembling response to his kisses, it was pretty clear she'd lived a slower life than he had—but she couldn't possibly forgive his lying to her all summer long.

"Change of plans," Ryan announced abruptly, and Jesse almost dropped the gas nozzle. He'd been so lost in thoughts of Vicki he hadn't even heard the man approach. "We need to start moving."

"Yeah, I heard you on the phone. What happened, anyway?"

Ryan shook his head in disgust. "*Odyssey* canceled a story for the March issue, and they're using Route 66 in its place. But they go to press two weeks from tomorrow. And... I couldn't buy any more time."

He sounded desolate, Jesse thought. A lot more upset than made sense, considering they could still pick up their pace and hit Los Angeles in time to sell the photos. It was practically a sure thing, as long as Marco was their only competition.

"What would've happened if you hadn't called them?" he asked.

"Then," Ryan said grimly, "I'd really be out of luck. This whole shoot would be a total loss."

The photographer sounded so bleak that Jesse kept quiet as the gas tank filled up. Ryan had to sell these photos, he knew, if he was ever going to get back into the business. But it didn't seem fair, moving up a deadline on someone who'd been shooting nonstop for more than a month.

"I've *got* to do this shoot," Ryan declared. "But how the hell we're going to fit Albuquerque and the Indian country and everything else into thirteen days, I don't know."

"We'll just shoot a lot more nights," Jesse suggested, before realizing that wouldn't leave him much time with Vicki. But already Ryan was shaking his head.

"The nights won't be any good without some kind of moonlight. Huey said not to worry about it. They won't use more than sixteen pages of photos, and they've already got California on file. But I still want to get every last shot I can... I just wanted more time to do it."

He seemed to be doing pretty well with what little time he had, though, Jesse noticed over the next few days. It helped that the country was so vivid, with a dramatic photo waiting at nearly every turn of the road. The sky seemed more blue and the clouds more white, the air more bright and the land more vibrant as they progressed across the Continental Divide, which ran down the spine of the nation and divided its waters into east and west.

This was the West, all right, and even as they scrambled for every possible photo, Jesse found it enchanting. Albuquerque, home of the Route 66 Diner and the El Vado Motel. The "Sky City" of Acoma, the oldest Indian pueblo in the land. San Fidel. Toltec. Baca. Names that spoke of magic, of mystery. Vistas that left him feeling strangely awed.

"It's different than seeing it on TV," he told Vicki when they met a few nights later near the Arizona border. "It's so big! You get the feeling this could be ten thousand years ago, and we'd never know the difference."

Ryan and Sarah seemed to feel the majesty, too. During the occasional hours when all three of them were traveling westward toward the next stop, they both stayed unusually quiet.

Sarah, though, had been quiet ever since they'd picked up their pace the other morning. For some reason she seemed even more upset than Ryan when he announced that the end of the trip was just two weeks away. Jesse had overheard them squabbling when he emerged from the rest room at the next stop.

"Don't think it'll make any difference if you get your test back sooner," she'd been saying.

"Damn it, that's not what I'm trying to do!" Ryan had retorted.

"Oh, sure, you can't wait to get this whole thing over with—" Sarah had stopped abruptly when she'd noticed Jesse, who had puzzled over their behavior until they came across the remains of the Long Horn Ranch, where shooting three rolls of film in ten minutes was enough to divert his attention.

There were plenty of diversions. Plenty of scenes they could have spent hours on, if only they had the time. The Petrified Forest with its ancient chunks of agate, carnelian and onyx. The Painted Desert with its rocks and soil arrayed in hues of azure, crimson and lavender. The legendary Wigwam Motel, with fifteen concrete tepees offering the comforts of air-conditioning, full baths and double beds. And the vast, wide-open stretches of land that seemed so much grander, so much more ancient than anything they had traveled before.

In a way it was almost a relief to arrive in Winslow, where Jesse had arranged to meet Vicki for the evening, and to drive down a main street that resembled those of a dozen other small towns he'd seen. He wouldn't dream of admitting it to her, not when photographers should be accustomed to all kinds of strange new vistas, but there was something comforting about the oilcloth-covered tables in the Grand Café which might have come straight out of Gilroy.

"Feels just like home," he observed, closing the plastic menu with the coffee-stained Daily Special announcement paper fluttering inside. And Vicki regarded him with interest as she took a sip of ice water from her gold plastic cup.

"Did you grow up in a small town?"

"Yeah," Jesse said, relieved that he could tell her the truth about something. "Place called Gilroy, not too far from Chicago. It's the kind of town that never changes."

"When was the last time you saw it?"

Oh, great. Try a little truth and see where it gets you. "Just last month," he said carefully, hoping he sounded casual enough. "My aunt still lives there."

"I always thought it'd be fun to live in a small town," Vicki observed. "You know, where everybody knows each other."

"Depends on what they know," Jesse muttered. But there was no point talking about his mother's disgrace, or how everyone expected him to follow in her footsteps. For once he was with a girl who liked him not because of his reputation as a troublemaker, or in spite of it, but simply for who he was.

Well, for who she *thought* he was.

"We got a lot of great pictures today," he told her abruptly, shifting his camera onto an empty chair. He was supposed to meet Ryan in an hour to shoot the neon cowgirl sign above the Store For Men, and he liked having the camera with him for Vicki to see. She still seemed impressed at the idea of a magazine filled with photos by someone she knew.

"Oh, I bet. That place with all the tepees—" She broke off as Ryan came hurrying up to their table.

"Hey, sorry to interrupt, but there's a train coming in behind the old Harvey House. Jesse, we've got to shoot this."

Of course they had to. The La Posada was a beautiful building in its own right, reminiscent of the haciendas that once graced the land of New Spain, and with the lights of a train in the background, they'd have another winner of a photo.

"Could I watch?" Vicki asked.

Ryan turned to her with a welcoming smile. "Sure. You're Vicki, right?" He offered his hand. "Nate Ryan."

She looked from him to Jesse and her eyes widened. "You guys look so much alike."

Good, Jesse thought. Maybe that distraction would keep her entertained while he figured out how to prevent a disaster. If she got any hint that he was only an assistant—

"All photographers look alike," Ryan told her, and Jesse breathed a silent sigh of relief as he dropped some money on the table and let Vicki precede him outside. Then she stopped short.

"I'd better leave a note," she said. "The Halls were going to pick me up here."

"Train station's three blocks east," Ryan offered, and as Vicki hurried back toward the cashier's stand, Jesse drew him aside.

"This is important. Can I shoot this photo?"

The photographer glanced at Vicki and then smiled. "Yeah, sure. It's kind of tricky lighting, but I don't suppose she'll know who's doing what."

Thank goodness, he didn't have to explain anything to Ryan. "One more thing," Jesse muttered as Vicki came back toward them, looking so excited that he felt his heart leap with anticipation. "I don't care about anything else, but please don't call me 'kid.' "

It might have been easier, Jesse thought the next morning, if Ryan had slipped and revealed him as a seventeen-year-old right from the start. But he hadn't, and now Jesse was in a worse predicament than before.

Now he had to deal with Sarah.

The shoot had gone beautifully last night, and Vicki had been fascinated with how they set up the camera, the lights and the reflectors. Ryan had given every appearance of working as equals, even referring her question to Jesse when she wondered what they planned to shoot tomorrow. "Because we're going to be in Flagstaff tomorrow night, and I'd love to watch you again. If it's okay."

"Sure, we'd love to have you," Jesse said grandly, recalling from Sarah's itinerary that they'd be at the Northern Arizona University campus around five. And then Ryan stepped in.

"There's supposed to be a great Mexican food place near there. You want to join us for dinner?"

In a way, Jesse could understand why he'd invited her without even questioning whether it was okay. The three of them had gotten along so well during the past hour, anyone would think they'd been friends for years. And Ryan could probably tell just by looking at them that Jesse wanted as much time with Vicki as he could get.

But not with his aunt as a chaperon!

"Oh, that'd be fun," Vicki answered, just as he started to protest that their plans weren't certain yet. And before he could think of a way out, the Halls had arrived and Vicki had left, with a promise to meet them at the El Charro Cafe tomorrow evening at six.

He had to think of something fast.

There was no way to lead into it gracefully, Jesse knew. But still he was relieved when Ryan asked him to drive the first shift and disappeared into the darkroom. At least he could confront Sarah alone.

They had driven fifteen miles out of Winslow, with each mile marker silently screaming, "Tell her!", before he worked up the courage to mention that Vicki had enjoyed watching last night's shoot.

"I wish I'd gotten to meet her," Sarah said. "We probably could've made it through one more day without my doing a load of wash."

He wasn't going to get a better opening than this, Jesse decided. "You can meet her tonight if you want. Ryan invited her to dinner."

He must have sounded more nervous than he realized, because his aunt looked at him curiously. "Did he? That'll be nice."

"Yeah. Well. The thing is, I kind of wish he hadn't. I mean—"

Sarah seemed to guess what he meant before he even finished the sentence. "Oh, hon, you don't need to worry about me embarrassing you. I promise I won't say anything about when you were a cute little kid."

They had once seen a movie where the boy's mother regaled his girlfriend with such stories, and Jesse couldn't help smiling at that. But Sarah didn't quite understand the problem.

"It's just...the thing is, Vicki thinks we're the same age."

He didn't even have to look up to know his aunt was getting that wrinkle of concern between her eyes. "How old is Vicki?" she asked in a carefully calm voice.

"I don't know, eighteen or nineteen. I mean, she's not a *lot* older. But she's already in college."

"Jesse, if she really likes you she won't care that you're not in college yet."

This was getting more difficult by the minute. "See, she kind of thinks I'm, like, a real photographer. You know, like Ryan and I are partners."

There was a silence. "You've been telling her quite a story, haven't you?" Sarah sounded disapproving, but at least she wasn't yelling at him. "Hon, if you're asking me to lie for you—"

"Uh, there's just one more thing," Jesse interrupted. "I didn't want her to know I was traveling with my aunt. I mean, it'd sound like I was a kid or something. So, I, uh...I told her you were Ryan's girlfriend."

Sarah gasped. "You told her *what?*"

"I had to explain why you were traveling with us."

"Jesse Corcoran—"

"It was the only thing I could think of!"

"How on earth could you—"

"What'd he do?" They both jerked around as Ryan's voice came from behind them. "Rob a bank?"

"No," Jesse muttered. Lord, this was going to be worse than he'd expected. "I was just asking Sarah to cover for me. See, Vicki thinks you and I are partners, and that Sarah's just along for the ride because she's your girlfriend."

Ryan broke into a slow smile. "You don't waste time with the small stuff, do you, kid?"

"It's not funny!" Sarah protested.

"Well, you gotta admit, it's—"

Jesse slammed on the brakes at the Tuba City exit and pulled onto the dirt road so he could face them both. "Look, it's just for one dinner, okay? I know I made a mistake—you don't need to tell me. All I'm asking is can't you please just back me up?''

Ryan and Sarah exchanged a glance, and then Ryan lifted his hands in a gesture of relinquishment. ''This one's your call, Corky. I'll go along with whatever you decide.'' With a teasing grin, he turned and headed back to the darkroom.

Leaving Sarah staring after him in disbelief. ''Thanks a *lot!*'' she called. And Ryan turned to give her a look of challenge.

''Hey, he's *your* nephew.''

''It's just for one dinner,'' Jesse reminded her, hoping to ease the tension Ryan had somehow left behind. ''You don't even have to lie. It's not like she's gonna ask if we're related or anything. If you could just, you know, not make it look like *I* was lying.''

Sarah shook her head. ''I can't,'' she said flatly. ''I can't do that, Jess. You'll have to figure out some other way.''

''Maybe I could tell her you and Ryan had a fight and you didn't want to come.''

''You will not tell her that! And maybe we should get moving again.''

Jesse started the engine, glanced over his shoulder and pulled back onto the road. ''Okay, but what's so bad about pretending you're his girlfriend instead of my aunt? It's not like Ryan's a big jerk or anything.''

Sarah swallowed. ''No. But . . . it wouldn't be the truth.'' She sat up straight, and her voice grew stronger. ''Jesse, I will not help you lie to this girl. I just won't.''

Why, *why* did his aunt have to be such a stickler for truth and honor and keeping one's word? She had probably never told a lie or broken a promise in her life. . . .

A promise.

''. . . *If you'll just stand up, I'll give you any reward you want. Anything you want, except quitting school. You can do it, hon.*''

He had. He had done it, and now was the time to collect.

Jesse turned to glance at her, thanking his lucky stars that Sarah would never go back on her word, and took a deep breath.

"You remember when we crashed into the ditch?"

She should have known. She should have guessed when she made that promise that it would come back to haunt her.

But how could she have imagined it would turn out like this? How could she have guessed she'd find herself sitting in a Mexican restaurant so close to Ryan that she could feel the warmth of his body burning into hers?

She was already pressed as far against the wall as she could get, and even so she was keenly aware of the scent of him, the sight of him, the sensation of him as he casually draped his arm around her shoulders and touched his margarita glass to hers.

"You doing all right, angel?"

He said it so naturally, the endearment almost didn't register. But when it did, she looked up and felt the warmth of his slow smile like a lingering caress, and she had to duck her head to hide the blush she knew was coloring her cheeks. How on earth could he do this to her so easily?

"Just fine," she murmured, still avoiding his gaze, and took a hasty sip from the icy, salt-rimmed glass. Half a margarita gone already, and they had been here no more than ten minutes. She had to get hold of herself.

"So, how did Brandon like Meteor Crater?" Jesse asked Vicki. "I kind of expected to see his leftover bubble gum on the biggest telescope."

"He threw Katie's troll over the edge and told her a meteor was going to fall on it," Vicki reported. "He had her convinced we were five minutes away from disaster."

"Kid sounds like he'd be a great photo editor," Ryan observed, slowly moving his fingers across Sarah's shoulder to caress the side of her neck. "If you ever want to get rid of him, I know a couple of magazines that would be glad to take him on."

"We're kind of down on editors right now," Jesse explained, either not noticing the caress or doing a good job of pretending such behavior was normal. "*Odyssey*'s not giving us nearly enough time to finish this shoot."

"That's terrible," Vicki agreed as Ryan trailed his fingers up Sarah's cheek, sending a jolt of sensation radiating from the center of her body.

"Worst part is," Ryan said huskily, "it's really not fair to Sarah. We can shoot twenty-four hours a day if we have to, but she's got to cram all her research into business hours." He slid his hand back to her shoulder and gave her a gentle squeeze. "I'll tell you, though, she's doing a hell of a job."

Vicki's eyes widened. "I didn't know you were a researcher, Sarah."

"Uh, yes." If Ryan would only move away from her, she could come up with a coherent sentence! "Yes, I am."

"She's the best," Ryan said, giving her another slow, compelling smile that intensified the core of warmth inside her. "I'm not just saying that," he added in a low voice. "You really are."

Good heavens, she was blushing again. This had to stop. Then, through a wave of heat, she heard Jesse say, "Pass the chips."

They both reached for the basket at the same time, and Sarah drew back as if his touch burned. With shaky fingers, she picked up her margarita and took another gulp.

"Easy, angel," Ryan murmured. "You doing all right?"

No, she was not doing all right! She was getting hotter by the minute, sitting this close to him, feeling the length of his thigh against hers, hearing the rough tenderness in his voice and wishing against all common sense that they could be alone....

"Yes," she managed to say. "Yes, fine."

Somehow, though, it was hard to remember she felt fine as the conversation flowed around her, with every sentence an effort to grasp. Ryan seemed to know just when to distract her with a light caress, just when to ease away before she lost all pretense of control and started squirming at the pleasure of his touch. This was crazy, Sarah told herself. He wasn't doing anything he shouldn't do in a public place. An occasional smile, a murmured remark, a casual drift of his fingers across her hand—and yet somehow she was on the verge of shivering, moaning, pleading for more....

She had to get hold of herself.

The arrival of dinner almost made her swoon with relief. Surely this would give her a chance to regroup. A chance to edge out of his reach. A chance to remember that no matter how much she might want this man, she couldn't have him and that was that.

"Truck driver in Albuquerque was talking about this place," Jesse told Vicki as the waitress set down their *chimichangas,* deep-fried tortillas stuffed with chicken and cheese and topped with sour cream, salsa and guacamole. "Said even though there's no atmosphere, this is the best Mexican food in Arizona."

It smelled wonderful. Even with her other senses loaded to the point of surfeit, Sarah could tell that much. "I've got to try cooking like this sometime," she said shakily.

Ryan eased his arm from around her shoulders and gave her a slow, teasing grin. "You like things hot, don't you."

"My mom got a Mexican-food cookbook one time," Vicki said. "But she couldn't find all the ingredients in Chicago. Sarah, where do you live?"

Before she could answer, Jesse broke in. "We're not that far from Mexico right now. Phoenix is only a few hours south of here, and that's practically on the border."

"I did a shoot in Phoenix once," Ryan recalled. "Great city to get lost in."

From the relief on Jesse's face, Sarah could tell the subject of their hometown was something he'd rather avoid. Good heavens, she was surrounded by pitfalls tonight. But far and away the most dangerous was the man at her side, whose nearness felt altogether too comfortable. Altogether too real.

"Too bad we don't have enough time to go down there," Jesse said. "I wouldn't mind spending a few weeks in Mexico."

He'd probably love it, Sarah thought. In fact, if Ryan had his way, Jesse would probably be wandering the streets of Tijuana alone a month from now. She sat up straighter, wishing she could get a little farther away from Ryan, and took another gulp of her margarita.

"Sarah," he said softly, "take it easy. Here, try some of this."

Before she could argue that it was impossible to take it easy with him so close to her, he dipped his finger into the guacamole on his plate and lifted it to her lips.

"Come on, angel. Try it."

For a moment all the sound in the restaurant seemed to swirl through her head, making her dizzy with some sensation she didn't want to claim. Then, as the compelling tug of warmth inside her grew even stronger, she felt a wave of recklessness urge her forward.

Slowly, deliberately, she took Ryan's finger in her mouth and leisurely licked it.

He almost gasped. She could feel the intensity of his response, a sudden electricity so swift and so hot there was no pretending it hadn't charged between them.

So there, she wanted to exclaim. *How do you like that, Nate Ryan?*

But she couldn't taunt him when the gesture had affected her even more sharply, even more intensely. Her heart was throbbing, her skin was tingling and she knew if she tried to speak, her voice would shake. Instead she looked down at her plate, willing herself to stop trembling, and felt him moving beside her.

"Pretty good, isn't it?" he murmured.

How could he even ask such a thing in public? She glanced up to see him lazily spooning some more guacamole onto her plate, and when he caught her gaze, he gave her a slow, knowing smile.

"Yes," Sarah whispered, and cleared her throat in hopes of achieving a more normal tone. "But that still doesn't mean I'm going to have it every day."

"You never know," he said, shifting to give her a little more room as she resolutely dug into her *chimichanga*. "You might like it."

Oh, he was right, she would! But she couldn't let herself abandon a lifetime of responsibility just because she liked this man more than anyone she'd ever known.

"The salsa's even better," Jesse said, passing the dish of finely chopped tomatoes, cilantro and chilies across the table. "I could eat this every day, no problem."

The what? The salsa? She had completely lost the thread of this conversation, Sarah realized. She had to get hold of herself.

"Could you really?" Vicki asked, gulping her iced tea. "You're more adventurous than I am. Sarah, do you think all photographers are that way?"

"I know this one is," she managed to answer, nodding at Ryan and feeling a quiver of amazement at how very relaxed he looked. How could he sit there so lazily when every particle of her body was charged with this fierce, demanding need?

If only, if *only* she could have gotten him out of her system that night in Amarillo. It was irresponsible to even think of indulging in a one-night stand—under the circumstances, it could never be anything more—but in a way, she still wished they could have finished what they'd started. At least then she wouldn't be hovering on the raw edge of desire whenever he so much as glanced her way.

It didn't help, as they progressed through dinner, that he seemed so very much at ease beside her. As if this were the real thing, and he had every right to smile at her with such comfortable intimacy. Every right to talk as if they had a future together. Every right to take her napkin and gently wipe a crumb of salt from her lips.

She was already so sensitized, so acutely aware of him, that his every gesture, even his every word, seemed to heighten the swelling warmth inside her. And yet she had no business feeling that way. He couldn't be deliberately trying to arouse her, not when he was conversing with Jesse and Vicki as if this were an ordinary evening on Route 66.

"The road between here and Kingman is supposed to be one of the best-used stretches," Ryan told them, lazily curling a strand of her hair around his finger as if such a touch was perfectly ordinary. "It's the last section we need to cover, and I'm hoping we can get a midnight shot of a truck heading west."

"I can't wait to see the magazine," Vicki said. "I'm going to tell everybody I know who took the pictures."

"You're just hinting for an autographed copy," Jesse teased, and she blushed.

"Well, if you get a chance..."

Jesse and Vicki were having a wonderful time, Sarah could tell as the evening moved along with aching slowness, aching sweetness. Ryan was having a wonderful time, too, judging from the ease of his voice and the warmth of his laughter. But then, *Ryan* didn't have to keep reminding himself how disastrous it would be to let this pretense of intimacy become real. Ryan didn't have to worry about whether Jesse might notice...

Ryan didn't have to worry about Jesse, period. That was the whole problem.

"You getting sleepy on me, angel?"

His low drawl sent another shiver of desire up her spine. "Yes," Sarah answered swiftly, not even caring that Vicki looked faintly embarrassed. Let her think they were hurrying home to bed together; what did it matter? At least the night air outside should cool things down.

She and Vicki stopped by the ladies' room while Ryan and Jesse dealt with the check, and when she glanced in the mirror, she was appalled at the heavy-lidded look of her eyes. She appeared as languorous as Adele used to after an evening with some man—*with Ryan, remember?*—and the idea that he could affect her just as strongly, just as powerfully, was enough to make her cringe.

She took two deep breaths, shook back her hair and squared her shoulders. Only a few more minutes to keep up this charade, and then she could put any fantasies she might have about this man straight out of her mind. Leaving Vicki at the mirror, she went back out and nearly bumped into him.

He was talking so intently to Jesse that he never noticed her behind him. "I know I said I'd go along with whatever Sarah decided. But I'm telling you, kid, this isn't the best way to play it."

"It's working, though," Jesse protested. "Vicki doesn't suspect anything."

"I know. But you can't build much of a relationship this way—not telling the truth."

Sarah caught her breath. Who was *he* to lecture Jesse about telling the truth, in light of everything he'd kept from her?

"Whatever," Jesse said, glancing up as Vicki emerged from the ladies' room. "Everybody ready?"

Ryan swung around and, with a smile that looked genuinely welcoming, drew Sarah to him. "I guess we're out of here."

She let Jesse and Vicki get well ahead of them on the way to the parking lot before she murmured, "I'm surprised you'd give advice like that."

"Like what?"

"About telling the truth." Realizing they were alone for now, she pulled away from him, trying to ignore an embarrassing sense of loss at knowing the show was nearly over. "Since when has that been a big priority of yours?"

He stared at her for a moment, and she could see a halfdozen answers battling in his mind. But what he said surprised her.

"We've got to talk."

As if that would change anything. "We have nothing to talk about," she told him.

"The hell we don't!" His vehemence startled her, and before she could react, he laid his hands on her shoulders, pulling her to face him. "You know we do," he said.

She ducked her head, trying to avoid his eyes, and wished she had never let Jesse and Vicki get so far ahead of them. This was no way to end an evening. "Ryan, please. Can't you just leave it alone?"

He let out his breath in a sharp sigh. "I can't do that. And you know why I'm not going to?" Before she could answer or pull away, he went on. "Because—and you tell me if I'm wrong—it felt so damn *right* being together tonight."

So he had felt it, too. She looked up at him, silhouetted against the amber light of the parking lot, and felt a shameful rush of agreement. But she couldn't let him know that.

"Didn't it?" Ryan prompted.

"So what if it did?" she retorted. "That doesn't mean anything!"

"You look me straight in the eye," he said softly, "and tell me that."

She made the mistake of looking into his eyes, and her throat closed up. No, she couldn't tell him that. But neither could she look away.

Ryan let the silence linger for nearly a minute, growing more revealing with every agonizing second, until he finally let her go and took a step back.

"We've got to talk," he repeated.

She could no longer argue with him. But some instinct made her counter, "Not in front of Jesse."

If he sensed he had won a victory, he had the grace not to show it. He only nodded, as if that was a reasonable request, and gestured toward the motor home, where Jesse and Vicki stood waiting.

"Tomorrow, when we get to Kingman, he can take some time off. Go play with Vicki, whatever he wants. But you and me, Corky..." He stopped, making no move to touch her, and waited until she looked at him before delivering a promise that left her nerves on edge. "We've got some things to straighten out."

Chapter Eleven

Ryan was wrong, that's all, Jesse thought as he paced the
gravel road near the Kingman campsite entrance. Sometimes you just couldn't tell the truth.

Not when you had only six more days together. Not when
she'd never speak to you again if she knew you were only a
high school kid. Worse yet, a high school kid who had
played fast and loose with the truth all summer long.

"It's your call, kid," Ryan had told him again this
morning, when Jesse tried to explain his reasoning. "I'm
not the world's greatest when it comes to giving advice. But
the way I see it, when you love somebody they ought to
know who you are."

That wasn't bad advice, Jesse had to admit. But with only
six days left until the end of Route 66, he couldn't afford to
ruin things with Vicki now.

She ought to be arriving any minute, even if the Halls
hadn't left Flagstaff until midmorning. The drive was a long
one, but there wasn't much to stop for along the way. He

and Ryan had gotten a few photos in Williams of the steam engine bound for the Grand Canyon, and had spent half an hour shooting an abandoned motel in Peach Springs, but aside from that the road had been kind of dull.

Although Brandon could probably get into trouble anywhere.

With any luck, Vicki would have the afternoon off and they could go exploring Kingman together. Jesse had already spotted a place not too far down the road that offered pool and video games, and while Sarah would shake her head if she knew he planned to stop in there, she hadn't asked about his plans. She and Ryan had to go over her research notes, anyway, which was fine with Jesse. He wouldn't have to feel guilty about taking the afternoon off.

He had enough to feel guilty about already.

It was a relief to see the Halls' motor home approaching the gravel drive. He needed to start moving, to work off some of the nervous energy that assaulted him whenever he thought too long about the story he'd spun for Vicki. Last night might have been a mistake, in spite of how flawlessly Sarah and Ryan had performed—they'd made it look so real that for a moment he'd wondered if they might have actually fallen in love without him noticing—but the evening had added so many more bricks to the wall of lies he was building that he could no longer hope to make things right.

Better just enjoy their last afternoon together, and then let Vicki go.

"Hey, Jesse!" Brandon yelled from the window of the motor home. "We're going to McDonald's, and you're not!"

That was the best news he'd heard all day. Ever since Ryan had mentioned after dinner last night that they wouldn't shoot much around Kingman, he'd been hoping Vicki could get the afternoon off. But in spite of her promise to ask, Jesse had worried that the Halls might send Brandon along with her.

Now they would have some time to themselves.

She emerged from the motor home looking as radiant as ever, and Mr. Hall—Dave, Jesse reminded himself, although he still felt weird calling Vicki's boss by his first name—waved at both of them. "Don't keep our girl out too late, Jesse!"

It was kind of sweet, how much the Halls seemed to care for Vicki, but then anyone who knew her would probably feel the same way. Jesse nodded and made a point of waiting until they were out of view of the campsite before kissing her as thoroughly as he wanted to.

"I missed you," Vicki told him when they finally came up for air.

"Yeah, I missed you, too." He wished they could be completely alone someplace, but things would probably get out of hand. With only six days left, it was better not to start something they couldn't finish. "I was looking around before you got here, and there's a place just up the road where we can get a soda, shoot some pool, whatever."

Vicki didn't drink. "My dad was an alcoholic, and you can't imagine how awful it was," she had told him back in Kansas. But she didn't seem to mind visiting the Red Horse, which was refreshingly cool after the fifteen-minute walk from the campground. Jesse ordered sodas for both of them, relieved at having an excuse for not revealing the age on his driver's license, and offered to beat her at a game of pool.

She played pretty well for a beginner, and it was a pleasure to show her the tricks he had picked up from Ryan. Halfway through the second rack, though, she leaned closer to him and whispered, "I think that guy is looking at you."

Jesse glanced across the room and saw Marco watching him from the bar.

"You're right," he told her, sinking a shot and feeling a smug sense of relief that it dropped in cleanly. "He's just some photographer who thinks he can shoot Route 66 better than Ryan and I can. Nothing to worry about."

She looked a little uncertain. "You think maybe he wants to talk to you? I need to stop by the rest room, anyway."

Given an offer like that, he couldn't help but agree. Marco looked distinctly uncomfortable at the sight of him, and that alone was enough to arouse Jesse's curiosity. Had the guy expected him and Ryan to conveniently disappear somewhere along Route 66?

He took his time strolling over to the bar, but no sooner had he gotten within a few feet of Marco than the photographer blurted, "So you and Ryan are still at it?"

This had all the makings of a great movie scene, Jesse realized. He halfway expected the guy to draw a gun, at which point Vicki would scream and Jesse would knock Marco through the slatted doors of the Old West saloon. But for the moment he only nodded, enjoying the sensation of holding the winning hand.

"Yep."

Marco shifted his considerable weight on the bar stool, looking even more uncomfortable. "He around?"

If the guy ever wanted to land a role in a Western movie, Jesse decided, he'd have to get in shape. "Nope. He's working on some research."

"Oh, yeah, he always did that." The recollection didn't seem to make Marco any happier. He swirled the ice in his drink and set it down again. "So he's made it the whole way, then. I never thought that'd happen."

If he had the nerve, Jesse thought, he wouldn't mind picking up the guy's drink and finishing it himself. But that might be taking this showdown business a little too far. "You win some, you lose some. Isn't that how it goes?"

"It's just that I didn't expect to lose this one," Marco said abruptly. "This is *Odyssey Magazine!*"

He sounded even more reverent about the magazine than Ryan did, if that was possible. "From what I hear, though," Jesse said, "you're doing all right without it."

Marco looked surprised, and then his mouth twisted. "It's not the money—even Ryan knows that much. It's the credit. Once you sell to *Odyssey,* you can write your own ticket.''

The money wasn't bad, either, Jesse knew. Especially if you were stretched as thin as Ryan, who had sold everything he owned to pay for this trip.

''Maybe you can try them again sometime,'' Jesse told him. ''You might get lucky.''

''You could, too, you know,'' Marco said, and his voice was imperceptibly softer. ''You and I could work something out.''

This wasn't a Western movie, after all. This was a wartime thriller, where the Nazi commander made a staggering offer to some underground spy, who pretended to consider it and then threw it back in his face.

''Yeah?'' Jesse asked. ''Try me.''

That was apparently the right response, because he could see Marco's face lighten with anticipation.

''I'll double what they're paying for the story,'' he said, ''if you can get me Ryan's photos.''

Jesse almost choked. The guy was offering him a fortune! Evidently he realized that Ryan's photos were his only chance of making a sale to *Odyssey,* and apparently he didn't mind spending whatever it took.

Marco must have taken the astonishment on his face for agreement, because he plucked a napkin off the bar and jotted down an address. ''Prints, negatives, everything you can get—except the research notes, I don't need those. I'll be here until tomorrow morning, so that'll give you time to work something out.''

''Uh-huh,'' Jesse mumbled, stuffing the napkin in the pocket of his jeans. Did Marco actually expect him to raid Ryan's darkroom? ''We'll see how it goes.''

''Got to be tomorrow morning,'' the photographer reminded him as he turned away. ''It'll take a couple of days to make it to L.A. from here, and I'll still have to make Huey's copy prints.''

"Copy prints?" Jesse swung back, startled. "What are those for?"

A look of regret stole across Marco's face. "I'll bet Ryan hasn't talked to Huey all week, has he? I should've guessed."

Good thing Marco hadn't guessed, Jesse realized. Otherwise he would have kept his mouth shut, and Ryan would never have known that Huey now wanted copy prints—whatever those were.

"Yeah, well," he said, trying to sound nonchalant as he caught sight of Vicki heading in their direction. "Anyway—"

"Cash on delivery," Marco interrupted, as Jesse started toward her. "Have we got a deal?"

"I'll let you know," he said, taking Vicki's hand and nodding toward the door. "See you around."

He was grateful that she didn't ask any questions until they were outside, but as soon as the door swung shut behind them, she stopped and asked, "What kind of a deal was he talking about?"

Jesse sighed. Already he regretted having listened to Marco's offer. He just hadn't expected to be confronted with such a staggering amount of money.

"This guy's not much of a photographer," he told her, trying to dismiss the uneasy temptation in his mind, "and he knows it. But he really wants to make this sale, and he's got a ton of money. So he offered to buy our photos for twice what *Odyssey*'s paying."

Her eyes widened. "Would that be a whole lot of money?"

Lord, would it ever. "It'd be enough to pay for another three trips like this one," Jesse said. He took her hand as they started down the road toward the campsite, and noticed with almost automatic awareness that the sky was darkening slightly. *Sky like this, we could get a great shot with the wide-angle lens. Maybe use another filter...* At that realization, he stopped. "But there's no way I'm gonna take him up on it."

He felt better, having said the words out loud. For a moment he was tempted to go back inside and tell Marco to kiss off, but there was no point making any further contact. Vicki, though, looked surprised.

"You're not even going to think about it?"

"No," he said, and felt a slowly growing pleasure at knowing how firmly he meant it. No amount of money could compare with everything he'd gotten from Ryan this summer. "I'm not. Ryan has too much riding on this story to give it all to Marco."

He started walking again, faster this time, and Vicki hurried to match his pace. "But what about *you?*" she asked. "It's your story, too."

He'd forgotten he and Ryan were supposed to be equal partners, Jesse realized. "Sure," he mumbled. "But for me, this is just another shoot. For Ryan, it's the only way he'll ever get back into the business."

Vicki reached for his hand, and when he looked down at her, he saw new understanding on her face. "That's really sweet," she said simply.

"Aw, well . . ."

"I mean, for you to turn down that much money. Ryan doesn't know how lucky he is, having you for a partner."

This was growing more awkward by the minute, Jesse thought as they headed across a vacant acre of land dotted with scraggly mesquite bushes. "He's done a lot for me, too. It's no big deal."

"Yes, it is!" Vicki told him. "I think it's wonderful, the way you look out for other people. It's not something you have to be modest about."

"You're giving me too much credit," he protested. "I don't want you to think I'm some kind of hero or anything."

"Well, you are," she insisted with a teasing smile. "Like it or not, Jesse Corcoran, you are a very nice person."

He looked down at her, smiling with such blithe confidence, and felt his heart twist. If only she knew! More than ever, he wished he had told her the truth from the beginning. Wished that she could say such things about the real Jesse Corcoran.

"It's nothing to get upset about, though," she offered, apparently reading his expression more accurately than he knew. "I mean, I didn't want to make you feel bad."

The quaver of apology in her voice was more than he could bear. With a surge of desperate yearning—if only he could make things right!—he pulled her into his arms, drawing her so close she was almost a part of him.

"Vicki, I love you."

He felt her grow very still, and when she raised her face to his, her eyes shimmered with happiness.

"I love you, too."

But you don't know me! he wanted to cry, and he heard again the echo of Ryan's words: *When you love someone, they ought to know who you are.*

He had to tell her.

Jesse drew a long breath, still holding her close. "Vicki," he said urgently, "no matter what, I want you to know I love you. That's the truth, okay?"

She hesitated, looking a little shaken. "Okay."

"And I want to keep on seeing you," he added, racing to get this over with before she could pull away. Now that he was committed, he needed to tell her fast before he lost his nerve. "But I'm not really a photographer."

She stared at him, as if wondering what that had to do with anything. "What?"

"I mean, not yet." He hurried on, relieved that at least she hadn't pulled away. She was bewildered, maybe, but she was still listening. "I'm just spending the summer with Ryan, helping out."

She swallowed and gave him a shaky smile. "Oh. I see."

"I'm not really even on my own yet," he continued, feeling his chest tighten with each word he forced out. This next part would be the hardest, but until he confessed it he would have no idea where he stood. "See, the thing is...I, uh...I won't be eighteen until April."

There was a silence. Then Vicki took a step back and ducked her head, so he could barely hear her whisper.

"I won't be eighteen until May."

Jesse felt himself reel. "You're—"

"I thought you were older!" she murmured, still looking at the ground, as if she couldn't quite meet his eyes. "I thought you wouldn't be interested in me if you knew I was still in high school. And I felt like such a baby, traveling with my family..."

He wouldn't have thought anything could shock him more than the news of her age, but he had never antici-pated this. "The Halls are your *family?*" Jesse repeated. She was traveling with her family?

"Well, my mom married Dave eight years ago, and then they had Brandon and Katie." For the first time, she looked up, and the uncertainty on her face made his heart swell with compassion. All this time she had been worried about tell-ing *him* the truth? "But I thought if you knew I was with my family," Vicki continued hurriedly, "you'd think I was just a kid—"

"No," Jesse interrupted, but she kept on going.

"And here you were already working. So when I realized you thought I was a nanny, it was like, okay, maybe he'll think I'm old enough for him."

"I was doing the same thing!"

She gave him a tentative smile, as if only now realizing he might still want her.

"Were you really?"

"Really."

Her smile leapt between them, and in a rush of pleasure he swept her back into his arms, wondering how on earth he could have gotten so lucky. To find out that she not only wasn't mad at him, but that they were in fact the same age, was a happier ending than he could have imagined. In fact,

Jesse realized as he bent to kiss her, this would make a better movie than either the Western or the wartime thriller. Right about now, the love-theme music should come up, and there should be sparkles in the air....

"You know," he told her when they could speak again, "this is the greatest day I've had all summer. I've been worrying for the past thousand miles what was gonna happen when we got to the end of Route 66 and I couldn't tell you the truth."

"I know! I was scared to say anything about going back to school, and I was so scared you wouldn't be interested in me...."

"I was interested in you the first time I saw you," he told her, as if the past half hour of celebration hadn't been enough to prove it. "I kept thinking about you, only in my mind I called you Aurora. Because one time I saw this movie, and there was a princess named Aurora—"

"Oh, I love that one! Katie has the video. We watch it all the time." Vicki blushed as he lifted her chin. "Now you're really going to think I'm a kid."

He'd never get a better opening than this, Jesse decided, for finishing his confession. "You want to hear about kid stuff?" he asked, guiding her toward the edge of the field, where a bright-roofed convenience store promised Icy Coolers 49¢. The air felt strangely parched in spite of the clouds hiding the sun, and it wouldn't hurt to get out of the heat for a minute before covering the last stretch home. "My aunt wouldn't let me come on this trip by myself. She...well, you met Sarah. She still thinks I'm about twelve years old."

Vicki gaped at him. "Sarah is your aunt?"

"Yeah." He gave her a hand over a clump of rocks, and they started across the baking asphalt of the Quik-Pik parking lot. "She was pretty upset when I made up that stuff about her being Ryan's girlfriend."

Vicki stopped short. "You mean she isn't really?"

"I had to talk her into going along with it," he explained, relieved that the distraction of the store was just ahead. It was high time they got down to choosing flavored ices and forgot all this other stuff. "I just thought, same as you did, that it'd look kind of dumb if I was traveling with my aunt."

She nodded as he opened the door for her, and for a few minutes they lost themselves in the air-conditioned comfort of selecting among Racy Raspberry, Bubble Yum and Cold Cold Cola coolers. "I can't believe it's this hot when the sky's so cloudy," Vicki said. "But, Jesse, I can't believe that about Sarah and Ryan, either. Anybody could see they're in love with each other."

"You're kind of a romantic, aren't you?" he teased, peeling the wrapper off her straw. "You see people in love everywhere you look."

She blushed as she took the straw from him. "But you saw them, too! Nobody looks at each other that way if they're just putting on a show."

Jesse fitted the plastic lid over his own cup and shrugged. "I don't know. They don't have a whole lot in common." Sarah didn't date all that much, but the few men she'd introduced him to had been a whole lot stuffier than Ryan. Besides, she would never let herself get swept away by anyone who'd once dated his mom—which was something they both seemed to view as a big secret, as if Jesse didn't already know what his mom was like. She'd been the kind of person men fell in love with as soon as they met her...not that it ever lasted.

"Would you mind if they *were* in love, though?" Vicki asked, following him to the counter, where a slow-moving clerk rang up their drinks. "I mean, they seemed to me like a really good couple."

"Sure, if that's what they wanted it'd be okay." Actually it would be great to have Ryan around, to spend more time together without having to get through college first, and to know Sarah would still have someone there after he left home. But the possibility of those two winding up together seemed pretty slim, in spite of Vicki's insistence on romance.

The heat outside seemed more intense after the air-conditioning of the store, but at least they had their Racy Raspberry and Cold Cold Cola. "Look at that lightning," Vicki exclaimed, gazing at the distant hills, which were bathed in lavender streaks. "My mom said this part of the desert gets these really dramatic summer storms."

"I guess it must," Jesse observed, wishing he'd brought the camera along. Maybe, if Ryan and Sarah had finished going over the research notes, they might get a few shots of these ominous clouds. "If it does rain, though, at least we're close to home."

"They're probably wondering where I am," Vicki admitted. "But I wouldn't have missed this afternoon for anything. Jesse, you have no idea how much I was dreading the end of Route 66."

"So was I," he told her. "I kept wondering how I could stay in touch with you when I was supposed to be traveling all over the country."

"Where do you live, for real? In that little town you told me about?"

"Yeah. It's not too far from Chicago."

Her eyes lit up. "So we really *can* still see each other? You know, I was so worried about what would happen if you wanted to visit me, and here I was living with my family...."

"Your family," he repeated, realizing for the first time what that implied. "Does that mean if I come up and see you, Brandon'll be there?"

She flinched. "Well...yes."

"Okay, then," Jesse said recklessly. "This'll prove I love you. I'm coming anyway. First chance I get."

"Really?"

"Try and stop me," he promised, and bent to kiss her again. This time she tasted of raspberry ice, and the cold sensation was surprisingly sweet. But this time, too, it was easier to let her go. Now they had all the time in the world stretching before them, and the prospect was a pleasure to contemplate.

He even felt a bit more charitable toward Brandon when the kid came dashing toward them brandishing a squirt gun and yelling, "Freeze, duckheads!" If the Brat From Hell was Vicki's half brother, Jesse was willing to cut him a little more slack. However, that didn't stop him from emptying the squirt gun before handing it back.

"We'll probably be driving straight through to Los Angeles tomorrow," Vicki told him as Brandon headed inside for a refill. "Dave said there's nothing worth seeing in the desert west of here."

"Good thing we had this afternoon, then," Jesse said. "If I thought this was the last time I'd ever see you—" He broke off. The thought was too awful to finish. "You've got my phone number in Gilroy, right?"

Vicki recited it from memory, making him wish he had done the same thing with hers. But he felt for the slip of paper she'd given him and found it in his pocket along with Marco's napkin.

"Oh, geez, I forgot to call *Odyssey Magazine.*"

"Why do you have to call them?"

"Marco said the editor wants something called copy prints—at least I think that's what he called 'em—and if that's true, I want to be able to tell Ryan about it." Besides, having another errand would make it easier to leave Vicki without feeling as if he'd had his guts ripped out. Still, as long as he knew he could see her again in Chicago, he could stand to say goodbye.

It took them fifteen minutes, though, and it wasn't until he tore himself away and headed back toward the pay phone at the Quik-Pik that Jesse realized Brandon and his squirt gun had been conspicuously absent from the scene. That was just as well. The best movie of his life shouldn't have to end on a close-up of the Brat From Hell.

He was still smiling at the thought when he reached the pay phone, and maybe some of the happiness in his voice communicated itself to the receptionist at *Odyssey Magazine.* For some reason she sounded absolutely delighted to hear from some photographer's assistant she'd never even met.

"So you're shooting with Nate Ryan? That's wonderful! He called in last week, and it was so nice to hear from him."

Too bad Ryan couldn't say the same thing, Jesse thought, remembering his frustration at learning that the deadline had been moved up. "Thanks. I'm calling because I heard Huey was looking for copy prints?"

Huey was in a meeting right now, the receptionist said brightly, but Jesse could leave him a message.

"No, thanks. I just wanted to know what copy prints are. Are we supposed to be making those?"

"Oh, no, the magazine takes care of that. Some free-lancers like to make their own, but it's really not necessary. Bless your heart! Ryan should have told you."

"Uh, he's busy going over the research," Jesse said. "I just thought I'd check it out. Well, anyway, thanks."

"No problem. Do you want Ryan's other messages? I know he got a letter here just this morning. In fact—" her voice dropped to a more confidential tone "—it was from a hospital lab in Amarillo. There's nothing wrong, is there?"

Oh, Lord. Not the hospital where he'd been. "I hope not," Jesse said slowly. Ryan must have asked them to send it to the magazine office, but why hadn't he mentioned that Jesse might be getting some test results? And could that be why Sarah had been so worried about him after the blood transfusion?

He gripped the phone a little tighter. "Actually," he said, hoping his voice sounded convincing, "I'm sure glad you mentioned that. Ryan would've been really upset if I forgot. He wanted me to ask you what it says."

"You mean, he expects me to read his mail?" She sounded a little doubtful.

"Yes," Jesse said. After all, these were *his* lab tests. "He specifically asked me to get the results from you. Said he doesn't want to wait another week to find out what they said."

"Well, I guess if that's what he wants..." His story must have been convincing, Jesse realized with relief, because she sounded like she believed him. "Okay, hold on a minute. Let me find the letter, and I'll read you what it says."

Chapter Twelve

"We've got some things to straighten out." The echo of Ryan's words had stayed with her all night and all morning, and now, with Jesse off to meet Vicki, there was nowhere to hide. Sarah made a careful pretense of concentrating on her notes, even though Ryan was still closeted in the darkroom. What would happen, she wondered, if she left the motor home before he finished his prints?

She didn't want to imagine his response if he emerged from the darkroom and found her gone. He would probably come tearing after her and force her into a showdown she couldn't win. No, better to wait and have it out with him once and for all. As long as she held fast to her resolve that nothing could make her give up Jesse, what was the worst that could happen?

Better not to think about that, either.

"Jesse gone already?"

Ryan's voice made her jump, although she had absolutely nothing to be nervous about. He set down a handful of black-and-white prints on the table across from her, and she saw that his knuckles were white.

Was he as edgy as she was?

"He left a few minutes ago," she answered, keeping her eyes on the page of notes before her. There was no point in looking up at Ryan. No point in letting him think *she* wanted to straighten things out.

He took a step back.

She fumbled for her pencil.

He flexed his hands together.

She stared blindly at the page.

He moved toward the window.

She bit the tip of her eraser.

He cleared his throat, and she dropped the pencil. "Look," Ryan said, turning away from the window and facing her across what suddenly felt like a very narrow distance, "I'm nervous about this. But I think it matters that we get some things straightened out. Because you're important to me."

It was hard to stay aloof in the face of an opening like that. "I..." Sarah began, and swallowed to clear her throat. "I'm nervous, too."

She saw the ghost of a smile flicker across his face. "Maybe that's a good sign." Then, as he gazed at her, his smile disappeared. "Do *I* make you nervous?"

"No," she lied. "No, I just... Uh, no."

Still watching her, he pressed his lips together, as if he had to fight back a smile. "All right, then," he said gently. "You want to go first?"

But she had absolutely nothing to say to him. "This was *your* idea," she protested. "I just want to get through the next six days and take Jesse home."

Ryan drew a long breath and slowly let it out. "All right, then," he said again, but this time his voice was grim. "So let's start with Jesse. Why are you so surprised I'd advise him to tell the truth?"

The man didn't believe in beating around the bush, did he? "Well..." Sarah's voice faltered, and she picked up the pencil to keep her fingers steady. "It seemed kind of ironic, considering the way you—"

"The way I what?" he interrupted. "You still think I've been lying to you, is that it?"

"Haven't you?" she demanded. If he wanted to raise his voice, then so could she. "Remember back in Amarillo? I asked if you'd known you were Jesse's father before we walked into the hospital, and you said—"

He took two steps toward her and she broke off, startled by the intensity on his face. "You want to hear the truth?" he demanded. "The first time I knew he was my son was when you said he had this rare blood type. I'm A-B negative, too, so that kind of clinched it. But, Sarah, I never once suspected I could be his father until that night when you mentioned Adele getting pregnant at the air show."

The night before the accident. She swallowed, remembering the events of that evening, but Ryan hurried on. "You see, Adele and I went to the air show the weekend before I left town. So when you mentioned that, I wondered for a minute if I might have been responsible. But it was just a suspicion, and I wasn't going to say anything," he concluded, "because...well, I know how you feel about Jesse."

He looked genuinely troubled, and for a moment she almost believed him. But he couldn't know how she felt about Jesse—or else he just didn't care. Because otherwise he never would have suggested that she send him off to the far corners of the earth.

"You still want to take him away from me, don't you?" Sarah accused.

Ryan sighed. "I want him in my life, yes," he said slowly. "But I want you, too."

She must have been holding the pencil more tightly than she realized, because it snapped in her fingers. Startled, she dropped the pieces on the table, trying to dismiss a sudden compelling vision of the two of them together, and looked up to find him watching her intently. "Ryan," she blurted, "it wouldn't work."

"Why not?" He sounded honestly curious, as if he couldn't imagine why not.

"A million reasons!"

The faint smile was back in his eyes. "Name one."

She should be able to name several, but for some reason she had to fumble. His smile was distracting her, and that wasn't fair. "Well...because...you travel all over the place!" Sarah told him, hoping her response sounded quick and definite. "You're always on the road."

"Yeah," he said, and she could tell from the growing smile in his eyes that she had made a tactical error. "So?"

She should have said she simply didn't want him, but it was too late now. "So I don't always want to be sitting home waiting for—"

"Come with me."

Her jaw dropped. "What?"

"I mean it. You're the best researcher I've ever seen— although that's not the only reason I want you—and you could make a lot more money managing stock photos than you could at the library."

"It's got nothing to do with making money," Sarah protested. Dear God, he must be serious. But she couldn't possibly stay with this man.

"All right, forget the money," he said abruptly. "What about the adventure? Sarah, come on. We could go anywhere—"

"I can't!" she cried, and hoped he couldn't hear the panic in her voice. "I've got Jesse to look after."

"He'll learn a lot more as an apprentice than he would at Gilroy Community College," Ryan stated firmly. "He can come on the road with us."

And there they were, back to the thing she most dreaded. "I'm not letting you have Jesse," she said flatly.

He gave a sharp sigh and turned away. For a moment he stood still, his body almost visibly crackling with frustration, then he swung back to face her.

"It always comes back to Jesse, doesn't it?" he asked. "Look, I know he's your family, but—"

"He's all I've got! And I'm not letting you ruin his life."

Ryan halted, obviously startled. "What makes you think I'm gonna ruin his life?"

"Because you're not responsible!" she cried. "You're always on the road. You live a whole different life from most people. And that's not what I want for Jesse!"

There was a pause, and then he nodded in acknowledgment. When he spoke again, his voice was very soft. "What about what Jesse wants for Jesse?"

Sarah stood up, feeling suddenly sick to her stomach. This conversation had gone on far too long, and she had to get out of here. "We've got nothing to talk about," she told him, and started for the door.

Ryan moved to block her way. "Yes, we do," he said, holding her in place with the sheer, demanding force of his gaze. "Tell me why you always, automatically, think the worst of me."

"I don't," she protested, but he took a step toward her and she backed toward the couch. This man was getting far too close, too fast.

"Yes, you do," he repeated, and although he spoke quietly, the accusation hit her like a shout. "You think I'm going to ruin Jesse's life. You think I'm not responsible." She tried to protest, but before she could find her voice, he moved even closer, his eyes burning into hers. "You think I've been lying to you. You think it would never work." *It wouldn't!* she wanted to cry, but still he wouldn't stop. "All I want to know is why you always think the worst of me."

"Because," she almost screamed, "I *have* to!"

There was a shattering silence, and as he took a step back, she collapsed onto the couch, burying her face in her hands.

Ryan leaned against the doorframe watching her, and wondered why he had never guessed until now that Jesse wasn't the problem. Maybe Sarah hadn't realized it, either—judging from the horror on her face, she probably hadn't—but Jesse was only the excuse.

It wouldn't do much good to point that out now, though. She looked like she was on the fine edge of losing control.

"You know," he said conversationally, moving to sit down on the other end of the couch, "it's kind of funny. Until I met you, there was no way I was ever going to get involved with anybody again."

She gave a shuddering gulp, but she didn't reply.

"I was afraid," Ryan continued. "I didn't want to risk losing anyone again, not after the way I fell apart last time."

Still no response. If only she would look at him. With her arms wrapped around her knees protectively, she seemed to be huddled into a shell.

"So you see," he offered, trying to keep his voice relaxed, "I can understand if you're afraid. I just don't understand why."

She moved then, sitting up a little straighter but still not looking at him. "I'm not," she said raggedly. "I got married, remember? I wasn't afraid."

The quaver in her voice gave her away.

"You are now," Ryan answered. "Did your husband hurt you that much?"

Still huddled over, she shook her head. "No," she whispered.

For some reason, he believed her. But something, somewhere, had made her unable to risk her heart. "Sarah," he said gently, "look at me."

She stared at her hands for an endless minute, and finally he realized she couldn't meet his eyes.

Why? Why couldn't she trust him?

Ryan drew a long breath. There was only one way to find out, and as much as he dreaded her answer, he knew he had to ask. "Is it because I was married?"

"No," she whispered, and in spite of the tremor he saw in her hands, he believed her. But there had to be some reason.

"Is it because of Adele?"

Her hands went utterly still. He could almost see her face freeze, almost hear her breath stop. Almost feel the blind, unreasoning horror that hammered at the walls of her heart.

"Aw, Sarah," he began, and then she cracked. As if her shell had suddenly collapsed, she gave a strangled cry and burst into tears.

"Please, just leave me alone!"

"I'm not gonna leave you alone," he told her, swiftly moving beside her and throwing his arm around her shoulders. "Sarah, what happened with Adele was eighteen years ago! It's got nothing to do with us now."

He didn't know if she even heard him at first, she was sobbing so hard, but then she tried to answer.

"She gave you—I wasn't—she always—"

"It's okay," he said, wishing he could somehow shield her from the pain he had never suspected lay inside her. Had she been carrying this around all summer? Or even longer. What was it she'd told him, that night in the field?

"Adele was always the adventurous one, and you were the responsible one," he said slowly, remembering her words. But what difference did that make? Surely she couldn't think he'd been in love with Adele. "Sarah, that has nothing to do with you and me."

She raised her tearstained face to him, and his heart twisted with regret as she whispered, "But she had your son. You loved her first."

"No," he said, hoping that for once he could make her believe him. "I slept with her first. I loved *you* first."

Her eyes widened, and he held his breath as a flicker of hope darted across her face.

Then she looked down again. "I want to believe you," she said shakily. "But—"

"Believe me," he told her, taking both her hands in his and trying to convey with the strength of his grasp how fervently he meant it. "Believe me! I wish that whole summer—" He broke off. He couldn't truly wish that whole summer had never happened, because then Jesse would never have happened. But he could wish, with all his heart, that Sarah didn't feel like his second choice. "I really wish," he said, his voice cracking with emotion, "I'd met you first."

She almost smiled at that, and from her reminiscent look he could tell she was envisioning such a meeting. A nineteen-year-old hell-raiser and a seventeen-year-old library clerk . . .

"You wouldn't have wanted me," she said simply.

Maybe he wouldn't have. Then.

"I want you now."

She ducked her head, and he could see a faint rush of color spreading up her cheeks. "I want you, too, but—"

"Stop!" he interrupted, forcing himself to stay still. "Stop right there. Say it again without the 'but.'"

It took every ounce of control he had not to coax her with a touch, not to remind her with his hands how gladly he could love her if she'd only say the word. But she had to realize it for herself, she had to want it for herself, and so he kept quiet as the silence between them grew steadily warmer, steadily more alive.

Finally she looked up at him, and the blush on her face was all the answer he needed.

"I want you, Sarah," he prompted.

Her voice was very soft, but she managed to whisper an answer. "I want you, too."

He felt a rush of gratitude, of wonder, so intense it nearly made him dizzy. But he kept his tone light, knowing this was still only the beginning. "There," he said gently, "that wasn't so hard, was it?"

Her cheeks grew even redder. "Ryan . . ."

"Now," he murmured, reaching for her hand and keeping his eyes on hers. Knowing this could make all the difference, that he could finally show her how much he loved her. "I want you to let me love you." And as he saw the mixture of doubt and anticipation in her eyes, he went on. "Not Adele. You."

She ducked her head, looking suddenly shy. Slowly, ever so slowly, he slid his fingers under her chin and tilted her face up.

She caught her breath.

Keeping up the gentle pressure so she couldn't lower her chin, he touched his lips to hers and felt her shiver.

Easy, Ryan reminded himself. Easy.

He traced her lips with his, exploring softness on softness, warmth against warmth. Tasting her shyness, her hesitation, her trembling acceptance as he continued slowly exploring, tracing only the outline of her mouth.

She lifted her face.

Ah...there, she was beginning to feel it for herself. The slow sensuality of lingering over a kiss, of taking it step by tantalizing step, of knowing they were still barely on the threshold of something bigger. The throbbing anticipation of knowing this would build, this would grow, this would spiral into a whirl of sensation in another minute or two. But for now, there was only the bare enjoyment of feeling her mouth against his, lightly, sweetly, softly inviting....

She opened her lips.

Taking his time, he circled the inside of her mouth with his tongue and felt her breath quicken, felt her shivering response. She was feeling it, too, he could tell, the building awareness between them, the growing recognition of need. His tongue met hers, searching, seeking, and he gloried in the trusting openness of her mouth, inviting him in. *Sarah, yes.* He thrust quickly and withdrew, making her gasp, and then he moved in more slowly. Teasing, confirming, celebrating—yes, she wanted this as much as he did, and, by God, he wanted it all.

He wanted her. With him, beside him, for the rest of his life. Now and forever...but especially now.

She no longer needed the pressure of his fingers to keep her face lifted to his, and he slid his hand along the side of her neck as he joyously plundered her mouth. He was almost beyond thought, almost lost in the flood of feeling, but in some corner of his mind he knew this was happening too fast, that he couldn't let them rush through what had taken a whole summer to build.

But when he heard her soft whimper of desire as he ended the kiss, he knew with a surge of pleasure that this was no time to stop. Not when they were both on the edge of a raging fire that had smoldered ever since the Fourth of July. Not when this woman looked at him with her eyes so wide, her breath coming in quick gasps, her hair on the verge of spilling into his tingling hands.

He reached for the stretchy loop that held her hair in place and slid it loose. With a rush of pleasure, he buried his hands in the soft abundance of hair, caressing her face and drawing his fingers through what felt like strands of satin against his skin.

No, they couldn't stop now. Not when she was writhing under his touch, sliding even closer to him, and as he heard the low moan of longing in her throat, he slowly moved his fingers from her hair to the top button of her blouse.

She caught her breath.

He kept his eyes fixed on hers, inviting her to speak. Daring her to speak. But she stayed silent except for a sharp, soft breath, and he set to work. Still holding her in place with a gaze that burned them both, he carefully unfastened the button without ever looking down.

She wet her lips.

He moved to the next, opening it by feel alone. The next. He could keep going forever, just watching her, feeling the warmth of her skin through the soft fabric in his hands and knowing that when he reached the last button—

"Oh, please," Sarah whispered.

His hands were already at her waist, where the last button was tucked into her shorts. Dropping his gaze for only an instant, he fingered both sides of the shirt and then slowly lifted it out of her waistband.

She gasped, and he closed his eyes as the scent of her skin washed over him. This was what he wanted, what he'd dreamed of, what he'd stayed awake remembering ever since that night in the grass, and this time nothing could come between them. This time she knew he loved her, and he could dare to believe she loved him.

He ran his fingers along the soft skin above her waist, along her sides, and savored the sensations that swirled around him. The feel of her against his fingertips, faintly dewy where the blouse had clung to her skin and now tinged with tiny goose bumps wherever his fingers traveled. The sound of her breathing more rapidly, more shallowly as she started her own exploration along the back of his neck and inside the collar of his shirt. The way she let out her breath in a rush as he smoothed his hands up her back and slowly unfastened her bra.

He felt her shiver, and when she spoke, her voice was husky and raw. "Should we... shouldn't we be in bed?"

Anywhere would be fine with him; anywhere would be wonderful. But if Sarah preferred a conventional setting, he'd be glad to move into bed. "Wherever you want," Ryan told her, and ran his hands down to her hips, keeping her within his grasp as they both stood up.

She swayed against him, dizzy with longing, and felt him reach to steady her. The intensity of her need was almost frightening, Sarah thought with the tiny core of reason she still possessed, but for once she wasn't going to listen to reason. For once she would throw off any sense of responsibility and let this burning intensity have its way.

Because she couldn't possibly stop now. Not with him so tantalizingly close behind her, holding her steady, sending her spinning into spasms of need. Spinning beyond all reason with the solid grasp of his hands on her hips, with the warmth of his body pressed against her as he gently guided her toward the bedroom.

How many times had she wished for him here? Wished for him standing beside her bed with his fingers lightly tracing the curve of her waist. Wished for him murmuring her name in that low, caressing voice. Wished for the touch of his hands on her shoulders, turning her to face him, lifting her chin for his lips to descend onto hers . . .

Like this. Exactly like this.

She gave herself up to the pleasure of his kiss, which rapidly surpassed even the memories she'd fantasized over. Because now there was an entirely new dimension that had never once entered her fantasies, a dimension that made all the difference. This time he loved her. Not Adele. Her.

But this was no time to think of Adele, and already he was making it hard to think at all. Hard to do anything but feel, but soar, but respond to the pressure of his hands on her hips, drawing her closer as she arched her back and thrust herself toward him. All she wanted was right here, right now, and his tongue was causing new swells of desire she'd never guessed were possible as he moved lower, lower, teasing and caressing and nibbling until she almost screamed. "Oh, Ryan, please!"

He must have felt the same urgency, the same hot and desperate need that burned inside her, because he swiftly gathered her in his arms and lifted her up, where she nestled for an exquisite moment against his chest before he gently set her down on the cool cotton sheets of the bed.

And stood staring down at her for what felt like an eternity, his face lit with wonder.

"Ryan," she pleaded, and he responded with an almost dizzying smile of promise as he reached for the waistband of her shorts and in one deft move yanked off the rest of her clothes.

Now her skin tingled as intensely as the core of yearning inside her, with the air washing over her from the shaded window above the bed. But she barely recognized any sensation beyond the sheer ache of desire as he stood again, just beyond the reach of her covetous hands, and rapidly shucked off his own clothes before kneeling over her and lowering his body onto hers with one long, intense kiss.

Finally he was with her, upon her, almost inside her, and she ran her hands down the length of his back, glorying, guiding him toward the hot, hungry center of her until with a sudden, savage thrust he was there, and she cried out with the pleasure of having him where she had dreamed of for so long.

This was better than dreams, better than fantasies. He was bigger, richer, more powerfully sensual than she had ever imagined, and he knew just how to move, just where to touch her, just when to slide his hands under her hips and lift her even closer as she gasped in acceptance, shivered with joy and almost tumbled into an endless ocean of color and light and sensation. But she held herself back, longing for more, and then he was giving her more, giving her everything, taking and sharing and celebrating until she no longer knew what was his and what was hers, only that they had melded and fused into a single, radiant burst of wonder and that someone was shouting and someone was sobbing and someone was whispering, "Yes."

Yes.

Oh, yes.

It seemed both a lifetime and an instant that they lay tangled together, slowly regaining their equilibrium and murmuring senseless sounds. Sounds that spoke more deeply than words, that promised and acknowledged and remembered and pledged. Sounds that pleasured. Sounds that thanked. Sounds that connected them, one to another, as a soft blanket of sleep stole over them in a lazy, sensual wave.

When she woke, it was more a drifting than an arrival. First there was the sweet shiver of bliss that still pervaded her body whenever she moved. Then the memory of what they had shared, and the dizzying realization that Ryan loved her. The drowsy contentment of reaching for him and the muted shock of realizing he was no longer there.

But she heard the soft click of his camera outside and saw with her last waking glance that the sky was a dramatic palette of lavender, turquoise and gray. That explained it, then. With another spasm of pleasure at knowing he would return, she curled herself around his pillow and slid back into sleep.

The next waking was more abrupt. It took a moment of confusion to realize that the voices in the front room belonged to Ryan and Jesse, and that they had been sliding in and out of her awareness for the past several minutes.

"See, I'd promised not to say anything until after the trip. But under the circumstances, I think it's okay."

That was Ryan, speaking softly. She stretched, sending a rush of blood tingling through her body, and missed the first part of Jesse's question.

"You know what that means? Now I can stay with you."

What? Surely they weren't discussing—

No. They couldn't be.

"I'll tell you, kid," Ryan said slowly, "we've got to talk about that. Only let's wait awhile. Sarah's...uh, resting...but she ought to be up any minute. We'll have to start making plans, uh, later."

"I still can't believe it," Jesse said, and his voice was dazed. "I mean, I always thought my dad was this guy in Europe. Only it's like—I don't know, if I could wish for anything I wanted...I would've picked staying with you."

This couldn't be happening. This had to be a nightmare.

"We've got a lot to talk about. But we've got all the time in the world."

"Yeah, I guess." Jesse sounded even more amazed than before. "That's why you came back to Gilroy, wasn't it? You were still in love with my mom."

But if this was a nightmare, why couldn't she stop it? Then, from the front room, she heard Ryan's soft response.

"I'll tell you, Jess, your mom was...she sure had a lot of sparkle. She was the kind of girl who—" He broke off, and there was a pause. "You know, maybe we'd better move outside. We don't want to wake Sarah." The door opened, and before it clicked behind them, she heard his voice again. "It's been a long time, you know? A hell of a long time...but I still remember Adele."

Chapter Thirteen

Nothing in her life had ever hurt like this.

Not hearing herself described by her sixth-grade teacher as "Adele Corcoran's sister. You know, the other one."

Not Phil's phone call after she learned there would never be another pregnancy. "Hey, sorry about that. I'll be home in a couple of weeks."

Not even her mother's attempt to cheer her up. "You've practically got a child of your own already. You know Adele will let you borrow Jesse anytime you want."

Those had all hurt, but this was beyond bearing.

She had to get away.

Sarah dragged herself out of bed and stumbled toward the bathroom, stepping on the clothes Ryan had dropped on the floor. Dear God, that she had let him ever *touch* her—

No. Don't remember. Don't even breathe.

"But I still remember Adele."

She clutched the edge of the sink, feeling a sudden knife-like pain in her heart.

Don't feel.

Her body wouldn't listen. It kept recording sensations—the numbness in her chest, the buzzing in her ears, the shudder in her stomach—random, formless sensations that stood between her and oblivion.

"Now I can stay with you, no problem...."

She had lost. In the space of a heartbeat, she had lost everything that mattered.

Her child.

Her future.

Her love.

All she had left was emptiness. Humiliation. And the cold seeds of a slowly growing anger. She *had* to get out of here...and she had to take Jesse home.

No matter what happened, she had to get Jesse home.

Ryan might follow them, but she would deal with that later. For now all that mattered was finding Jesse, finding the fastest way out of Kingman and forgetting about everything else.

She would have to call a cab to get them to the bus station or the airport, whichever was closer. She would have to pack up their things, but that wouldn't take long. Jesse and Ryan were probably walking around the campsite right now....

"...A lot to talk about. But we've got all the time in the world."

Not if she could help it.

With a few quick swipes of water, Sarah rinsed away the last evidence of Ryan's betrayal. If only she hadn't let him convince her—

Don't think about it!

Just move. Just grab anything. The blue blouse, fine. The white shorts, okay. Don't even look at the mirror.

Adele would be there. Adele, who had won again.

Avoiding any glance at the mirror, she dragged her carryall and Jesse's duffel bag out of the closet and rapidly filled them with the contents of the dresser drawers. Everything else could stay behind—the research notes, the taco chips—

Don't think, she ordered herself. Don't feel.

Just go. Just close the zipper, call the cab, find Jesse and get out.

Forget about explaining. Forget about the research, forget the entire trip. Forget Ryan and—

Stop thinking about him!

Just move.

Just leave.

Just go.

"So," Jesse repeated, "were you in love with her or what?"

Ryan winced. He hated having to explain that Adele had been nothing more than a nineteen-year-old's idea of fun, and yet he didn't want to lie about her. Especially with Sarah still so fresh in his mind.

"The thing is," he said carefully, "we were both just kids. She was working in the doughnut shop, and I was waiting to report to basic training. I mean, we weren't really thinking about the future, you know?"

"I already figured that much," Jesse muttered, sounding a little bitter. He kicked a rock off the bare dirt path that led to the edge of the campsite and then turned to face Ryan. "Just one question, all right? Where the hell *were* you when I wanted a dad?"

Oh, Lord. He should have expected this. After all, he would have liked to ask the same thing of his own father... if he'd ever run into him.

"Jess," he said slowly, knowing he might get only one chance to explain a lifetime absence, "believe me. If I'd known your mom was pregnant, there's no way I would've ever left her. *Or* you." He swallowed, envisioning all the years he had missed, and wished again that Adele had tried to contact him even once. "But I never knew, and I'm sorry. We both missed out."

To his relief, Jesse evidently recognized the honesty and the regret behind his words. He hesitated for a long moment and then swallowed. "I guess stuff happens."

Ryan felt a rush of relief. If his son was old enough to understand that, the rest would be a lot easier.

"I'll tell you," he offered, "I couldn't be happier about the way you turned out."

Jesse gave him a dubious grin. "Yeah? Well, you haven't seen everything yet." They started walking again, not with any destination in mind, but simply so they could keep moving while they adjusted to this new relationship. Acknowledging themselves as father and son, Ryan realized, was a hell of a lot different than seeing themselves as traveling companions. And yet nothing had really changed. This was still the same kid he'd enjoyed all summer. The kid he wanted to keep in his and Sarah's life.

Thinking of Sarah made him smile, and before he realized it his steps had quickened. He couldn't wait to see her again.

"You know what?" Jesse said as they completed their circle around the campsite. "This'll make things a lot simpler when we finish the shoot. Now I can stay on the road with you."

Ryan slowed down. "Actually," he began, but the kid hurried on.

"You said before that you wanted me, remember? And now if Sarah knows you're my dad, she can't really say no. I mean, she won't be quite so, uh..."

But Sarah would never relax her insistence on what was best for Jesse. "You know better than that," Ryan told him.

He shrugged, kicking another rock off the well-worn path as they started another lap. "Still, you're my father, right? And we haven't ever gotten to do much stuff together...."

The kid knew right where to hit, Ryan realized. But there was no way he could go against Sarah's wishes now. Not when she had finally started to trust him.

"Jesse, look," he said. "Two years from now, if you want, we can start working together again. The way we are now. But in the meantime, it won't take you that long to get some kind of associate degree."

"But who *cares* if I get a degree?"

"Sarah does."

"But—"

"And I care about Sarah." Understatement of the year, Ryan thought with a twinge of amusement, though he couldn't very well tell Jesse what an incredible woman his aunt was. Not without giving away something she might rather keep private.

"So do I, but—" The kid broke off, looking suddenly incredulous. "Wait a minute. You're not, like... I mean, Vicki had this idea you guys were really in love or something."

From the half apologetic, half hopeful sound of his voice, Ryan could tell Jesse had already wondered about the possibility.

"Vicki's a smart girl," he said lightly.

Jesse stopped dead and turned to face him with a look of amazement. "No kidding? You and Sarah... Does she know?"

Ryan almost laughed, remembering the way she'd turned his name into a litany of passion, but that was a memory for the two of them alone. "Yeah," he said. "We kind of talked about it this afternoon."

Jesse shook his head in wonder. "You and Sarah, huh? That's really something." He hesitated, as if wondering how to ask the next question. "It's not just because she reminds you of my mom, is it?"

Oh, Lord, not Jesse, too! "No," Ryan said firmly, wishing again that Sarah and Adele had been anything other than identical twins. "It's got nothing to do with your mom, Jess. They're completely different people."

"*I* know that!" Jesse sounded indignant. "I've lived with both of them, remember? What I mean is ... well, I just don't want Sarah to get hurt."

So the kid felt responsible for Sarah, did he? "Good for you," Ryan told him, feeling a sudden swell of pride and pleasure in his son. "You don't have to worry, though. I love her more than I've ever loved anyone."

Jesse looked at him appraisingly for a moment and must have recognized the truth in his eyes, because he nodded an acknowledgment. They started walking again, this time toward the west, where the occasional darts of lightning had disappeared from the sky. "So, Vicki was right, huh?"

He sounded kind of pleased about it, and Ryan was glad. There would be no problem convincing Jesse that they belonged together, which he knew would matter to her. "Yeah," he said. "Anyway, one way or another, it looks like you and I'll be spending a lot of time together."

"I guess so!" The kid still looked a little dazed, but of course, he'd been hit with a lot today. When Jesse had sauntered in with a half embarrassed, half defiant question about paternity testing, Ryan had nearly choked. But a single instant of consideration was all it took for him to decide that here was the time for truth. Given the circumstances, Sarah would understand why he had to do it now.

Besides, he realized with a new twinge of pleasure as he remembered the moment of decision, he no longer had to worry about her thinking he'd broken his word. She knew at last that he loved her, and what a difference that made. Now that they'd finally cleared up the obstacle of Adele— if only he'd known a long time ago how much that bothered her!—there was nothing left to keep them apart.

They could start planning for the future, for a lifetime together. A lifetime of love, wherever they were. Jesse would be out on his own before long, although he'd probably still come home every now and then. Home to the two of them ...

"...In Gilroy?" Jesse asked, and Ryan jerked himself back to the present.

"We'll have to work it out." If Sarah really wanted to stay in Gilroy, he'd just have to find a way. "I'm hoping, though, that I can convince her to take over my stock-photo business. Unless she can't stand to give up her job."

"I don't think she loves it that much. She needed to get a job someplace, and the school was hiring."

That was a relief. "Good, because I'd really like to turn the business over to her. Then we could spend part of the year on the road and the rest wherever she wants."

"She loves Chicago," Jesse said immediately. "The only reason we moved to Gilroy was because Sarah's parents left her the house. And she had all these bills from her husband's credit card."

There was a lot he didn't know, Ryan realized, about the woman he loved. But then, they had the rest of their lives to share stories and memories, laughter and dreams.

"So anyway, that's the plan," he said, and heard a soft huskiness in his voice that hadn't been there before. "What do you think? Can you live with that?"

Jesse shrugged. "I guess. There're colleges all over Chicago, and besides—hey, I didn't tell you what happened with Vicki!"

The story took another five minutes of circling the campsite, and by the time they started back down the lane toward the motor home they were both slightly giddy with elation. Talking father-to-son, Ryan thought, was somehow more satisfying than talking photographer-to-assistant. "Been quite a day all around, hasn't it?" he observed, and Jesse grinned.

"Yeah. It's not every day you get to...oh, there was something else I wanted to tell you. You know who Vicki and I ran into?"

So, Ryan reflected as Jesse described Marco's offer, the rumors about his competitor were true. Maybe tonight he'd call the guy on it, ask what the hell he was trying to pull, but for now he felt too good about Sarah and his son to worry about a lousy photographer.

"I couldn't believe he'd offer that much money. But I guess he realizes he's out of the running otherwise," Jesse concluded. "Hey, look at that sky."

Postponing any thought of calling Marco at the Red Horse, Ryan instinctively reached for his camera. Good thing he had it with him, because suddenly the sky had turned strangely golden, with streaks of lightning radiating in the distance, and already he could envision how this dramatic sunlight would shimmer through the field of cholla cactus behind the campsite.

"We've got to get this one," he said. "Go grab the reflector, will you? I'm gonna set up over there."

The kid nodded and ran back toward the motor home, leaving Ryan to shoot what might be the most spectacular nature photo he'd gotten all summer. He didn't even need the reflector, he realized as the light grew more intense. Still, Jesse would be back in a minute, and they could enjoy their first shoot as father and son.

After five minutes, though, there was still no sign of Jesse. Ryan finished the roll of film and loaded another into his camera before realizing the eerie light was gone. The kid must have run into Vicki—funny how they had both found the woman of their dreams on the road to paradise—or else he had gotten distracted talking to Sarah....

She must be awake.

Striding back toward the motor home, Ryan felt a tug of longing that surprised him with its fierce intensity. For the first time all summer, he realized, he could walk in and greet her with a hug as well as a hello. She would look up, the way she always did, with that smile in her eyes. Then he would lean over the table or meet her by the sink, and kiss her with the pleasurable ease of knowing they belonged together. Nothing long, nothing passionate, not in front of the kid. Just a quick, friendly kiss of welcome, of acknowledgment, of reminding her she was wanted and treasured and loved.

When he flung open the door of the motor home, though, he was greeted with silence.

"Corky?"

The bedroom door was open, and Ryan moved cautiously toward it. No reason to be nervous, of course. She and Jesse must have gone outside for a minute, maybe looking for him on the other side of the campsite.

But he felt a quiver of uneasiness even before he saw the bedroom.

What the hell?

Every drawer was open and empty, as if someone had hurled all Sarah's and Jesse's clothes into a suitcase with no thought for organization. A wet bath towel lay crumpled on the floor, alongside the bed they had shared barely an hour ago, and the room almost screamed of emptiness.

But that didn't make sense.

Ryan hurried back to the front room, where a pile of research notes lay on the table. She wouldn't have packed up and taken off someplace with Jesse, would she? No, not when they had just shared the best afternoon of the summer.

"Sarah?" he called again, and another prickle of uneasiness darted across his spine. Maybe he shouldn't have left her.

But she'd been sleeping so cozily when he saw that dramatic sky, it seemed better to grab the photo and come back. Then, just as he'd started toward the bedroom again, Jesse had arrived with his question about the paternity test....

Oh, Lord.

Ryan closed his eyes, trying to remember what Sarah might have overheard. Even though it didn't make sense, he felt a wave of foreboding. Surely she wouldn't walk out just because he'd told Jesse the truth. Not when they'd finally broken through the wall of fear, not when he'd finally convinced her that his affair with Adele had nothing to do with them now.

Surely she knew he loved her. Surely she couldn't still think all he cared about was Adele's son.

Could she?

He didn't know. But the heaviness in his chest felt colder. If she had packed up and taken Jesse with her—only a week before the end of Route 66—she must have been upset beyond all reason.

Ryan almost sprinted for the pay phone near the manager's office, hoping he'd run into her and Jesse just returning from the laundry room. Instead he ran into a kid with a squirt gun who fixed him with a threatening gaze and ordered, "Freeze, duckhead!"

"Brandon!" Vicki came tearing around the corner after the kid and stopped at the sight of Ryan. "Oh, hi. Brandon, you put that away right now."

The kid reluctantly lowered the squirt gun. "Jesse already left," he announced. "Otherwise I would've got him right between the eyes."

Here was salvation. "You saw Jesse?" Ryan asked. "Was he with someone?"

Brandon looked smug. "They went in a taxi. Him and some lady." Then, with a grimace at Vicki, he added, "But he wasn't kissing *her*. He was pretty mad."

"When was that?" Ryan demanded, and the kid shrugged.

It couldn't have been more than ten minutes ago. Damn, if only he hadn't sent Jesse back for the reflector! If he had known Sarah was getting ready to bolt, he would have locked her in the motor home until he could convince her that she wasn't just a substitute for Adele.

With a mumbled apology to Vicki, who looked completely bewildered, he turned and ran back to the motor home. He could probably make it to the airport before they left town, and he had to move fast. He had to reach Sarah before she could resurrect that wall around herself. Before she could shut him out of her heart again.

He'd lost one love already.

Damned if he was going to lose Sarah, too.

"Sure, I can take you up," the ponytailed charter pilot told him, shifting a wad of chewing gum from one side of his mouth to the other. "Missed the plane to Vegas, huh?"

Ryan swallowed, gazing out the window at the small-town airfield, where a lone, single-engine Cessna swayed in the evening breeze. He couldn't let himself relax yet.

"I missed it by eight minutes, and I've got to get there before they connect with a flight to Chicago."

"No sweat," the pilot assured him. "We'll just take care of the paperwork, and then we can be on our way. You looking for somebody?"

"Yeah." The tightening in his gut was twisting harder with every wasted minute. It had taken nearly half an hour to find the pilot, and with the sunlight rapidly fading, they still hadn't made it off the ground. "How soon can we leave?"

"Just need to file a flight plan. This isn't a regular route, you know. So it'll cost you."

He hadn't even thought about the cost. "Sure, whatever," Ryan said, although any amount over the eighty dollars he had left would present something of a challenge. "Let's get going."

"I can take a check if it's local. Otherwise it's gotta be cash."

Oh, hell. "Look, can we worry about that after we find them?" He could probably get an advance from Huey tomorrow morning when the *Odyssey* office opened. But the pilot shook his head.

"No way, Jose. I'm not taking off for Vegas without four hundred in cash up front."

Four hundred? Cash up front? He might as well ask for four million, Ryan thought. Who the hell would carry that kind of money—?

Then it hit him. For a moment, remembering how Jesse had described the offer from Marco, he felt as if he were floating in a sea of ice.

But there was no choice. If he didn't reach Sarah tonight, he might never get through to her again.

"The money's no problem," he said deliberately. "I just need to make a phone call, and I'll have it in fifteen minutes."

The pilot stared at him, looking so uncertain that Ryan had to clench his fists in his pockets.

"You sure you want to go there tonight? It's a lot to pay when there's another commuter flight tomorrow afternoon."

Ryan drew a long breath. He knew what was at stake. If he turned his photos over to Marco, he could forget about ever selling to *Odyssey*. And with Huey the only editor willing to give him another chance, he might as well get rid of his camera.

It was a sickening thought. But the thought of losing Sarah was even worse.

"Yeah," he told the pilot. "Let's go."

Chapter Fourteen

"You're crazy," Jesse said as they crossed the landing strip into the hubbub of Las Vegas's McCarran Airport. "You know that, don't you?"

"I don't want to talk about it," Sarah repeated for what felt like the fiftieth time. If they could just get home, she could manage to organize an explanation that wouldn't leave Jesse feeling as if this was all his fault. Because it wasn't her nephew's fault that she had trusted Ryan—that she had fooled herself into believing he loved her.

"Ryan's gonna be really upset."

She had expected him to return with Jesse, so she could tell him in person that she never wanted to see him again. But when Jesse had come in alone just as she saw the cab arrive out front, the only logical choice had been to leave without a word.

"He'll get over it," Sarah muttered, looking around for an airline counter where she could ask about the flight to Chicago.

Of course, Ryan would probably show up in Gilroy within the week, demanding his son. But by then she would have gotten the feel of him out of her mind. By then she would no longer remember how sweetly he had promised her, teased her, lavished her with assurances that she was nothing like Adele.

The one with "a whole lot of sparkle." The one he had never forgotten.

"And it's gonna be expensive," Jesse added, pointing to the line of people at the ticket counter. "When Vicki flew to see her dad without making reservations, it cost three times more."

"I know," Sarah said, wishing she could put her hands over her ears. Jesse wasn't making this easy—not that she could expect him to understand. He seemed to believe Ryan could do no wrong, that the man he'd always wanted for a father deserved to have Sarah thrown into the package as well. "Jesse, will you please just let me think?"

"You're not thinking," he muttered. "You're acting crazy. I don't see why you're mad at Ryan, anyway."

"Because—" Sarah broke off. *Because the only reason he made love to me was so he could keep my sister's son!*

"He said he loves you," Jesse persisted. "Doesn't that count for anything?"

Of course Ryan wouldn't tell her nephew how he'd fed her the exact lines she longed to hear. "I don't want to talk about it," she repeated, fumbling in her purse for the credit card she had used to charge their flight out of Kingman. Getting home was going to cost more than half of what she'd earned this summer—if Ryan even decided to pay her, which he might very well forget. After all, she wasn't completing the trip. "What time does it say up there?"

Jesse glanced at the schedule board behind the ticket agents. "Flight 279 to Chicago leaves in half an hour. But we wouldn't get in till almost midnight their time. You're not going to call Eileen to pick us up at midnight, are you? When she'd have to drive all the way in from Gilroy?"

"If I have to," she snapped. "Jesse, do me a favor. Go get a drink or something. But don't go too far."

Rolling his eyes, he gestured toward the bank of pay phones down the concourse. "Maybe I'll call the campsite and see if Vicki's still there."

"Fine." He was twenty feet away before she thought to call after him, "But I don't want you phoning Ryan!"

He didn't even look back. It wouldn't matter anyway, Sarah realized. Ryan wouldn't take off for Gilroy until his shoot was finished, not when he knew Jesse would be there waiting for him. And by the time he showed up at their front doorstep next week, she would have herself under control.

She would never again let him convince her that she mattered more than Adele.

Eight more people ahead of her in line. She could see Jesse talking on the nearest phone, his duffel bag looped carelessly over his shoulder, and for a moment she could almost see Ryan in the way he stood, the way he gestured. . . .

Dear God, would she ever be able to look at Jesse again without thinking of his father?

Seven more people. No, Sarah pleaded to herself, of course she wouldn't always see Ryan in her nephew. Within a few days, surely, she would have herself back to normal. She wouldn't still be feeling the soft, persuasive heat of his fingers against her skin. Shivering at the memory of his body, so solid, so strong against hers. Hearing his rough, compelling voice cutting through the clamor of the airport. . .

"What the *hell* do you think you're doing?"

Sarah spun around. Ryan was charging straight toward her through the crowd of people, and he looked as though he was ready to hit anyone who got in his way.

"Going home," she told him, hoping her voice sounded normal. How on earth had he gotten here so fast? He was wearing the same clothes he'd worn this afternoon, the same shirt and jeans he'd dropped on her bedroom floor only a few hours ago, and the memory of it was still enough to make her dizzy.

"Corky—" he began, and she hastily cut him off before the memory could sink any deeper.

"Look, you didn't have to come after us. I know you want to see Jesse, but—"

He stared at her incredulously, reaching forward to grasp her shoulders before she could pull away. "You still think all I want is Jesse?" he demanded, searching her eyes with his. "Hasn't anything I've said gotten through to you?"

She took a step back, almost bumping into the woman ahead of her in line. This was no place to make a scene, but Ryan didn't seem to care. "I heard you with him," she stated, deliberately keeping her voice low. "You promised not to tell him anything until after the trip, remember? And then I wake up and you're saying that under the circumstances you can tell him he's your son."

Ryan flinched, and another unbidden vision flashed through her mind of the way he'd looked this afternoon in bed. "He asked me, damn it! He found out about the paternity test, and he walked right in and asked me. What was I supposed to tell him?"

She gulped. It had never once occurred to her that Jesse might have demanded the truth.

"I know I should've waited for you. If I had it to do over again—" He broke off, and a reluctant grin suddenly flashed across his face. "Hell, if I had it to do over again, you and I would still be in bed."

"Ryan!" She threw a startled glance over her shoulder and was relieved to see a gap between her and the woman ahead in line.

Ryan didn't appear at all abashed. "We'll get back to that. Meanwhile... I'm sorry I didn't wake you up, okay? I should have, the minute he asked."

But then she never would have overheard him telling Jesse about how he still loved Adele. "It wouldn't have made any difference," Sarah said stiffly, backing up a few more steps and wishing Ryan would remain where he was. "I can make him stay in school until he's eighteen, but then..." She swallowed, fighting back a rush of tears. "We both know he's going on the road with you."

The tension in his body seemed suddenly tighter, as if he had been holding himself together by sheer force of will. "I was hoping," Ryan said softly, "it'd be with *us.*"

Tears were clogging her throat, but she knew she couldn't let them spill. If this man saw her crying over him, she would lose every last bit of pride she possessed. "Oh, that'd be real convenient," Sarah snapped. "You could have everything you want."

"What I *want*," he said in the same low voice that had mesmerized her this afternoon, "is you."

But she knew better than that. "No, you don't," she told him, feeling the familiar burning in her chest again. "You want Jesse and you want Adele. Well, you've got Jesse. But I won't stand in for Adele."

The shock, hurt and anger on his face made her wince, but before he could reply, Jesse's voice rang out. "Hey, you made it!" He came bounding back from the pay phones, looking as if he'd just spent a wonderful ten minutes with Vicki. "How'd you get here so fast?"

"Chartered a plane," Ryan said shortly, as if the subject wasn't worth discussing. "Jess, your aunt and I need to talk."

"We've got nothing to talk about," she protested. He couldn't seriously think she'd jump on his chartered plane and pick up the Route 66 shoot as if nothing had ever happened. Could he?

"We damn sure do," Ryan told her, moving so he stood between her and the ticket counter. "Because, Corky, I'm not letting you go."

The man was too big, too solid, too compelling—not only his body, but his face, his eyes, his voice—to walk around. But she would have to. No matter what it took, she would have to get herself and Jesse onto that plane. "We're leaving for Chicago in twenty minutes," Sarah whispered.

He glanced over his shoulder at the three people ahead of them in line and then turned back to her. "All right, I'll come with you."

Jesse started to speak, but she cut him off. "You can't, remember? You've got your shoot."

"Not anymore," Ryan said. "Besides, you mean more to me than—"

Jesse drew a sharp breath of surprise. "You didn't sell Marco the photos!" he blurted.

"—Any shoot in the world," Ryan continued, and for a moment Sarah felt such a wave of longing that she nearly moaned out loud. But Jesse was already stepping between them, facing down the photographer with an incredulous demand.

"After this whole summer? What for?"

"To pay the pilot," Ryan said, sounding suddenly older and more tired than she had ever heard him. "Jesse, will you please just give us a minute?"

With a quick, searching glance at both of them, he nodded and moved off toward the snack bar, leaving Sarah staring at Ryan with a mixture of horror and hope.

"I had to find you," he said softly, as if wondering how to make her believe him. "I couldn't let you go."

"You gave up your *Odyssey Magazine* photos? To—to come here?"

He only shrugged, but she already knew the answer. He had sold his summer's work.

He had sacrificed his dream.

"Oh, Ryan," she whispered, stepping away from the ticket line and feeling her heart contract. "You did that for me?"

"No," he said, looking into her eyes but making no move to touch her. "For us, Corky. I did it for us."

The slow, surging flood that swept through her almost hurt, it was so rich and so intense. She took two uneven steps forward and, with a soft gasp, stumbled into Ryan's arms.

He caught her in an embrace so tight, so welcoming that she felt the tears stuffed behind her throat overflow in a rush. But this time they were tears of wonder, of happiness, of realization. He loved her. He loved her!

This was what she had dreamed of, what she had rejoiced over this afternoon before she overheard him talking to Jesse. Now, though, she knew it was for real. No one who loved Adele more would make a sacrifice like that.

No, he truly loved her. Her, the responsible one. The unadventurous one. And to think she had almost left him.

She would never, Sarah resolved, make that mistake again.

"Ryan," she murmured, and without a glance at the ticket-line crowd he guided her to a sheltered alcove, where he pressed her closer to him in silent confirmation. Yes, they belonged together. Yes, they would have the rest of their lives together. "Oh, I love you."

She felt his body tremble in response, and he swiftly, urgently pulled her against him, as if to share the joy of hearing it. Then, as she lifted her face to his, he kissed the tears on her cheeks until she guided him to her lips, where she could taste the salt that lingered on his.

He pulled back before she was ready to let him go, but with his eyes so full of gladness she knew there was more to come. He brushed a strand of hair off her cheek and then took both her hands in his before blurting a question. "You'll marry me, won't you?"

She felt herself reel in amazement. How could he have known so quickly what she had barely let herself fantasize?

"I should've asked you before," he continued. "I was sort of taking it for granted, but that was a mistake. Sarah, I don't ever want to lose you again."

"You won't," she promised. No matter what lay ahead, they would share it together. "Even if you wind up in Alaska, I'm staying with you."

The happiness on his face radiated between them until she could almost feel it flowing into her. "Alaska, huh?" Ryan said with the slow, compelling smile she loved. "I'll keep you warm."

For once she could let herself enjoy his teasing without worrying what anyone might think. "I'm counting on you," she told him, and his grin grew broader, then vanished.

"I want you to count on me," he said, suddenly serious. "Even though this didn't work out with *Odyssey,* I promise I'll take care of you."

He would, she knew. At least in every way that he could. But there were some areas—like making a home—where she would have to care for him. "I'll do it for you, too," Sarah promised, and his answering smile told her he understood what she meant. They would both give and both receive. "Jesse, too," she added, before realizing her nephew had been right all along. "Oh, dear. He kept trying to tell me you loved me, and I didn't listen."

"You're listening now, though, right?" Ryan ran his hands down her cheeks again, as if reassuring them both that it was now okay to touch her. "I love you, Sarah. I always will. Even when Jesse's off at college, that isn't going to change."

She caught her breath in surprise. What made him think Jesse was going to college?

"We already talked about it," Ryan explained, as if reading her mind. "This afternoon, while you were resting. I told him he can go on the road with us, but first he's got to get through school."

Was that what he'd meant when he told Jesse they had to start making plans? He must have expected, even then, that the three of them would be a family. If only she had known . . .

"Is that okay with him?" Sarah asked faintly.

"It sure is. Even so, we'll have to talk about what *we're* gonna do. I don't want to drag you off to Chicago to manage stock photos if you want to stay at the library. It's just—" He broke off, looking suddenly shaken. "I forgot, I won't be getting any more assignments. But I'll figure out something. Maybe I'll work for a newspaper. I don't know. I'll find something."

Even though he spoke casually, hiding any sign of regret, she felt her heart twist with compassion. "I wish you hadn't given up your chance at *Odyssey*. I'm so sorry you did that for me."

He pulled her back to him, lifting her chin so he could look into her eyes. "I'd do it again. In a minute. So don't ever think it was a bad choice, okay?"

"Okay," she whispered, and just as he bent to kiss her again, she saw Jesse come sauntering back from the snack bar.

He stopped dead at the sight of them.

Then she saw him smile. "So," he said, making Ryan jerk his head up in surprise, "you guys want me to come back in a couple hours?"

Still with one arm around Sarah, Ryan reached to grab Jesse by the shoulder and draw him into their circle.

"No way, kid," he said, and his voice was rough with love. "No way. We're all three of us in this together."

All three of them were together in a way they'd never been before, Sarah realized with growing pleasure as they covered the last stretch of desert on the way to Los Angeles. Although they no longer had the *Odyssey* mission to keep them going, they had a future to plan. They had a family to build.

"I'm not gonna have to wear a tux or anything when you get married, am I?" Jesse asked the morning they left Kingman, after a short night's sleep. And she gave him a hug, realizing this was his way of asking whether the marriage was going to happen.

"You can wear whatever you want," she told him. "Except your Stryker shirt!" They hadn't even started planning a wedding, but she had the feeling Ryan would be glad to leave the details to her. "Maybe you'd like to invite Vicki."

Jesse grinned, adjusting the rearview mirror as a truck moved into their lane. "I have to tell her she was right all along. She said anybody at that restaurant in Flagstaff could see you guys were in love."

Sarah blushed. "She probably knew it before I did." Then she caught herself. There was no need to tell Jesse how her envy of Adele had complicated matters so badly. After all, Adele *was* his mother... and a sister she could finally think of without that automatic sense of inferiority. Ryan had given her back the twin sister she loved. "Anyway," she said gently, "Vicki's a nice girl. I'm glad you'll be seeing more of each other."

There were so many things to be glad about, she thought as they stopped for the night outside San Bernardino. Ryan had chosen a campground far enough from the city that the stars were clearly visible in the desert sky, and the three of them climbed up to the motor-home roof, where they could see the stars overhead and the city lights in the distance.

"Be a great photo if we used the wide-angle lens," Jesse commented, crunching into a taco chip and passing the crinkly bag to Sarah. "All those lights."

"Let's wait till the moon gets a little farther up," Ryan suggested. "But you're right, kid. You've got a good eye."

He must have gotten it from Ryan, she thought with a sweet twinge of pride. The man was a born photographer. Even with the Route 66 story completely lost, he was still looking at everything with the eye of an artist.

If only she hadn't caused him to give up his photos.

Jesse, she knew, thought they should visit the *Odyssey* office anyway. "At least you can tell them you *had* the story," he'd urged Ryan during lunch at a Needles diner. "I'll back you up."

Ryan had spent a long time swallowing a bite of his meatball sandwich. "Thing is," he said finally, in a voice that brooked no argument, "I promised Huey I could deliver the photos, and either I can or I can't. If I can't, it doesn't matter why not. They'll have to use whatever Marco brings in."

"Even if he brings in your photos?" Jesse demanded, and Ryan flinched.

"Jess, I can't deliver *Odyssey* what I promised, and that was the problem in the first place. I already called and told them I'm off the shoot. There's just no reason to go by there."

Remembering that now, Sarah set down the bag of taco chips and moved behind him to smooth her hands across his shoulders. He looked up at her with an appreciative smile, and she began gently kneading, coaxing the tension from his muscles.

She knew, without even questioning how she knew, that Ryan couldn't go back into Huey's office and beg for another chance. He'd already gotten another chance and given it up, and she respected the pride that kept him from demanding yet one more.

But still, she wished they were on their way to *Odyssey Magazine*.

He sighed deeply as she dug her fingers into the corded muscles of his shoulders, and she felt him beginning to relax as she kept up the steady pressure.

"Ah, yeah," he muttered. "Thanks, Corky."

Still kneading, she smiled at the nickname. "You know, my name won't be Corcoran once we're married. You're going to have to come up with something else."

He brought her hands down to his chest and kissed one finger. "You'll always be Corky to me, love. Jess, does that moon look about right?"

Jesse straightened up from the taco chips and squinted at the sky. "Pretty good," he agreed. "Can I do this shot?"

"Sure," Ryan told him. "Make it a good one. This'll be our last photo on Route 66."

It was hard to believe they'd covered almost every mile of the road to paradise. But tomorrow they would reach the end, where the legendary highway hit Santa Monica's Ocean Avenue and turned into the Pacific Coast Highway heading north.

"I'm going to miss this road," Sarah said.

Ryan kissed her hand again, then let her go. "There'll be other roads," he promised. "But I know what you mean. This one's kind of special."

Kind of special. She thought of his words half a dozen times the next day, as they wound their way through Asuza and Pasadena and into the Los Angeles basin along the Arroyo Seco Parkway. Even though the California air seemed lighter, somehow, the streets were more crowded than any they'd seen since leaving Chicago.

They had seen so much, she marveled, letting the vast array of images sift through her memory. Downtown Chicago, where they would start looking for their new home as soon as they got back. The Illinois farm towns. The ice-cream stand in St. Louis. The Fourth of July picnic near the creek in Oklahoma. The lighted oil derricks. The flatlands outside Amarillo. The majesty of New Mexico and the vast deserts of Arizona. And now, two miles from the ocean, it was almost at an end.

"You guys want to hang out at the beach for a while?" Jesse asked as they approached the Santa Monica pier, its boardwalk gaiety an odd contrast to the serenity of the surf. "Because I, uh, I have to go meet Vicki in about twenty minutes. I could run and see her and then come back."

Sooner or later, Sarah knew, they would have to see about getting a flight from Los Angeles to Chicago and figure out some way to get the motor home back to Ryan's friend, who had already found himself another project. But for now it was curiously pleasant to have no mission, no deadline looming over them. And Ryan evidently felt the same way.

"Take your time," he told Jesse, who pulled off to the side of the road in front of a No Parking sign. "Where is Vicki, anyway?"

"I'm pretty good at finding places to meet." Jesse gave them both a cocky grin. "I'll be back here in a couple hours, okay?"

Ordinarily she wouldn't dream of letting her nephew navigate the Los Angeles freeways alone, but he had shown remarkable competence in getting them here. And besides, he was probably better at taking care of himself than she had ever been willing to admit.

"Have a good time," Sarah told him, and Ryan took her hand as they watched Jesse guide the motor home back into the traffic on Ocean Avenue.

"Nice going, Sarah."

She knew immediately what he meant. "I just figured he can probably take care of himself."

"You're right," Ryan told her, and they started across the street toward the beach. "Good for you."

It was a breezy afternoon, and the smell of the salt air wafted toward them from the ocean even before they reached the sand. "Somewhere around here is a plaque," Sarah recalled, "in honor of Route 66. I copied down the words, back in Tulsa."

"Yeah? You're a hell of a researcher, you know that?"

But it hadn't done any good. Even though he had insisted he would still pay her, saying a deal was a deal, she couldn't help feeling guilty that her notes, which were supposed to help sell his story, wouldn't make a bit of difference.

"I wish my research could've sold your story," she told him as they started across the sand, and Ryan sighed.

"Stop worrying about it. I'll do something else."

He probably would. But still she wished she could make up for him having lost his dream. "You think maybe some new magazine might—"

"Sarah," he interrupted, taking her hand and nodding toward the sea, "forget it. We'll worry about that later, all right? Right now it's summer, we're in California, we're at the beach and we gotta go wade in the ocean."

"All right," she agreed. It would take some effort to stop grieving over his loss, but if he could manage it, then so could she. Sarah yanked off her shoes and then gasped at the heat of the sand under her feet.

"Whew," Ryan muttered, sounding equally startled. "Race you down to the water."

In fifteen seconds they were at the edge of the surf, where a cold wave lapped over their ankles. Sarah shrieked and he grinned at her. "Can't win, huh?"

"I just wasn't expecting it to be this cold!" She scooped up a handful of water and threw it at him. "So there."

"Oh, she wants to play rough." He scooped up two handfuls and she darted away, running at the edge of the water, where the sand was damp. "You're gonna get it now."

"No!" she protested, but when he caught up to her and grabbed her from behind, there was no more water in his hands. Instead he spun her around to face him, and she saw on his face a mixture of laughter and tenderness.

"I love you," he murmured.

Another wave splashed over their legs, but neither of them felt it. They might have been floating or flying, for all the sensation that registered as they stood together, pressed against one another, heart-to-heart and soul-to-soul.

The waves were up to their knees before either of them realized how long they'd been standing in the same place. "We're going to get stuck if we don't move pretty soon!" Sarah told him, and he made a show of yanking first one foot, then the other out of the squishy sand.

"Whew," he said. "That was close."

She laughed. Everything seemed lighter, suddenly—easier and more fun. And they were certainly in the right place to enjoy a mood like this. "Let's go look around the pier."

They climbed the rickety wooden steps to the top of the pier, where sightseers and fishermen shared the railing in easy harmony. They strolled along the boardwalk, where a profusion of shops and restaurants offered seaside memorabilia and surprisingly good hot dogs. They wandered to the far end, where the benches overlooking the ocean invited them to linger for another hour as the sun slid lower into the shining water and the distant boats glided slowly past.

When a cluster of teenagers with skateboards trooped by, Sarah glanced at her watch. "I hope Jesse's doing okay."

"He is," Ryan told her, and put his arm around her shoulders. "I have to tell you, you've been doing a great job of not worrying about him."

He sounded sincere, but that seemed like a strange compliment. "I'll always worry about him!" Sarah protested. "But I know I've got to let him do things on his own. Even when he's fifty years old, though, I'll probably still be hoping he's all right."

Ryan looked at her thoughtfully for a moment and then smiled. "I bet you will, at that," he said, and she could tell from the tenderness in his voice that he appreciated how she would always care for Jesse. "I guess that's just what mothers do."

She nestled her head against his shoulder, enjoying the scent and the warmth of him beside her in the ocean breeze, and then sat up straight as she heard footsteps pounding toward them. It was Jesse, looking more excited than she'd seen him all week.

She waved, and Ryan turned, but before they could stand up, Jesse came racing across the wooden deck and braced himself against the railing facing them. "You guys ready for this?" he demanded. "Huey wants to see you tomorrow morning. He's got an assignment for you."

Beside her, Ryan went absolutely still. "What?"

Jesse plopped down on the bench next to Sarah, turning so he could address them both. "I went to *Odyssey Magazine*. I know you didn't want to go there, but you never said I couldn't. And Marco had already been there, with *your* photos, and he told everyone they were his."

Sarah caught her breath and felt Ryan wince. But all he said was, "Yeah?"

"So Huey had gotten the message you were off the shoot, and he bought everything Marco had. He said they couldn't believe how much better it was than anything the guy had ever shot before. I told them it was because you'd shot them."

Ryan let out his breath in a soft rush. "And they believed you?"

"They had to," Jesse said, practically wriggling off the bench. "You know the shot of the kids in Joplin, where we used the extra filter? And the Winslow train station, with all those lights? And that church in Tulsa, and the Club Cafe billboard, and the oil rig—they loved that one. Once I explained how you set 'em up, and the film speed, and the lenses we used—" He broke off, his words almost tumbling over one another. "Yeah. They believed it. And Huey said even though they've already paid Marco for this shoot, the guy will never work again. They're giving you the photo credit, because Huey wants you back."

"My God," Ryan murmured again, sounding as though he'd just been given another life. He stood up, looking out over the ocean for a moment and blinking rapidly, then turned back to Jesse and Sarah. "I don't know what to say."

"Well," Jesse suggested, "why don't you see what Huey offers you? He said they're doing this one story about small towns in the Midwest, but that sounds pretty boring. There's one in Mexico that might be—"

"Small towns in the Midwest?" Sarah interrupted. The entire premise sounded too good to be true. "Jesse, are you sure you're not making this up?"

"Are you kidding?" he protested. "If I was making this up they'd be doing a shoot in Hawaii. Or Montana. Someplace like that." He shrugged and grinned at them both. "Someplace good."

So it was true. Her nephew had actually salvaged Ryan's dream, and he had done it all on his own. Sarah scooted over to give him a long hug, and Ryan moved back to the bench, resting his hands on both their shoulders.

"Thank you," he said hoarsely. "Jesse, thank you."

"Hey, no problem. Call it a wedding present or something." His tone was light, but underneath it there was a new seriousness. "Anyway, you guys have done a lot for me."

She felt a rush of tears burn her throat, but Ryan answered for them both. "That's what parents are for."

Sarah reached for his hand on her shoulder, and he leaned down to kiss her. "Right, Corky?"

"Right," she whispered, feeling more like a mother than she ever had in her life. "I love both of you so much."

"Aw, Sarah." Jesse sounded embarrassed. "Don't start crying."

Ryan sat down beside her and propped his feet up on the deck railing. "Tell you what," he said. "Why don't we sit here and watch the sun go down, and then find someplace for dinner."

"No stewed tomatoes," Jesse said immediately, making Sarah laugh in spite of herself.

"No stewed tomatoes," she agreed. It was hard to believe how far they'd come since the morning they'd loaded those grocery boxes into the motor home. More than two thousand miles and into a whole new life. "We've come a long way, haven't we?"

"Yeah," Jesse said, slouching forward to prop his feet up on the railing alongside Ryan. "We actually made it. You know what this is, right here? The end of the road to paradise."

Ryan draped his arm around Sarah's shoulders and gave her a slow, gentle squeeze that set her heart soaring once again. "You know, actually," he said, "it's the other way around. The road to paradise starts right here."

Epilogue

"Will you take this woman to have and to hold, to love and to cherish..."

Sarah reached for Ryan's hand, and he smiled down at her.

"...In good times and in bad..."

He squeezed her hand, and she swallowed a lump in her throat. What had begun on the road to paradise was now culminating in a sunlit Chicago chapel, and she wished she could make the day last forever. There was so much to celebrate, so much to treasure...even more than she had anticipated that day on the Santa Monica pier.

"...For richer, for poorer..."

It would likely be richer, with so many assignments coming in. Ryan's Route 66 story had captured the attention of editors all over the country, and Ryan and Jesse had been working steadily ever since. Even with Jesse taking classes at the University of Chicago and Sarah managing Ryan's stock-photo orders, there were plenty of weekend shoots to keep them enjoying the pleasures of the road.

"...For as long as you both shall live?"

She blinked back an unexpected rush of tears as Ryan smiled at her again. They already knew the answer, but hearing the words was giving her chills.

"I will," came the reply.

The minister reached for Jesse's and Vicki's hands and joined them together. "Then, by the power vested in me, I now pronounce you husband and wife."

Applause echoed throughout the church as Jesse kissed his bride, and Ryan gathered Sarah into his arms.

"Watching them," he murmured, "makes me want to get married all over again."

She knew what he meant. There was nothing like a wedding to illustrate how wonderful marriage could be. How incredibly exciting and how very sweetly satisfying.

"Maybe," she whispered, "we could do it again for our fiftieth anniversary."

"Sounds good to me." They shared a quick, confirming kiss before Jesse and Vicki started down the aisle, and watched with soaring joy as their son and his wife moved forward together. "I hope," Ryan said hoarsely, "they'll be as happy as we are."

"They will be," Sarah promised. "After all, they met the same summer we did...and look how well it's turned out for us."

"Same place, too," he observed, brushing his fingers across her cheek. "Remember the end of Route 66?"

"Every time I look at the picture." On their wedding day, nearly five years ago, Jesse had presented them with a photo he'd shot at the Santa Monica pier, with Ryan and Sarah in each other's arms against a brilliant sunset sky. "You were right, you know? You said the road to paradise started right there."

"We're still on it, Corky," he said, and his face crinkled into the familiar smile she loved as he laced his fingers through hers. "Every day we're together...it's still the road to paradise."

* * * * *

Silhouette®

SPECIAL EDITION™

COMING NEXT MONTH

Celebration 1000! Begins With:
#991 MAGGIE'S DAD—Diana Palmer
Celebration 1000!
Returning home, Antonia Hayes was determined not to fall again for Powell Long. But the single dad was sexier than ever—and he had *definite* ideas about their reunion!

#992 MORGAN'S SON—Lindsay McKenna
Morgan's Mercenaries: Love and Danger
Rescuing a little boy hit close to home for high-risk expert Sabra Jacobs. Mercenary Craig Talbot knew they faced perilous odds on this mission—but the real danger was losing his heart to her....

#993 CHILD OF MINE—Jennifer Mikels
Ambitious and practical Alex Kane needed one thing: to get his son back. But that meant marrying carefree and outgoing Carly Mitchell, and once they'd said their vows, it was obvious this marriage would *not* be in name only!

#994 THE DADDY QUEST—Celeste Hamilton
Precocious Zane McPherson was on a quest to find a daddy who'd be the perfect match for his mom, Holly. Tough cop Brooks Casey never entertained the idea of being a family man—but one look at Holly had Brooks changing his mind!

#995 LOGAN'S BRIDE—Christine Flynn
The Whitaker Brides/Holiday Elopement
Samantha Gray knew Logan Whitaker was trouble the moment she saw him. She'd only wanted a secure future for her children, but falling for the sexy rancher seemed inevitable—and resisting his tempting offer of marriage was even harder....

#996 BRAVE HEART—Brittany Young
No-nonsense lawyer Rory Milbourne didn't believe in fate. But Daniel Blackhawk knew it was destiny that had brought Rory to him—and that she was the other half of his heart he'd been waiting all his life to find....

It's our 1000th Special Edition and we're celebrating!

Join us for some wonderful stories in a special celebration with some of your favorite authors!
And starting the celebration is

Diana Palmer
with
MAGGIE'S DAD
(SE #991, November)

Returning home, Antonia Hayes was determined not to fall again for Powell Long. But the single dad was sexier than ever—and he had *definite* ideas about their reunion!

Celebration 1000! kicks off in the month of November—don't miss it! Watch for books by Lindsay McKenna, Jennifer Mikels, Celeste Hamilton, Christine Flynn and Brittany Young. You'll fall in love with our next 1000 special stories!

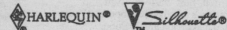

Become a Privileged Woman,
You'll be entitled to all these Free Benefits. And Free Gifts, too.

To thank you for buying our books, we've designed an exclusive FREE program called *PAGES & PRIVILEGES™*. You can enroll with just one Proof of Purchase, and get the kind of luxuries that, until now, you could only read about.

BIG HOTEL DISCOUNTS

A privileged woman stays in the finest hotels. And so can you—at up to 60% off! Imagine standing in a hotel check-in line and watching as the guest in front of you pays $150 for the same room that's only costing you $60. Your *Pages & Privileges* discounts are good at Sheraton, Marriott, Best Western, Hyatt and thousands of other fine hotels all over the U.S., Canada and Europe.

FREE DISCOUNT TRAVEL SERVICE

A privileged woman is always jetting to romantic places.

When <u>you</u> fly, just make one phone call for the lowest published airfare at time of booking— <u>or double the difference back</u>!

PLUS—you'll get a $25 voucher to use the first time you book a flight AND <u>5% cash back on every ticket you buy thereafter through the travel service!</u>